THE NORDIC TRANSLATION SERIES

Sponsored by the Nordic Cultural Commission
of the governments of Denmark, Finland,
Iceland, Norway, and Sweden

ADVISORY COMMITTEE

Einar I. Haugen, Harald S. Næss, and
Richard B. Vowles, Chairman

THE BLACK CLIFFS

THE BLACK CLIFFS

GUNNAR GUNNARSSON

SVARTFUGL

Translated from the Danish by Cecil Wood

With an Introduction by Richard N. Ringler

1967

THE UNIVERSITY OF WISCONSIN PRESS

MADISON   MILWAUKEE   LONDON

Published by
The University of Wisconsin Press
Madison, Milwaukee, and London
U.S.A.: Box 1379, Madison, Wisconsin 53701
U.K.: 26–28 Hallam Street, London, W. 1

Originally published by
Glydendalske Boghandel Nordisk Forlag
Copenhagen, Denmark
Copyright © 1929
by Gyldendalske Boghandel Nordisk Forlag

Printed in the United States of America by
George Banta Company, Inc., Menasha, Wisconsin

Library of Congress Catalog Card Number 67-25943

INTRODUCTION

I

Gunnar Gunnarsson was born May 18th, 1889, on the parsonage-farm Valþjófsstaður in the Fljótsdalur region of eastern Iceland.[1] His father worked as farm overseer for Gunnarsson's uncle, who was the local priest. When Gunnarsson was seven his parents moved north to the farm Ljótsstaðir in Vopnafjörður. Like many Icelandic writers he was much attached to his mother and greatly shaken by her death, which occurred soon after this move. It was also in the best tradition of Icelandic authorship that he started writing very young: in 1906, only seventeen years old, he published in Akureyri two small collections of poems in his native tongue, *Remembering Mother* (*Móðurminning*) and *Songs of Spring* (*Vorljóð*). The following year he sailed for Denmark, determined to follow in the footsteps of his viking forebears and seek fame and fortune abroad. His first story in Danish was composed on shipboard. He spent two winters at the Askov Folk High School in southern Jutland, which has been attended by many Icelanders both

[1] I want to acknowledge my debt to the works about Gunnar Gunnarsson which are mentioned in the bibliography—particularly to those by Andrésson, Einarsson, and Gelsted—for the factual material and some of the interpretations in the first section of this introduction; also to the American Council of Learned Societies for treating me to a year in Iceland—an experience which underlies any understanding I may have of Gunnarsson's work; and finally to my colleagues in the Department of Scandinavian Studies at the University of Wisconsin for many helpful suggestions.

before him and after, and did garden work during the summers. After leaving school he worked for a time pouring concrete at Askov, then on a farm out in the country, and finally settled in Århus in the autumn of 1909, hoping to support himself by writing for the local newspapers. The net result of this hope was frustration and poverty, which pursued him to Copenhagen when he moved there in the spring of the following year.

His thoughts at this time centered on becoming a writer, and he realized that writing in his native language would neither support him financially nor gain him a European audience. Even today potential book sales in Iceland (pop. 193,000) will not support a career of creative writing —and the language is formidably difficult for non-Scandinavians. Gunnarsson's decision to write in Danish, though it has undeniably made him one of the important figures in modern Danish literature, has also had the unfortunate result of setting him between two stools: his Icelandic origins and subject matter often lead Danish literary historians to exclude him from consideration as a Danish writer, while the fact that he writes in Danish brings him in for very sketchy and superficial treatment by Icelandic critics. In the earlier part of his career, especially, his decision to write in Danish subjected him to frequent abuse from his countrymen, since Danish was the language of the "enemy": it was at precisely this time that Iceland's battle for independence from Denmark was being prosecuted with the greatest vigor.

Gunnarsson's first book in Danish, *Poems (Digte)* came out in 1911. Then in the spring of 1912, when he was still in his early twenties, he wrote *Ormarr Ørlygsson*, the first part of his novel *The Family from Borg (Af Borgslægtens Historie)*. It was published later that year. On the proceeds from this work—300 kroner—Gunnarsson married a Danish girl, Franzisca Jørgensen. The three later volumes of the novel followed fast on the heels of the first: *The Danish Lady at Hof (Den danske Frue paa Hof*, 1913), *Guest the*

One-Eyed (*Gæst den enøjede*, 1913), which Gunnarsson finished in two or three weeks and which enjoyed an immediate critical success, and *The Young Eagle* (*Den unge Ørn*, 1914). The completed work established Gunnarsson's reputation in Scandinavia. It was the first of his novels to be translated into English, under the title *Guest the One-Eyed* (1920), and became the first novel by an Icelander to be made into a motion picture (1919).

It is a large-scale attempt to write a modern Icelandic family saga, tracing the rise and fall of a powerful family through several generations. Sensational incidents and colorful, if somewhat stereotyped, characters throng its pages. With roots deep in the author's homesickness for Iceland and in the widespread optimism and idealism which preceded the First World War, it is a romantically shaded portrayal of rural life in Iceland, of a type not at all uncommon in Icelandic literature.

The war cast a shadow over Gunnarsson's optimism and brought him face to face with one of the major problems of literature in the contemporary period, indeed in any period: How is man to hold to his idealism—his faith in God and humanity, his hope that life will prove in the last analysis meaningful—in the face of the ample evidence furnished by modern life and modern science that evil and chance are governing factors in the universe? Gunnarsson grappled with these problems in a number of pessimistic books which in their overall sourness and emphasis on the malevolence of fate are very reminiscent of the novels of Thomas Hardy.

The first of these was *The Shore of Life* (*Livets Strand,* 1915). Gunnarsson wrote the first draft of this novel at night, in the lulls between bouts of depressed reflection and chain-smoking. "But whether I was waking or sleeping, reading or writing, sitting quietly in the solitude of the night or chattering in the company of friends, pain and yearning howled in my breast: the pain of a man expelled from the paradise of peace and trust, the yearning of an intelligent creature for more comprehensive understanding than is generally allotted to mankind." *The Shore of Life* is the story of a devoted but doubt-ridden clergyman whose wife almost dies giving birth to their first child, Blithe (Blid). Since it would be fatal for her to have more children, sexual relations between her and her husband must be suspended. However, after ten years they resume them, trusting in the priest's mystical conviction that God is good and kind, that he will not let his creatures come to harm, and that men must cast themselves completely on his mercy and providence. The wife becomes pregnant, of course, and dies in childbirth; and some years later Blithe is drowned in a tragic accident. "Oh God, oh God—you devil!" cries the priest, carrying his daughter's body up onto a headland to bury her with a good view of the sea, according to the old pagan custom. He does not want her to rest in consecrated ground. "In those days," Gunnarsson wrote later, "it had not begun to dawn on me that mankind is one soul and one body, that our mutual involvement is unavoidable, our mutual responsibility total—and that the soul is scarcely less related to the body than the skies are to the sea and the earth." In *The Shore of Life* Gunnarsson attempts, as he explained long afterward, to evade this mutual responsibility by placing the blame for all things on God.

In 1918 appeared the first of Gunnarsson's historical novels, *The Sworn Brothers* (*Edbrødre*). It deals with the earliest Norse settlers in Iceland, Ingólfur and his foster-brother Hjörleifur. Like fellow Icelandic novelists who write in a second language, notably Kristmann Guðmundsson, Gunnarsson has produced a number of historical novels. Icelandic history—especially the history of the settlement and saga periods—has always awakened considerable interest in the Scandinavian countries and Germany, and Icelandic writers who refashion this material, trying to recreate its physical milieu and especially its psychological constellations, have had no difficulty finding markets and popularity. Other novels of Gunnarsson's which deal with this earliest and most romantic period in the history of Iceland are *Land* (*Jord*, 1933); *The White Christ* (*Hvide-Krist*, 1934) and *Greyman* (*Graamand*, 1936). Concerned with events from later periods are *The Black Cliffs* (*Svartfugl*, 1929); *Jón Arason* (1930), which tells the heroic story of the last Catholic bishop of Iceland; and two novels written in Icelandic after Gunnarsson's return to his native land, *Sorrow on the Moors* (*Heiðaharmur*, 1940) and *Requiem Mass* (*Sálumessa*, 1952), both of which deal with life in late nineteenth-century Iceland. Gunnarsson considers that these eight historical novels form a loosely knit cycle called *The Settlement* (*Landnám*). This title reflects his conviction that the settlement of Iceland is a continuing process that has not yet come to an end.

Returning to Gunnarsson's pessimistic period after the First World War, we may take note of the novel *Seven Days' Darkness* (*Salige er de Enfoldige*). Written in Rapallo in 1919, it was published in Copenhagen the following year and translated into English in 1930. Its scene is Reykjavík in 1918, during an epidemic of Spanish flu lit fitfully by an eruption of the great volcano Katla. The book portrays the struggle between a man of noble character and a Satanic adversary. Evil triumphs in the end, and the moral imperative registered by the book is the simple one, that men ought to be good to one another. The novel has been praised as a model of construction and condemned as psychologically unconvincing. And indeed there is often a tendency in Gunnarsson's earlier works to depict characters with sensationalized or sentimentalized motivation who are not sufficiently complex, manifold, and ambiguous in the subtle interchanges of daily life to persuade us of their psychological and artistic plausibility.

Gunnarsson's next major project was the writing of an extensive, fictionalized autobiography, *The Church on the Mountain* (*Kirken paa Bjerget*), which came out in five volumes between 1923 and 1928. It is probably his major, and certainly in many respects his most mature and successful, work. Recollection of his youth, his family, and his homeland seems to have tempered the pessimism of the wartime and post-war years, bringing him to a more unconditional acceptance of life with all its richness and contradictions. The first volume, *Playing with Straws* (*Leg med Straa*, 1923), is based upon memories of Gunnarsson's childhood in Fljótsdalur. With its idyllic account of childish occupations and preoccupations, washed in the more mature and melancholy light of recollection, it often puts the English reader in mind of Edwin Muir's *Autobiography*. Like this latter work, it strongly suggests that the memory of a happy childhood—and the optimism and basic trust engendered by it—can help a man weather the moral turmoil of his mature years and give him faith in himself and mankind, even if the whole world is falling in ruins about him. The second volume, *Ships in the Sky* (*Skibe paa Himlen*, 1925), recounts the family's move to Vopnafjörður and the death of Gunnarsson's mother. Severe characterological imbalances follow this event: weakening of trust in his real environment and retreat into the more secure and less whimsical world of imagination. These themes persist in the third volume, *The Night and the Dream* (*Natten og Drømmen*, 1926). The last two volumes, *The Inexperienced Traveller* (*Der uerfarne Rejsende*, 1927) and *Hugleik the Hard-Sailing* (*Hugleik den Haardtsejlende*, 1928) deal with Gunnarsson's early years in Denmark and his development into a successful writer. An English version of *The Church on the Mountain* by Evelyn Ramsden appeared in 1938, the first two volumes translated under the title *Ships in the Sky*, the last three under the title *The Night and the Dream*. The translation is adequate, though it gives an effect of cuteness which is quite foreign to the original.

Immediately after completing this great hymn to life, and while still in the grip of its optimism, Gunnarsson ad-

dressed himself to telling the story of one of the blackest
and most brutal crimes in modern Icelandic history. This
conjunction of a positive author and a negative story has
resulted in a curiously ambiguous novel, *The Black Cliffs*,
which here appears for the first time in English translation. The place which it occupies in the sequence of Gunnarsson's work goes a long way toward explaining the
book's peculiar atmosphere. But more of this in a moment.

Gunnarsson lived in or near Copenhagen until he was
fifty. Then, in the spring of 1939, he returned to Iceland.
During the war years he busied himself farming at
Skriðuklaustur in Fljótsdalur, not far from the place of his
birth, and afterwards (1949) he moved to the capital,
Reykjavík, where he now resides. Since returning to Iceland he has written in his native tongue, and also worked
on the Icelandic-translation edition of his complete works
(21 volumes, 1941–62). To the latter he has contributed a
number of postscripts which describe how his novels came
into being, and often attempt to reconstruct his state of
mind at the time of their writing. They are a mine of autobiographical information.

II

Sailing north from Reykjavík on a coastal steamer you
swing around the tip of the Snæfell Peninsula, dominated
by its majestic, snow-clad volcano—the Snæfell Glacier—
and enter the vast bay of Breiðafjörður ("Broad Fjord"),
dotted with many islands. Far away across this bay looms
the rocky shoreline of the Northwestern Peninsula, a great
lobster-shaped chunk of land, deeply cut by fjords and
joined to the Icelandic mainland only by its narrow tail.
The entire area is remote, isolated and mountainous, and
permits human habitation only in thin strips and pockets
along its coast. The stretch of coast at the extreme south-
west of this peninsula—the lobster's left claw—is known as
Rauðisandur ("Rødesand" in Danish, "Red Sand" in English). Here is Saurbær, the parish church; farther to the

west is Keflavig; and off to the east, isolated amid all this isolation, are the ruins of the farm Sjöundá ("Syvendeaa" in Danish, "Seventh River" in English) where, in the year 1802, one of the most sensational murders in Icelandic history was perpetrated.

Gunnarsson himself, at the time of writing *The Black Cliffs*, his historical novel about this famous crime, had never explored the Rødesand region on foot, had only seen it from the deck of a coastal steamer.

Until 1918 I knew of the business at Sjöundá only by hearsay, though I had made the acquaintance of the Steina cairn five years earlier and sometimes paused next to it on my solitary, early-morning hikes up Öskjuhlíð, before most of Reykjavík was on its feet. Then, in the spring of 1918, I was en route to Vöpnafjörður, travelling west, north and east along the coast aboard the *Sterling*, which made a stop in every single harbor and unharbor (how different it was sailing along the coast in those days, when no one was in a hurry!) and even chugged a little way up into Gilsfjörður, if I remember correctly. We were travelling west along Barðaströnd, which, seen from the sea on a spring day, bewitches a man with its majesty and dreamlike beauty, when it so happened that we sailed close in beneath Skor. I was anxiously reciting Matthias' poem about Eggert to myself when someone nudged me and drew my attention to a group of dimly discernible ruins in the overgrown fields up beyond Skor Cliffs, some distance from the sea. It was Sjöundá. I no longer remember whether I noticed any signs that the farm was inhabited, but I do distinctly recall seeing the vestiges of an enclosed hayfield.

I am ashamed to confess that this tiny green patch on the steep slope, bathed as it was in some of the grimmest memories from the Icelandic past, riveted my gaze much too much for me to be able to give Saurbær, and the Rauðisand coast in general, the attention they deserved. No little tatter of hayfield is so wretched that it won't be turned into a pleasure ground by the sunlit laughter of buttercups and dandelions on a spring day; no recorded human life is so miserable that radiance of some sort does not emanate from it. Looking out toward Sjöundá and remembering the Steina cairn, I was seized by the conviction that here was the substance for a story—a story which I would be capable of telling. I would not be able to tell it exactly as it happened (that is never possible), but as it *might* have happened and even—were I to be entirely successful—as it *ought* to have happened. Who can do more than that?[2]

Ten years were to go by, however, before Gunnarsson wrote the book which had been suggested to him by this glimpse of Syvendeaa in 1918. During these years he wrote *Seven Days' Darkness,* a distillation of his pessimism and lack of reconciliation with the world, and later underwent the therapeutic experience of writing *The Church on the Mountain,* with its God's plenty of people and places, its ambient, overarching optimism. Often during these years he thought of returning to the Syvendeaa material,

> plucking up my courage and going to work on Rauðisand. But always, at this crucial point, I began to have doubts that I was sufficiently ready. I didn't like the idea of telling the story without knowing the locale better than one can know it by seeing it from out at sea. On the other hand, I was afraid of coming too closely into contact with the setting of a story which was itself so remote in time.

He studied the area with the aid of maps and travel books, telling no one about his plans and wondering whether the book would ever materialize. Finally in the winter of 1928–29 he decided to go at it in earnest. He spent the winter in the Danish National Archives, where many of the records of the trial were deposited, taking down copious notes which he typed up when he came home in the evenings.

> So the winter passed. In the spring I got to work and started telling the story—telling it the way that seemed most natural to me. Hitherto it had always been called *Sjöundá*

[2] Gunnarsson's remarks on the genesis and meaning of the novel, quoted here and elsewhere in this Introduction, are to be found in "Sjöundá og Arnarhváll," his postscript to the ninth volume, *Jörð* (Reykjavík: 1950), of the Icelandic collective edition of his works.

in my mind's eye; when I finally began to grapple with it, it was under the title *Svartfugl.*

The germ of the novel sprouted in Gunnarsson's mind during his most pessimistic period, and it is not surprising that the subject would appeal to him in that mood. We can only imagine how different the book would have been had he actually gone ahead and written it in 1918. But he resisted the temptation to tell the story prematurely, and it grew in his mind during ten years of increasing artistic confidence and burgeoning optimism. The novel in its final form betrays traces of this gradual unfolding in two contradictory psychological climates, and its moral ambiguity is perhaps ultimately attributable to the circumstances of its growth. It is in this sense no less autobiographical—no less an index of its author's moral and psychological development—than *The Church on the Mountain.*

The precise subject of the novel has often eluded critics. At its first appearance it was taken by some reviewers to be little more than a detective story, a courtroom drama à la Perry Mason. But it is clearly much more than that. So simplistic an explanation does enormous violence to the novel's complexity and fails to account for its peculiar tension, a tension which has little to do with the accumulation of evidence and the identification of the murderers. From the outset no reader can be in doubt—simply from the atmosphere of the book and from Eiulv's oblique comments—of Bjarni and Steinun's guilt. What little suspense there is derives from wondering whether they will be *proved* guilty, and here Judge Scheving's preconceptions furnish a fairly unambiguous forecast of the ultimate event. The material evidence which is brought forward is remarkable either for its irrelevance or for the ease with which it can be misconstrued: the long rigmarole about Jon Thorgrimsson's trousers leads nowhere, and the hole

xvi

in his neck is wilfully misinterpreted by Scheving to the very end. The cloud of witnesses who appear at the trial supply very little useful evidence: their artistic purpose is pretty clearly to establish the unhealthy psychological atmosphere at Syvendeaa and to illustrate the character of the two victims. In sum, the simple mechanics of gathering together evidence and establishing circumstantial guilt are not Gunnarsson's major concern.

Any consideration of the meaning of the novel must begin with its richly symbolic title, *Svartfugl*. The Icelandic word *svartfugl*—literally "black bird"—is the generic name for the family Alcidæ (or, in English, Alcids). This family consists of auks, murres, guillemots, and puffins, and its members are (generally speaking) black on top and white underneath. They are very sociable birds, the various species nesting freely alongside one another, in vast colonies, on the precipitous bird cliffs (*fuglabjörg*) along the Icelandic coast.[3] They and their eggs are hunted by the Icelanders in the spring, and it is dangerous work. "The bird cliffs are often steep and treacherous; Látrabjarg for example is between twelve and fourteen hundred feet high. All over these cliffs are platforms and ledges where the birds nest and lay their eggs, often sitting so thickly that bird jostles bird for a considerable stretch."[4] It is this sort of bird cliff that is described by Eiulv in the passage which is so critical for the interpretation of the novel:

I remembered with great clarity the day Bjarni had spoken of . . . A sheer, ocean-sprayed mountain wall that looked from a rocking boat below like something growing into the sky. A storm of shrieking birds—a white-shining, black-spark-

[3] See Roger Tory Peterson *et al.*, *Fuglar Íslands og Evrópu*, tr. and adjusted to Icelandic conditions by Finnur Guðmundsson, (2nd ed.; Reykjavík: 1964), pp. 201–4.
[4] Jónas Jónasson, *Íslenzkir þjóðhættir* (3rd ed.; Reykjavík: 1961). p. 196 f. Jónas gives a long and interesting account of fowling techniques on these *fuglabjörg* (pp. 197–99).

ling cloud of sea birds which, like a continuation of the breakers, swirled up at the black cliffs and disappeared in the mists of the mountain. When as a child I saw that sight for the first time, I did not have a moment's doubt that it was the angry sea itself capriciously spraying winged fish from its belly. Even last year it gave me a chill to come up against the cliffs' fantastic, relentless, ineradicable life—that storm of life where, amidst noise and stink and filth, existence triumphs, life renews itself, springing young and fresh and blood-warm from the sterile rocks. Every summer.

Erlendur Jónsson interprets the symbolism of the passage as follows: "Nowhere is life as many-sided and dizzyingly active as in the cliffs where the Alcids make their home. And nowhere is life squandered so recklessly. Blind urges, demanding gratification and fulfillment, draw no distinction between life and death."[5]

From a certain point of view, one which is crucial for the interpretation of the novel, the human community is a bird cliff and all men are *svartfugl*: here are two symbols for man's unregenerate animal nature. There is an ever-present possibility of civilized life reverting to this dimension, this lowest common denominator. This is the crime of Bjarni and Steinun. Judge Scheving finds the crime unforgivable precisely because he is so afraid of this tendency in himself. Eiulv too has this element in himself:

"Don't do it," Amor Jonsson answered. "Let it alone. Every bird has to fly on its own wings. But I can believe that you're getting dizzy—in the midst of the dark birds."

Eiulv at his most pessimistic even wonders whether mankind's desire for truth is anything more than one of the "blind urges" of the bird cliff.

Faith in truth's strength and triumph, in its grace and its curative powers—at that moment it ebbed from me. Truth! Was not the need for truth one more of the thirsty werwolves of the mind? One of the most insidious, possibly . . . Truth!

[5] *Íslenzk Bókmenntasaga 1750–1950* (Reykjavík: 1962), p. 104.

Was it not also one of existence's dark, hoarse, voracious vultures? Was not its law, like that of the rest of life—to multiply and destroy? . . .

The bird cliff, then, is a symbol for human life at its animal level: for a world which is beyond good and evil, since it is too primitive to distinguish between them, and has no conception of guilt and innocence. For this reason it is important to remember that the Alcids are parti-colored birds, both black and white, both guilty and innocent, "a white-shining, black-sparkling cloud," as Eiulv describes them. Their nature is both black and white, and it is Eiulv's triumph to perceive and understand this fact. Scheving gets no farther than their name—*svartfugl*— "black birds"—and assumes, literalist that he is, that their nature is unrelievedly black.

And in fact, perhaps the central theme of the book is how different psychological types react to the events and personalities at Syvendeaa, to the element in human nature which is symbolized by the bird cliffs. The spectrum of possible reactions is furnished by three characters: the narrator Eiulv, his ecclesiastical superior Jon Ormsson, and Judge Scheving.

What chiefly characterizes the reaction of the Reverend Jon Ormsson is its non-reactiveness. His is a simple and unexamined faith, which retains its stability only because it is constantly in flight from any real contact with the darker aspects of life. He cannot stand being home when one of his cows has to be slaughtered: by fleeing from violence he denies its existence. "He did not want to know." This ostrich-like refusal to notice anything unpleasant also characterizes his view of morals: "In the Reverend Jon's world there was no real sin. Human beings were children —at the worst, full of bad habits." He wants at all costs to avoid finding out anything evil about human nature, looking into its depths—which is what both Eiulv and Scheving, in their quite different ways, have a calling and compulsion to do. And what of the Reverend Jon's theology?

Its poles are "the Trinity . . . in cloaks of heavenly blue and crowned with suns" and "a cheerful hairy devil, horned and with a tongue of fire," the innocuous pantheon of Icelandic folklore. Whatever God and the Devil may be, they are certainly not this. There is nothing in the Reverend Jon's spiritual or psychological arsenal which can help him face the trouble at Syvendeaa: " . . . piety and childish faith are one thing; something quite different is the icy blast of lonely death." The indictment against the Reverend Jon does not end with this charge of looking the other way. There is more—and worse. The moral cowardice of look-the-other-way leads directly to the practical cowardice of let-well-enough-alone, which soon embroils the Reverend Jon in a concrete dereliction of duty and makes him partly responsible for events at Syvendeaa. Nothing in the book is more touching than the way in which Gudrun, with typical Icelandic shyness and indirection, tries to suggest to Reverend Jon that she is deeply troubled; nothing more appalling than the way in which he wilfully ignores her feeble SOS. If he had listened to her, she might never have been murdered—or if he had gone on a "pastoral visit" to Syvendeaa (as he should have done) when the rumors of adultery became widespread. It is entirely appropriate that Reverend Jon should stand between Bjarni and Steinun when their sentence is read, guilty along with them, convicted along with them.

Judge Gudmund Scheving and Eiulv Kolbeinsson, the narrator, are also guilty and convicted, though the former refuses to acknowledge this fact and writhes and twists his way through the book in order to avoid facing it, while the latter's recognition of it is his greatest triumph and our pledge for his reliability. Scheving and Eiulv stand at the center of the book, its two protagonists, struggling over the meaning of Bjarni's tragedy, perhaps over his soul itself. It is no accident that one of them is a judge and the other a priest, for they are judge and priest par excellence: one is the letter which killeth, the other the spirit which giveth life. For Eiulv, to understand all is to forgive all; for Scheving, to collect all the evidence is to pronounce judgment. Eiulv is humility, Scheving is pride. And ultimately—and most significantly—Eiulv is faith, and Scheving is doubt.

Gudmund Scheving is a complicated and ambiguous character precisely because he is trapped in his own inner inconsistencies, doubts, and fears, harrowed by his own private *angst*. Unlike the Reverend Jon, he suspects what sort of forces operate beneath the veneer of civilization in other men and in himself. For this reason he is all the more determined to control these forces, and a rigid legality is the sort of control he finds most satisfactory. The forces he fears are the forces of chaos: the mutability, inconstancy, and flux of all things in the world, including human love and motivation. "I wasn't born yesterday," he says. "Man's motives . . . Chaos, I give you my word. Chaos that even the Devil himself couldn't find his way through." He cannot bear the thought that the world is a bird cliff and that all men are *svartfugl*. He is tormented by man's inability to escape from his animality. "We have to die—all of us—like what we are *not*: men." He has the materialist's genuine horror of his materialistic world and a desperate yearning for something better. By the end of the book Eiulv has come to understand him thoroughly, as shown by his reflections upon all men's desire for constancy: "Everybody, everybody seeks it. Even the Unbelievers, who, like Gudmund Scheving . . . have no hope that God is anything else but man's dream of constancy which they yearn for with every fiber, and find nowhere." Scheving is by turns irreverent, coarse, heartless, wisecracking, irascible, temperamental, bullying—"a capricious man." But is all this caprice anything more than a desperate dance on the edge of the abyss of his own human nature, which Scheving is afraid to look into because he knows it is full of demons? And his attitude of moral bravado, his cocky pose of being beyond good and evil—is it not more of the same? It is easy to understand why he feels threatened by Bjarni and consequently hates him: Bjarni's behavior suggests that human motivation is fate or chance, something for which you cannot be arraigned; that the demons will sometimes rise from the abyss of their own free will without even being conjured. Both Bjarni and Steinun contend that they are not really guilty: somehow it all just "happened," as in a dream. "I had the bad luck to kill Jon Thorgrimsson," says Bjarni. Such a doctrine is anathema for Scheving, who must always be able to point to someone who is to blame, who has made a conscious decision to do evil. This is why he acts in such a "malignant and threatening" and merciless way towards Bjarni: he is unable to tolerate the ambiguity of the situation. A murderer must be completely black and his crime must be premeditated. The actual death of Jon, with its chancy elements, its Gordian knot of who is to blame and for what, goes against Scheving's need for clarity and order: hence he insists, somewhat hysterically, on the stabbing and on premeditation. He rejects Eiulv's suggestion that Gudrun died of fright, not of strangulation, for the same reason.

It is also fairly clear that Scheving projects his own fantasies onto Bjarni: objectifies in Bjarni what he finds most frightening in himself, sentences it, executes it.

"The like of that cold-blooded, stupid, nerveless animal . . . He went ahead and stabbed the man down, no matter how the hell he carries on about it. And then he buries him—over across from the farmyard. And then sleeps the whole winter with his wife—wall to wall with the corpse, so to speak. And bed to bed with his own wife."

The sexual excitement and revulsion in these thoughts, in this way of looking at things, is Scheving's and not Bjarni's. Hence Scheving's great concern and alarm about the fact that Bjarni and Steinun have engendered fantasy, have conjured up the demons:

"It pretty nearly seems to me, that even more horrible than what has been done are the fantasies which the suspicions about it have awakened. The black thoughts and dreams that have been aroused can be washed away by only one thing. The two must die. I almost said: whether they killed or not."

How enormously threatening Scheving finds Bjarni—threatening precisely because he awakens a sympathetic stirring in the badly ordered chaos inside Scheving himself—is indicated by this speech to Eiulv:

"How have you been able to live in that hell—in that fire of fiendishness and malice—month after month," he whispered. "It's a riddle to me . . . You aren't infected yourself yet—are you?" he asked, and inspected me closely. There was a certain hidden fear in his piercing, not quite certain, eyes. "I'll tell you—for my part I am pretty near to getting—desperate . . . I try to—amuse myself. To keep it at a distance . . . My head's swimming, right at the moment. This whole hopeless confusion of guilt and shame and terror . . . It's more than a man can breathe in . . . They must die."

I would like to point, finally, to a very revealing moment in the depiction of this man whose God is a "dream of constancy," a rigid, legalistic deity made in his own image. Bjarni tells how after he had killed Jon Thorgrimsson, Steinun seemed angry with him. He could not understand this. " 'I asked God about it often.' Judge Scheving dropped his fist when Bjarni mentioned the name of God. He sat biting his lips, silent as a stone." He finds the remark blasphemous: God's name on a murderer's lips! Yet murderers too are God's children, and any viable concept of God must be broad enough to embrace Bjarni and Steinun. Let us hope it is also broad enough to embrace Scheving himself, for if we adopt the *Rubaiyat's* definition of hell as "the Shadow from a Soul on fire" then Gudmund Scheving is in hell. "Salvation and damnation are not something outside," not something external to a man. "Salvation and damnation are in you yourself."

Eiulv Kolbeinsson is perhaps not in heaven—not, certainly, in Reverend Jon's tinseled heaven—but he is probably as close to heaven as man, with his two feet planted in the dung of the bird cliffs, can ever get in this life. Putting the story in the mouth of a priest was a masterstroke on Gunnarsson's part. For even if there is much self-doubt in Eiulv, he never once has any doubt about God, not even on the night before Bjarni's confession: "That night was like an abyss of misery, through whose impenetrable darkness faith and hope glimmered only faintly, like distant stars" Their glimmer may be faint, but for Eiulv it is never in doubt. Consequently he supplies a strong center of faith, a ground tone of optimism, against which are counterpointed the ghastly events of the story and the doubt of Gudmund Scheving.

Eiulv is a great self-doubter. Like most really good people he is entirely unconscious of his own goodness. He is humble and self-deprecating, frequently complaining about his "impotence." Though he has had fifteen years to reflect upon his and other people's behavior, his modesty keeps him from recognizing that in the year 1802 he reached his maturity and was changed—by his implication in events and implication with people—from a passive and withdrawing spectator of life into a strenuous participant. From the outset he realizes that Reverend Jon is acting irresponsibly in not investigating the rumors from Syvendeaa, but he half hopes that his superior's refusal to accept responsibility will excuse his own. He is curious but wants to remain uninvolved: "I was willing to listen, but not to become involved." Finally he is forced by events and his own deepening involvement in them to accept the "spiritual responsibility" which his superior has abdicated and write the momentous letter to Gudmund Scheving.

He will never entirely get over a feeling of guilt for having stood by idly at the beginning; and even doing his duty turns out to make him feel guilty. He is in fact guilt-prone. Yet in spite of all of this he changes from a spectator to a participant: his growing self-confidence and his sense of being responsible for Bjarni to God lead him to such dizzying heights of activity as suborning the court reporter and leaving Bjarni and Steinun alone together on the night before their confession. He has a feeling, justified by the event, that this will induce them to tell the truth; so his action is practical. Yet at the same time it is the kindest thing anyone does in the book, one of the *only* kind things. Eiulv Kolbeinsson has become a man who knows what to do.

Furthermore, his experiences in 1802 and the years following are Eiulv's initiation into life, into the intricacies of his own character and that of his fellow men. His great discovery is that he is Bjarni and that Bjarni is he. It takes a remark of Steinun's—a curious moment when she speaks to Eiulv as if to herself—to make him realize that all men are one man and that this man's feet are planted on the bird cliffs:

> Her fate, as it had developed and would develop, touched mine. Was woven together with mine. Were all men's fates woven together? Was a man blind if he did not see this? Insensitive if he did not feel it? . . . Yes, that was it. I knew that suddenly . . . And there I stood—in the midst of a threatening, endless blackness. In the midst of blood and horror and the numbing tolling of a sinful heart.

And yet this conviction has been growing on him gradually. He has a remarkable ability to empathize with others. He sees others in himself, an introjecting tendency which sets him poles apart from Scheving, the projector, who sees himself in others. Yet there is more than mere empathy and introjection: there is something concrete. Eiulv's own experiences put him in a position to understand Bjarni, to identify with him, to be his "secret sharer" very much in the sense of Conrad's novel of this title. There is a strange bond between them from the moment of their first meeting: "The man meant something to me—there was no mistaking that." Like Bjarni, Eiulv has had the experience of coveting—and stealing—his neighbor's wife. That is the whole point of the courtship episode in which Eiulv takes Olof from his brother Pall. Eiulv himself has known "smouldering yearning, vague fears, new hate. And new, ungovernable love." He has seen the jealousy and reproach in his brother's eyes just as Bjarni saw it in Jon Thorgrimsson's. He has hurt his brother—and Bjarni killed his brother man. Eiulv's momentary identification of himself with Cain is no accident. In view of these factors—Eiulv's empathy and his own parallel experiences— it is hardly surprising that he should have "a vague feeling of complicity" and should devote all his energies to unravelling the knot of Bjarni's guilt. Nor is it any wonder that Bjarni is simultaneously afraid of Eiulv and drawn to make him his confidant. "I have always known that I have a friend in you, Eiulv. Only I didn't know—what a terrible friend . . ." It is interesting to note that Eiulv finally sets to work recording the events of 1802 on the day of his own son's death fifteen years later. It is as if the final piece of his puzzling relationship with Bjarni has fallen into place, as if perfect identification and understanding are now possible. For it was over the coffin of Bjarni's own two sons that Eiulv first made the acquaintance of this man who "touched my heart more than I can say: it was just like being put eye to eye with your fate . . ."

Returning once more to the antithesis between Eiulv and Scheving, between faith and doubt, we notice that opposed to Scheving's rejection of life the way it is—a rejection rooted in despair of anything better—there is Eiulv's acceptance. He cannot in the last analysis wish that things were different. Crossing the hills behind Rødesand on his way to the trial he muses:

"Was it possible for me to bargain with God so that Bjarni and Steinun, and the two who were dead—oh, all those dead —were just a product of my imagination? . . . No, it was not possible for me. Anything but that."

And whereas, for Scheving, the penalty for rejecting life is doubt and darkness, for Eiulv the reward of acceptance is faith and illumination:

I stopped and caught my breath. The sea down below was black, with sparks of gold. Where I stood was a steep, glistening slope, dizzyingly high but still with cliffs towering over me. Suddenly a feeling of joy, of dark, hot joy rose in me. God had put me in a difficult post. I would not betray Him. Intoxicated with the cliffs, the freezing cold, and the night-dark sea I went on. But now with God at my side.

I V

We come finally to a consideration of the murderers and their victims. And here Gunnarsson himself supplies us with a useful point of departure, in remarks which go a long way toward explaining why the murderers are sunlit and attractive people while their victims are shadowy and repellant.

Every time I remembered sailing along Skor Cliffs—and recollection of that day popped up often enough from the depths of my mind—I would see the luckless couple before my eyes. It was somehow as if Bjarni and Steinun had their place in the sunlight, in spite of everything. True enough, the sunlight over Syvendeaa was not like other sunlight, or so it seemed in remembrance: it had the beauty of sorrow, as befits an abandoned farmstead and a wasteland of lost and vanished life. But it was sunlight nonetheless, and the light of the sun is never completely joyless. Love is love, even in sorrow and murder. Criminals are human beings. And not only that: they are often far from being mere scoundrels, but men who have somehow become entrapped in crime.

Sometimes, through fog and drizzling rain, I would catch a dim glimpse of Gudrun Egilsdottir and Jon Thorgrimsson. I assume that there are all kinds of weather on Barðaströnd, just as everywhere else—and rough weather was the habitat of those two. The enchanted storm which destroyed them had swallowed them up forever: not even the blessed sun was strong enough to release them from the enchantment, the injustice which had been perpetrated against their innocence. It is hard to exaggerate the inequity of life. Did the two of them never enjoy the sun? Yes, doubtless—like all other human beings who live and breathe. But the shadow of the sacrificial knife often falls most blackly on the victim. It is true enough that the happiness of Bjarni and Steinun was not unmixed and that the block and the cairn lay in wait for them, but nonetheless there was radiance playing about them—the sorrowful light of guilty love; the longing for happiness, which drew them from the beaten path; stolen pleasure, for which they paid the full price.

Like Conrad's Lord Jim, Bjarni is "one of us": not an unpleasant misfit, not an inherently criminal type. It is this fact which implicates us in his crime and traps us so firmly in the moral problems of the book. Bjarni is impulsive and open—"headstrong, dumb"—the sort of man who is adored by children. Tested to the uttermost, however, he loses his moral balance: the loss of his "farmers" crushes him, leaves him "alone in the world." After their deaths he suffers through "two long years," and then Steinun enters his life. She is attractive in much the same way as he, with her "calm steady glance, strong and silent." They are beautiful people. They "deserve" to be lovers and to be happy. The pathos of "what might have been"—that old delusion —is never far from their consciousness. As Bjarni puts it, "The unlucky thing was that Steinun and I didn't meet each other when we were young."

Unfortunately, when young they married two lesser beings who have since clouded their lives and deprived them of sunlight. Self-pity is the strongest element in both Gudrun Egilsdottir and Jon Thorgrimsson. Bjarni's wife is a grumbling hypochondriac, a hysterical woman who thinks the world has cheated her completely and is perpetually ready to blame and complain. Steinun's husband is weak and pathetic, crabby, grouchy: "Jon Thorgrimsson didn't amount to much—in any way." It is clear that the unpleasant atmosphere at Syvendeaa is the creation of these two: the quarreling and wrangling, the fear and suspicion, the fright and despair, which have impressed themselves so deeply on that grotesque threesome of hostile, withdrawn children. The character of Gudrun and Jon—and the pestilential atmosphere of Syvendeaa, "isolated and invisible" —is amply suggested at the trial by the long string of witnesses. And there is more: with striking psychological insight, Gunnarsson suggests that the idea of adultery occurred to Gudrun and Jon long before it occurred to Bjarni and Steinun, that the fact of adultery was simply an inevitable result of the projection, the diseased and self-pitying imagination, of Gudrun and Jon. Bjarni in his simplicity has only a dim inkling of all this:

"They knew about it?"

"No, they didn't know anything . . . but they noticed something . . . they couldn't miss it I guess . . . Long before there was anything—they seemed to notice something. It was as though they pushed us into it."

"Long before there was anything, you say . . . Are you sure of that?"

"Oh yes; I know what I'm talking about. Because it was that—that caused . . ."

"Caused what?"

"No, it doesn't matter," Bjarni murmured tiredly. "I can't work it out anyhow. I never could."

It is not surprising, therefore, the Bjarni and Steinun should claim that fate came upon them from outside, that they were not to blame for what happened. They are curiously united in this. Steinun cries:

"I'm—simply not like . . . like everybody must believe. I've done—terrible harm . . . But I'm not like that . . . It just all—happened..."

And Bjarni says:

"I decided to kill him. I made up my mind. I talked a lot with Steinun about it."

"You were agreed?"

"We were agreed, yes . . . For a while we almost didn't talk about anything else. It was—it was like a dream."

"A dream? What do you mean?"

"Yes—I can't explain it . . . But we talked so much about it. I'd really made up my mind . . . I think."

So Bjarni and Steinun attempted to disperse the clouds which had gathered about them, to wrestle from life the sunlight which each man believes to be his inalienable right, to snatch happiness. And for a while they did achieve happiness and "there was radiance playing about them." But in the end . . . "Happiness—you don't get it with a hard hand, Eiulv," Steinun acknowledges ruefully.

v

"What was evil, what was good?" Eiulv asks. The question is still unanswered at the end of the book, which is not after all a moral treatise but a study in character and psychology. On the other hand, from its study of character emerges a very clear hint for practical morality. Opposed to Bjarni's occasionally (and Scheving's uninterruptedly) pessimistic view of life as a bird cliff ("We cannot help one another—we can only kill one another") there is throughout the book a continuing reaffirmation of the moral of Gunnarsson's earlier novel *Seven Days' Darkness:* men ought to be good to one another. But here this moral is not simply a dry text: it is incarnate in the person and actions of Eiulv Kolbeinsson—just as Gunnarsson's earlier, despairing attitude after the First World War is incarnate in the person and actions of Gudmund Scheving. To be able to see one's former psychological state objectively, to embody it in a fictional character, to grasp it in its entirety—this is the certain criterion of having advanced beyond it. The character of Eiulv shows how far Gunnarsson has come. "Our inner peace depends on the dreams we have," Eiulv says—"on the kind of life dream that is ours." For

Eiulv life is a dream of heaven, for Scheving a dream of hell. And what after all, asks the *Rubaiyat,* is

> Heav'n but the vision of fulfill'd Desire,
> And Hell the Shadow from a Soul on fire?

We project our own inner certainty or doubt, our own madness or sanity, on the universe.

Eiulv is not like the priest in *The Shores of Life,* who, curiously enough, formulates his doubt and despair in bird imagery very like that of *The Black Cliffs:*

> He heard a gull shriek and the next instant he saw a solitary gull winging above the fjord, heading out to sea.
> "Searching gull," he said. "Searching gull, what do you see in the deep? Do you understand the meaning of life, oh bird of prey with your cold heart, your vigilant eyes, your insatiable greed? Do you understand the meaning of life? Is the deep not deep?—and life not life?—and death not death? Your only reply is a shriek—ask a foolish question and get a foolish answer! On you fly, and your questioner keeps on asking: What do you see, searching gull?"
> And as he stood there all at once it seemed to him that he himself was a gull in flight.

The voice which poses these unanswerable questions is weak and hysterical, and the interrogator loses his mind when no answer is forthcoming. Eiulv asks the questions in a firmer voice, and though he too receives no reply, he understands, as Gunnarsson himself had come to understand, that "mankind is one soul and one body, that our mutual involvement is unavoidable, our mutual responsibility total," and that even in the silence—even here on the bird cliffs—he and all men dwell in the peace of God.

RICHARD N. RINGLER

Madison, 1967

BIBLIOGRAPHY

BY GUNNAR GUNNARSSON

Collective Editions

Rit Gunnars Gunnarssonar (Writings of Gunnar Gunnarsson). 21 vols. Reykjavík: Útgáfufélagið landnáma, 1941-62.

Skáldverk (Works). 19 vols. Reykjavík: Almenna bókafélagið, Helgafell, 1960-63.

Individual Works

Vorljóð (Songs of Spring). Akureyri: Oddur Björnsson, 1906. (Poems).

Móðurminning. Nokkur kvæði (Remembering Mother. Some Poems). Akureyri: Oddur Björnsson, 1906.

Digte (Poems). Copenhagen: V. Pio, 1911. There are English translations of several of these poems in *The Locomotive* (Copenhagen), IX (1913), 51-53, 115 and XX (1914), 51 f.

Sögur (Stories). Reykjavík: A. Sveinbjarnarson, 1912. There is a translation by Jacob Wittmer Hartmann of "Rauði fossinn" ("The Red Fall") in *The International,* X (1916), 43, 63, and of "Systurnar" ("The Sisters") *ibid.,* 319-20.

Ormarr Ørlygsson. Af Borgslægtens Historie [I]. Copenhagen: Gyldendal, 1912. (Novel.)

Den danske Frue paa Hof (The Danish Lady at Hof). Af

Borgslægtens Historie [II]. Copenhagen: Gyldendal, 1913. (Novel.)

Gæst den enøjede (Guest the One-Eyed). Af Borgslægtens Historie [III]. Copenhagen: Gyldendal, 1913. (Novel.)

Den unge Ørn (The Young Eagle). Af Borgslægtens Historie [IV]. Copenhagen: Gyldendal, 1914. (Novel.)

Borgslægtens Historie (The History of the Family at Borg). Collective edition of the four novels cited above. Copenhagen: Gyldendal, 1915. English (abridged): *Guest the One-Eyed*, tr. by W. W. Worster. London: Gyldendal, [1920]; New York: Knopf, 1922.

Livets Strand (The Shore of Life). Copenhagen. Gyldendal, 1915. (Novel.)

Smaa Historier (Short Stories). Copenhagen: Gyldendal, 1916. This is a Danish translation, with substitutions and additions, of *Sögur* (1912). Two of these stories have been translated into English: "De mørke Bjerge" ("The Dark Mountains") by W. W. Worster, in *Denmark's Best Stories*, ed. Hanna Astrup Larsen. New York: Norton, 1928, pp. 363–77; and "Kirke findes der intet Spor af" ("And of the Church not a trace") by Mekkin Sveinson Perkins, in *The American-Scandinavian Review*, XXV (1937), 67–70.

Varg i Veum (A Wolf in the Sanctuary). Copenhagen: Gyldendal, 1916. (Novel.)

Smaa Skuespil (Short Plays). Copenhagen: Gyldendal, 1917.

Drengen (The Boy). Copenhagen: Gyldendal, 1917. (Novella.)

Smaa Historier. Ny Samling (Short Stories. A New Collection). Copenhagen: Gyldendal, 1918. "Da likkan gik J. J. Snóksdal forbi" ("Fortune passes by") has been translated by W. W. Worster in *The American-Scandinavian Review*, XII (1924), 475–83.

Edbrødre: Roman fra Islands Landnamstid (The Sworn Brothers: A Novel from the Time of the Settlement of Iceland). Copenhagen: Gyldendal, 1918. English: *The*

Sworn Brothers. A Tale of the Early Days of Iceland, tr. by C. Field and W. Emmé. London: Gyldendal, [1920]; New York: Knopf, 1921.

Salige er de enfoldige (Blessed are the Poor in Spirit). Copenhagen: Gyldendal, 1920. (Novel.) English: *Seven Days' Darkness,* tr. by Roberts Tapley. New York: Macmillan, 1930; London: G. Allen and Unwin, 1931.

Ringen. Syv Historier (The Ring. Seven Stories). Copenhagen: Gyldendal, 1921.

Dyret med Glorien (The Beast with the Halo). Copenhagen: Gyldendal, 1922. (Dramatic poem.)

Den glade Gaard og andre Historier (The Merry Farm and Other Stories). Copenhagen: Gyldendal, 1923.

Leg med Straa (Playing with Straws). Af Uggi Greipssons Optegnelser [I] *(From Uggi Greipsson's Notes).* Copenhagen: Gyldendal, 1923. (Novel.) English: see *Skibe paa Himlen,* below.

Skibe paa Himlen (Ships in the Sky). Af Uggi Greipssons Optegnelser [II]. Copenhagen: Gyldendal, 1925. (Novel.) English: *Ships in the Sky,* tr. by E[velyn]. R[amsden]. Indianapolis: Bobbs-Merrill, [1938]; London: Jarrolds, [1938]. This title includes both *Leg med Straa* and *Skibe paa Himlen.*

Natten og Drømmen (The Night and the Dream). Af Uggi Greipssons Optegnelser [III]. Copenhagen: Gyldendal, 1926. (Novel.) English: see *Hugleik den Haardtsejlende,* below.

Den uerfarne Rejsende (The Inexperienced Traveller). Af Uggi Greipssons Optegnelser [IV]. Copenhagen: Gyldendal, 1927. (Novel.) English: see *Hugleik den Haardtsejlende,* below.

Det nordiske Rige (The Nordic Domain). Copenhagen: Gyldendal, 1927. (Speeches.)

Hugleik den Haardtsejlende (Hugleik the Hard-Sailing). Af Uggi Greipssons Optegnelser [V]. Copenhagen: Gyldendal, 1928. (Novel.) English: *The Night and the Dream,* tr. by Evelyn Ramsden. Indianapolis: Bobbs-

Merrill, [1938]; London: Jarrolds, [1938]. Under this title are translated *Natten og Drømmen, Den uerfarne Rejsende,* and *Hugleik den Haardtsejlende.*

En Dag til overs og andre Historier (A Vacant Day and Other Stories). Copenhagen: Gyldendal, 1929.

Svartfugl (The Alcids). Copenhagen: Gyldendal, 1929. (Historical novel.)

Rævepelsene, eller Ærlighed varer længst: Komedie i fire Akter (The Foxes, or Honesty Wins in the End: A Play in Four Acts). Copenhagen: Gyldendal, 1930. (A play based upon *Bandamanna saga.*)

Jón Arason. Copenhagen: Gyldendal, 1930. (Historical novel.)

Verdens Glæder: En Tylft Historier (This World's Pleasures: A Dozen Stories). Copenhagen: Gyldendal, 1931.

Vikivaki: Jake Sonarsons efterladte Papirer (Vikivaki: Jake Sonson's Posthumous Papers). Copenhagen: Gyldendal, 1932. (Novel.)

Jord (Land). Copenhagen: Gyldendal, 1933. (Historical novel.)

De Blindes Hus (The House of the Blind). Copenhagen: Gyldendal, 1933. (Novella.)

Hvide-Krist (The White-Christ). Copenhagen: Gyldendal, 1934. (Novella.)

Sagaøen (The Saga-Island). Copenhagen: Martin, 1935. (Illustrated history.)

Graamand (Grey Man). Copenhagen: Gyldendal, 1936. (Historical novel.)

Advent. Copenhagen: Gyldendal, 1937. (Novella.) English: *Advent,* tr. by E. C. Ramsden. London: Jarrolds, [1939]; *The Good Shepherd,* tr. by Kenneth C. Kaufman. Indianapolis: Bobbs-Merrill, 1940.

Trylle og andet Smaakram (Trylle and Other Trifles). Copenhagen: Gyldendal, 1939. (Animal stories.) English: *Trylla, and Other Small Fry,* tr. by Evelyn Ramsden. London: Hutchinson, [1947].

Heiðaharmur (Sorrow on the Moors) [Urðarfjötur I]. Reyk-

javík: Menningar- og fræðslusamband alþýðu, 1940.
(Historical novel.) Danish: *Brandur paa Bjarg: Roman
fra Island.* Copenhagen: Gyldendal, 1942.
Ferðafélag Íslands: Árbók 1944: Fljótsdalshérað. [Reyk-
javík: 1945]. (Travel book.)
Árbók 45 (Yearbook for 1945). Reykjavík: Helgafell, 1945.
(Poems, essays, and short stories.)
Árbók 46–47 (Yearbook for 1946–47). Reykjavík: Helgafell,
1948. (Essays and short stories.)
Sálumessa (Requiem Mass). Urðarfjötur II. Reykjavík:
Útgáfufélagið landnáma, 1952. (Historical novel.) Dan-
ish: *Sjælemesse.* Copenhagen: Gyldendal, 1953.
Brimhenda (Sonata by the Sea). Reykjavík: Helgafell, 1954.
(Novella.) Danish: *Sonate ved Havet.* [Copenhagen]:
Gyldendal, 1955.

ABOUT GUNNAR GUNNARSSON

Bibliography

Sigurðsson, Haraldur. *Skrá um bækur Gunnars Gunnars-
sonar á íslenzku og erlendum málum. . . . Sérprentun úr
Ritum Gunnars Gunnarssonar XXI.* Reykjavík: 1962.
Also in *Skáldverk XIX.* Reykjavík. Almenna bókafélagið,
Helgafell, 1963.

Biography and Criticism

Andrésson, Kristinn E. *Íslenzkar nútímabókmenntir 1918-
1948.* Reykjavík: Mál og menning, 1949. Swedish: *Det
moderna Islands Litteratur 1918-1948,* tr. by Rannveig
and Peter Hallberg. Stockholm: Kooperativa förbundets
bokförlag, 1955. Pp. 147–53.
Arvidson, Stellan. *Gunnar Gunnarsson islänningen.* [Stock-
holm: Seelig,] 1962. Icelandic: *Gunnar Gunnarsson,* tr.
by Jón Magnússon. Reykjavík: Útgáfufélagið landnáma,
1959.

Björnsson, Sigurjón. *Leiðin til skáldskapar. Hugleiðingar um upptök og þróun skáldhneigðar Gunnars Gunnarssonar.* Reykjavík: Bókaútgáfa Menningarsjóðs, 1964.

Einarsson, Stefán. "Gunnar Gunnarsson," *Skírnir,* CXII (1938), 138–60.

————. *A History of Icelandic Literature.* New York: Johns Hopkins Press, 1957. Pp. 285–87. Icelandic (augmented edition): *Íslensk bókmenntasaga 874–1960.* [Reykjavík:] Snæbjörn Jónsson & Co., 1961, Pp. 365–68.

————. *History of Icelandic Prose Writers, 1800–1940.* Ithaca: Cornell University Press, 1948 (*Islandica* XXXII–XXXIII). Pp. 144–52.

Elfelt, Kjeld. *Gunnar Gunnarsson: Et Essay.* Copenhagen: Gyldendal, 1927.

Gelsted, Otto. *Gunnar Gunnarsson.* Copenhagen. P. Haase & Søn, 1926.

Gislason, Bjarni M. *Islands Litteratur efter Sagatiden.* Copenhagen: Aschehoug, 1949. Pp. 79–84.

Hesselaa, Peder. *Essays.* Copenhagen: Gyldendal, 1924. Pp. 9–48.

THE BLACK CLIFFS

For all good men who may chance to see these pages, I, Eiulv Kolbeinsson, humble curate of Saurbaer church in the parish of Rodesand, Bardestrand, invoke God's blessing and my own.

The Lord did upon this day, which is All Saints' Day, Saturday, the first of November in the year of our Lord 1817, to our, his parents', great sorrow and anguish summon to Him Hilarius our son, in the fifteenth year of his life, together with, to our further sorrow, five of our faithful servants, in that the boat in which they had rowed out to the fishing grounds was found washed up on shore, empty.

Lord have mercy upon the dead and give comfort to the living upon whom sorrow bears so heavily, each according to the nature of his heart. And look with compassion upon thy humble servant on the morrow, which is All Souls' Day and the twentieth Sunday after Trinity, that, in the absence of my honored and ailing Dean, I may speak with a clear conscience and in fit and proper piety to my afflicted fellow sufferers and to the other members of the parish on the day's text, Matthew 5, in which is written: Jesus proclaimeth salvation.

My beloved helpmeet Olof said, when her respected uncle, Amor Jonsson, farmer in Hoenevig, with evident sorrow and honest sympathy had reported finding the boat, she said, "The wind and the sea are beyond my reach, but it's a hard thing to have Hilarius drowned like a pup and know that he'll go unavenged."

"On whom would you avenge him, my dear niece?" asked Amor Jonsson, that worthy man.

But I, knowing the impetuosity of my wife in adversity and in prosperity alike, and knowing that she said this only out of the overwhelming bitterness of a mother's pain, I said, "We will speak no more of it."

And we did not.

There were no tears to be seen in my wife's eyes. I saw naked death in her eyes, and I was ashamed. And her good uncle . . . for the first time I realized he was just an ordinary human being, not a wizard at all, saw that his black beard was shot through with gray, and his yellow, visionary eyes weak and wavering. That was when he whispered to his niece after we had sat there a while, silent in our sorrow, "Try to cry, my child."

Olof stood up then, Young Olof, as they called her back home in Keflavig to distinguish her from her mother, Madame Olof, and answered, "I'll save my tears for God; He will have them in full measure."

Then she left. Not for nothing is she Monsieur Jon Palsson's daughter.

But I was not worried about my wife Olof; not even in the inmost reaches of her soul will God, who sees into our hearts, be able to find anything evil or unworthy.

It is worse with me, the poor, confused "Publican," as they used to call me here in the old days, and probably still do call me, my salty, sea-going farmers.

The Reverend Jon Ormsson, in Sauthlauksdal, our Dean, they call "the Sinner." You might imagine from this that they think worse of him than of me. But they do it as a joke. Nobody can be less inclined to sin—unless out of the goodness of his heart—than the Reverend Jon, who will leave his home and wander restlessly among his parish flock, if only for the slaughter of an old cow.

As for me, they mean no harm by calling me the Publican—or maybe harm enough. In any case, they mean it. And the reason is that half the parish tithes and taxes are mine, as the owner of Saurbaer farm and church. That is to say, they are my church's for division between the Dean, the Reverend Jon, and the church. And this much I can say: not a penny of the Lord's money, to say nothing of the Reverend Jon's, have I in any way, at any time, turned to my own advantage. But my old church, which in its day was the principal church in these parts, is not going to suffer, or be slighted, or be paid in false or debased coinage, merely because it is a farmers' church—so help me God! Nor is the Reverend Jon Ormsson, that all too good-hearted man, going to suffer the loss of any part of the tithe for which I am answerable to him.

Am I not supposed to respect the church God has given my unworthy person? If I did not, I would think myself the most miserable creature that ever walked on two legs. Long before I came here the first time, I had seen this church of mine in a dream, been in it with a congregation and alone, even preached in it. And I always woke from the dream in tears. And since I have been here . . . oh, you house of sorrow, house of children, of sinners, and of innocents. Death you have seen, and crime. Murderer and victim. Sin and the wages of sin.

There was nothing I could do to defend my church, buffeted by the storms of souls, but I have served it to the best of my poor ability. With my own hand I painted it so that the candles and the sun would light it twofold, so that the handsome altar piece, the apostles on the pulpit, and the old silver chalices could come into their own. I did it the summer after Hilarius, on that day, the thirteenth of January, was sent to us by God. But it was not just because of that. The truth is, I read for the ministry and took my vows only because I wanted to serve the old house of God that distant, unknown relatives' death had unexpectedly left me as an inheritance—to serve it with my tongue as well as my hand. The Lord has seen my intentions . . . as he has seen my impotence.

Not that I have been in any way remiss with my

church's means.What I could not collect because I let justice wait upon mercy, or because from some bankrupt estate there was nothing to be had, I have regularly made good out of my own pocket, and in hard cash. Verily have I been for Baer church a zealous publican. What men may think or say about that, they themselves will have to answer for. In that respect I have never felt, or had reason to feel, any impotence.

My impotence, God knows, was a good deal more significant than anything like that. It appeared where the matter was not of fish or cloth, but of blood. Not of silver or gold, but of souls. You have seen that, Lord. But until this day, only You.

Are You calling me to judgment now, throwing my only son Hilarius, like a poor plaything, to the elements?

So here I am. Give my hand the strength to strike a spark of truth from the dark stone I carry in my breast.

II

My son Hilarius could have been the victim of worse
forces than the wind and the sea, which are cool and salt,
and still have an honest, fraternal severity. Surely You
knew what was best for him, Lord. What did I know of
his heart?—although his dear heart was for me like the
young morning sun. But no grown man can ever find his
way back into the wilderness of youth. And so palpably
that I ought to remember, You have shown me in due
course how terrible it is to sink beneath the blood's dark
waves.

No one could have been less fit to find himself standing
in the midst of hard and terrible events than I was fifteen
years ago, young and inexperienced, a boy in his twenties
two years ordained. And a newlywed—such arrangements
had been made for my marriage.

How shall I begin? Shall I begin with Bjarni of Syvendeaa? Or with my brother Pall? Or with myself? No, let
me begin with Amor Jonsson, the wizard . . . Still, it has to
be Bjarni.

I had never met a man like Bjarni, nor have I since, his
yellow, curly beard fluttering in the spring breeze, and his
blue eyes sparkling as though made of pure crushed crys-
tal . . . standing there tall and powerful, a creature rolled
from the blue of the skies and bright cloud banks . . .
standing there beside the rude little coffin he had come
with, a short, wide box—a strange receptacle for death.

He touched my heart more than I can say: it was just
like being put eye to eye with your fate. And it may have

been that what I thought was spontaneous affection was nothing but a tick in my mind, a danger signal. But one thing was certain, the man meant something to me—there was no mistaking that. And so I stood there across from him, beardless, a newly ordained curate—almost a minister. And that was my first encounter with the practical business of my calling.

What a day that was. One of these new spring days with few clouds in the heavens and the broad fjord blue-black beyond our red shoreline. Why cannot a life like Bjarni's be encapsulated in one such day, such a blessed day of sorrow and light? Why? And yet the day still lives, as it once lived. Lives in me, transitory publican. Should it live less and more faintly in God's eternal heart? But then . . . the other days. The then still-unborn days. Those days . . . And I stand here as before, with bloody knuckles at a wall of darkness.

The day that Bjarni of Syvendeaa, with his yellow beard and his blue eyes, came wandering into my existence, that day I will remember as long as I live. I can not only feel it in the depths of my heart, I can even feel its sun on my skin. For it was one of those days of youth when the painful joy of living gnaws at you, when promise and fulfillment empty and fill the heart like the ebb and flood tides.

"It's an odd coffin." It burst out of me as though I were still a boy, and not an ordained minister at all.

The strange farmer looked at me carefully. "Are you our new curate? What's your name now?"

I acted as though I had not heard him. "Whom do you have in the coffin?" I asked solemnly—for even if it were the remains of a bed-ridden cripple and the body couldn't be straightened out, even if it were some poor legless torso, I thought it not very proper of the big farmer to pinch pennies on the lumber.

The golden-bearded giant was in no hurry to tell me.

"My name is Bjarni Bjarnason—I'm a farmer at Syvendeaa here in the parish," he replied formally. He had put

8

down the coffin on one of the little green mounds in the churchyard, on one of the graves. "The ones I've got in the box, they're my farmers . . . That's what I called them. Their names were Bjarni and Egill, seven and eight years old. They caught cold a few days ago . . . My wife, now, she's coughed ever since we've been married, and that was eleven years ago. But the boys here, they died all at once. Children are children . . . and it's only practice makes perfect. You mustn't think it was to save money I put them in one coffin . . . It doesn't hurt anything, does it?"

"Certainly not," I said, ashamed.

"Well, that was the . . . Will you let them stay in the church until Sunday?"

Although I had been told that there was a man outside with a dead body, I had forgotten to take the church key with me. I ran in to get it, ran. For by now I had forgotten that I was any kind of minister.

When Bjarni started to put the box down in the middle of the church, I stopped him and gave him to understand that he should put it in the choir—right in front of the altar.

"That's only for my betters," he objected.

"This is my church," I said.

He looked at me then a long time . . . Afterwards he sat down in one of the pews, pulled his cap off, and sighed heavily. And at the same time surreptitiously, the way you sigh in a house where there is someone you are reluctant to wake.

I sat down, too. When we had sat a while in silence, I asked, "You have several children, Bjarni?"

"Uhhuh . . . I've got one more boy—Gisli—he's six," Bjarni answered, without taking his eyes from the coffin. "But it's a funny thing with him. You never see him. He's always down at the shore. You've known kids like that, they can't stay away from the ocean—until they end up in it."

How often I was to remember these words of Bjarni.

He went on. "And I've got the two daughters . . . girls."

9

What was I to reply to that? What could I say? The man had obviously lost what he felt was his world, his farmers.

When we finally left the church, he gave a troubled glance back—asked: "The Reverend Jon'll come Sunday, I hope?"

"As far as I know," I answered, a little offended.

But as I was turning the key in the lock, I already regretted my heedlessness. And to Bjarni, who had seated himself on the churchyard wall, who was sitting and looking toward the door, breaking off one grass stalk after another and chewing them slowly, I said, "Come along in and have something to eat, Bjarni."

He did not hear me, until I touched his shoulder and repeated my invitation. Then he went along. As though in his sleep.

Only when he had eaten—in silence, while I watched him—did it seem as though he woke up.

"I could dig the grave right now, you know," he said, getting up with relief. "Then that'd be done."

I followed him out. South of the church I showed him a place—his boys were going to have all the sun there was. And besides, the water at flood tide came stealing in over the shallows, nearly encircling that part of the churchyard, enclosing it in polished or hammered silver, depending upon the weather. It is so beautiful. I loaned Bjarni a spade, and I stayed with him while he dug the grave.

When we had laid out the plot I said, "Since they are in one coffin, your boys, you can have the burial plot for twelve alen—the same as for an adult. For two boys at that age, it is normally nine for each," I stammered awkwardly. I had learned all these details carefully. "If they had been a few years younger . . ."

"I'm not that poor a stick," Bjarni broke me off short. "Lay out a plot for twenty-four alen, my farmers are going to lie there free and clear!"

Later I understood that it was, among other things, this

kind of answer that made people call him difficult. And dumb.

The care he took with that grave . . . The sides were smoothed with the spade again and again, and the last of the loose earth at the bottom was scraped together with his bare hands. In one motion he was up without my seeing how he did it; stood and rubbed the dirt off his palms, stood and looked down into the grave, reached for a clump of earth and crumbled it. And rubbed the palms of his hands together again.

"Well now, I'd better get back home to Syvendeaa," he said after a long while—and could not figure out what he had done with his cap.

He looked for it where he had eaten—it was not there. Could he possibly have left it behind in the church?

We found it on the pew where he had sat. Although he had certainly left it there deliberately, or perhaps just for that reason, he hardly looked this time toward the short black coffin that held his farmers.

. . . On Sunday the Reverend Jon Ormsson was held up at the last moment. So I turned out to be the one who came to commit Bjarni's farmers to the dust.

Unasked, I spoke a few words at their coffin.

I said, "I don't know you, you two boys lying here, haven't ever seen you, my small friends. But from your father's bereavement, it's clear to me that you were good boys. And so it is a joy to me to bid you welcome here in this place for God's children, my unknown brothers, my first guests to the grave. May the sorrow that follows men returning to the dust be as pure and simple for every burial to come in Baer churchyard. Then we will all come to rest easy hereafter . . . "

Who could suspect how terrible the words were that God had put into my mouth . . . terrible, for they were as though minted for the grievous events of sin and death which we were later to stand face to face with, right here in my poor house.

III

Not until eighteen months later did rumors begin to spread out from Syvendeaa.

As far as I was concerned, what had happened in the meantime was that I had met the woman, Olof Jonsdottir, of Keflavig, who in that year of fortune and misfortune—1802—became my beloved wife. Woman! Young Olof was at that time still only a child. Like myself. And like Pall, my brother. She was nineteen, Pall twenty, I was twenty-five.

But with her nineteen years, she was her parents' daughter through and through. Which is to say, completely herself.

Unfortunately, it took quite a time before I knew that I was in love with Young Olof. It took all too long. Because when it did finally dawn on me, I had already noticed for some time, and actually approved, my brother Pall's seeking out her company. And they each other's.

She did not need to kiss Pall, as they went by each other on the ice, for me to know that I was not the one she ran a forbidden mile to meet at Stakka Pond, where we tried skating with homemade bone skates. But she made no secret of that part of the game, and once, when I came racing right at them and could not miss seeing it, she called out to me, laughing, "We're nibbling . . ."

I was so heavy-hearted, and I didn't know why. I actually believed it was only because their behavior was offensive to me. To make a joke of kissing—that struck me as the same as singing psalms to a dance tune. These meetings on the ice in the romantic night, in the white moonlight under twinkling golden stars, began gradually to torture me. Before, they had sung within me like lonely, distant music. To skate there with the roaring ocean just beyond, the silent, threatening cliffs behind—it was not only like being separated from your body to live in a poem, a folksong, to live in simple, rhymed stanzas, blissfully reposing in an endless ecstasy. It was like a church service, too. It was as though God's sleeping breath approached you—calmingly, from far out in endless space.

So—I began to stay away from these night games.

But when I did go one evening with Pall, I noticed that he and his friend were continually nibbling. They did nothing but nibble. And then, to my horror, I realized that I hated Pall, my brother. And hated her . . . Yes—I thought I did . . . at any rate, a fury I did not want to acknowledge but which I could barely manage to control threatened to burst my heart.

It was that—that it was just a game with them—that was unbearable for me.

Anyhow, it was obvious to me that my brother was too poor to be able to think of marriage, generally speaking; but specifically too poor to be able to think of being the son-in-law of Monsieur Jon. Not even Young Olof would be able to get him recognized as a son-in-law at Keflavig. The thought was certainly not uncomfortable for me. But still—he was my brother . . . Turn over the farm to him and live on my calling in poverty for God—that I could not do. I simply could not. I dared not. No power on earth could have made me give away the destiny the Lord had prepared for me. But help him with my money, support him while he studied—that I could do. And some of our best bishops had begun poorer than he would be with me behind him. Perhaps this way he could, my brother Pall, approach heights of distinction that I would never reach myself. Yes, and did not seek.

After many doubts and internal struggles whose nu-

13

cleus was an unsolved puzzle within me, I called Pall in one day to see me in my little room where I usually spent the days alone, very much alone, and I introduced the subject. I said, "You're twenty years old, Pall, and you're strong and healthy, thank God . . . But do you ever think about your future, boy?"

"What do you mean by that, brother?" he answered with a glint in his eye—quite untouched by the tension holding me like a vise; apparently even without any suspicion that what was at stake was his life and his happiness.

There was bitterness running through my heart, sharp, black bitterness. He was my brother; Cain's eternal cry—without any real awareness of it on my part—lay unspoken in my mind too. But I controlled myself. And I searched for and found exactly the words I wanted to have spoken. My brother Pall meanwhile stood there with a smile, looking at my books and papers, looking at me, at my cassock hanging on the wall. And when I said nothing he answered, "You think I would fit the black robe, brother?"

What happened to me in that moment I don't know, but from the depths of my being there arose, cruel and secret, an evil relief. Since then I have not hated my brother. But I felt pity, certainly, a disdainful pity. And I answered him this time, gently, and my concern was genuine enough: "What have you thought about your future yourself?"

Then quite suddenly Pall was uneasy. It was a good feeling to see a little human fear in his eyes. He asked, "What do you mean? Can't I stay here? Have you any complaints to make about me as a foreman?"

"Not any," I flared up. "But do you really think it's the kind of a position you can get married on?"

Then Pall turned red behind both ears. I might as well have struck him full in the face. He answered, "Well—there'll be some way to manage it—when the time comes."

"Possibly," I cut in spitefully. It was plain to me that it was not only our ages that stood between us. "But there's

an old saw that you need a strong line for a big fish . . .
But as I was saying, if you should get the idea you want
to read for the ministry I'll support you and help you in
any way possible."

"And I would have to go away?" he asked.

"Unless you can make the seminary come to you, certainly."

"Couldn't you . . . Couldn't you let me have the money
it would cost you—with other conditions?"

"Of course. Any time. With any conditions you want to
set."

Pall left. And I was left alone.

I was so troubled that I sat there with my head in my
hands, not feeling a thing. I could not very well send him
to school against his will. That is what it means to be a
human being, that we are to follow our inmost urges—and
take the consequences. By using my authority as a brother
I could make a minister of Pall, in time. But hardly a man.

As I sat there I began all of a sudden to see Olof before
me—Young Olof. I wanted to go to her—talk with her
about Pall. And I began to talk to her . . . sat there in my
room and talked and talked . . . But soon I forgot that it
was Pall we were supposed to be talking about. Before I
realized it, I was sitting there talking with her about—myself. Speaking the way men never speak with their
tongues. Or in any case not before they come to bliss at
God's throne.

. . . Not long after that we, Olof and I, had our first and
last conversation that summer.

It was a Sunday morning that I saw a boat come flying,
with the sails set as though it were a matter of life or
death or there were a mad man at the tiller. I ran down to
the shore. It was either the luck of the innocent or a mira-
cle; out of the green breakers shot Olof and her boat—it
unharmed, she as soaked as a drowned man.

"I came to listen to you, curate," she called through the
strands of her dripping hair—I was supposed to speak in

the church that day. "I couldn't because of Monsieur my father and Madame my mother. They had to use the horses themselves. So I saddled a sea horse; I took the only boat that I could budge. It wasn't a bad little trip. And so now I have the pleasure of saying hello to Jon Palsson."

She ran on like this as we went together up from the muddy shore. I said not one word.

She began to look at me sideways. But she went on. "I could use a pair of trousers and one of Pall's jerseys. Dry clothes would feel good."

"A good switch would be still better," I said—but that was all, though a good many angry words were burning my lips.

She was silent for a moment and then she burst out, "Is that to be my thanks for risking my life to hear you?"

And then I could no longer control my tongue and answered coldly, "Up to now it hasn't been *my* lips you were sucking honey from."

She turned blood red. And then she fell silent too . . .

I am certain that she showed up in church that day just to irritate people with her men's clothing. And certainly she managed to do it. In any event it couldn't be to hear me, for in the middle of the sermon she left, very stiff-necked. When the service was over it turned out that she had stolen her father's horse from the stall, mounted it astride as if she were still a little girl, and ridden home.

That was in August. After that I did not speak to Young Olof, in fact we hardly saw each other until a good six months later—the day when I got engaged to her; "bought" her, as I said to tease her.

IV

"For you I'd rather do a good turn than a bad one, Eiulv,"
Bjarni of Syvendeaa said to me, pressing my hand, the
day his farmers were buried.

I could find no answer for him. Because a little to one
side stood a stranger, a man with black, smooth hair and
beard and two small golden eyes in a dead-white face
staring steadily at Bjarni and me. Particularly at Bjarni.
The man was dressed in black—tall, slender, very little
like the other farmers and seeming not to belong among
them. I could not take my eyes from a whip of bone and
silver he held in his hand.

Bjarni's wife, Gudrun Egilsdottir, came up to thank me
too, but I could not tell what she said for her crying and
coughing. She was a little woman who the whole time
held her hands over her mouth and coughed, coughed.
In spite of the mild weather she had a woolen scarf over
her head and she was wrapped in shawls. I had to be told
twice before I believed it was Bjarni's wife. The damp
hand she gave me made me involuntarily draw my hand
back. On the whole the woman filled me with a peculiar
sense of uneasiness. And with pity. A pity that transferred
to Bjarni and robbed him of some of my earlier warm
sympathy.

When Bjarni and Gudrun left, the black man came up
to me and gave me his hand. "Greetings to you, young
prophet," he said in a friendly manner—although a little
caustically—and pressed my hand firmly. "My name is
Amor Jonsson—my father, of sinful memory, was a man

17

who always stood by his actions, whatever they were. Welcome to Rodesand."

I stammered my thanks. And in that way and no other I met my first and only friend.

Although friend . . . I will make no secret of the fact that in the beginning I was afraid of Amor Jonsson, more or less. Everytime we met I gave a start, my blood took on another rhythm. When I was with him everything seemed possible. And—everything was possible. But friend . . . He was not honest with me nor I with him. But at any rate he was the only human being who, in the early days, sought me out, who even stayed overnight with me at Baer just to be with me.

But I could never understand him—When was he talking in earnest? When was he joking?—until much later it dawned on me that he never joked.

I remember one Sunday with the afternoon sun low over the fjord and the shore dark red against the white foam of a light swell. We were sitting on the church wall where I had gone with him. His white horse, saddled and bridled, was grazing at our feet.

"How can you possibly warn the people of Rodesand not to build their houses on sand?" said Amor jestingly. "Of the twelve houses here along the shore, eleven of them, among them your own—the church and churchyard included—are built on sand. Built on sand washed up from Bredefjord, with a little layer of dirt. Bjarni of Syvendeaa is the only one of the parish farmers whose house is built on rock, off to one side and well hidden way out in Skor Cliffs . . . isolated and invisible . . . Whether that farm stands firmer than the others—only God knows."

The voice which spoke into the sparkling evening sun— whose light already was breaking up into sparks in the air —was dark and smoldering. I remembered suddenly that I had noticed that Amor Jonsson never spoke a word to Bjarni; only looked at him earnestly, almost inquisitively, but not really unfriendly. All the same, the memory of his manner with Bjarni—together with these words about the farm's isolation—made a shudder run through me.

"The foundations for Rodesand were chewed by the industrious lumpsuckers in the fjord, grain by grain." Amor Jonsson went on, "If I were a minister I would bless their appetite every Sunday morning from the pulpit. There they are—right at this very moment—side by side above the sea weed, with their blunt snouts turned toward the land, munching. Obscure cuneiform of the deep—obscure and changeable."

We were silent.

"Well—without the lumpsucker's tooth, the mussel's shell, and the insatiable appetite of both, there simply wouldn't be any Rodesand, my son," my guest concluded, and got up. "Shall I tell them hello for you in Keflavig?"

He did not look at me when he asked the question, nor did he wait for my answer. The hoof beats over the hard turf echoed fainter and fainter until they disappeared in the thickening darkness.

I went toward home, inwardly stung by vipers I did not know: evil premonitions, smoldering yearnings, vague fears, new hate. And new, ungovernable love.

V

There began to be no little talk in the parish about the lack of harmony at the lonely farm in Syvendeaa—between both family heads, even between the couples themselves.

The story was that after the death of his boys, Bjarni had rented out the half of the farm to Jon Thorgrimsson, who had moved in from Skapadal at Patreksfjord with his wife, Steinun Sveinsdottir, and their five children.

The first year everything had gone well; Bjarni and Jon were both peaceable men. Bjarni might have been a little irritable, but in return for that, extremely easy to make up with; Jon was an inoffensive grumbler people avoided when they could—but who could be put up with.

The women . . . Gudrun Egilsdottir certainly never did harm to any living creature intentionally. Though it was probably hard enough in daily comings and goings to have to put up with her endless complaints, her coughing, and her detailed accounts of the capricious chest pains that plagued her. And Steinun was a woman with a calm, steady glance, strong and silent. Quarrelsome she certainly did not appear to be.

Perhaps I did not hear everything that was said about the life of these people together at Syvendeaa. But what I did hear I would a lot rather not have heard.

Did I believe what people were saying? . . . Who can really make up his mind what he believes and what he does not believe of what people say? What I believed about Bjarni at that time—I couldn't say. And besides, the uncertainties and beliefs of those days have been obscured long since by the blind darkness of events. But this much is certain. The Bjarni I knew, or thought I knew, the Bjarni I liked to see and meet—that was the one who brought his farmers to the grave, with the spring wind tousling his golden, curly beard. Could you think so ill of this man—think that he trod God's plain commandment under foot, and public decency? In his own home? . . . But the truth probably is that deep inside me there lurked a doubt—What was evil? What was good?—although really I do not understand and can hardly believe in that doubt.

So, that is the truth? Although I was at no time aware that I thought that. Although at this moment I dare not maintain that I did. Or is it just something that I suspect myself of having done?

The Reverend Jon Ormsson, our Dean—he did not want to know. Even a reference to the story in his presence, and his pale face in the white frame of beard and hair would turn bright red. And when the fire rose in the Reverend Jon's gentle eyes people preferred to keep quiet.

But I wonder if I did not think, after all, that the Reverend Jon was the minister at Rodesand, while I was just his curate. And that the responsibility was therefore his. Yes, I did, I know that I did. And so I did think that there was responsibility to be assumed in the matter. Responsibility that was not assumed.

However, I was so occupied with what was happening in my own heart that there was only occasionally any room for other thoughts and feelings. What was happening in me? There is nothing I can say about it. Less than nothing . . . But—Amor Jonsson seemed to know.

That winter—the worst one I ever lived through—more snow fell than I would ever have believed could be in the heavens. It began to snow at Michaelmas, and it went on that way the whole winter. And still you could say with a kind of truth that you never set foot in snow the whole winter. For just as soon as the snow had piled up, there would follow a thaw that would melt it, and on top of the thaw there would follow a biting frost each time, that froze the melting water to ice. The whole country was iced over gradually, sank deeper and deeper under a layer of smooth gray ice. Even from the dizzying crags behind the town there was ice hanging—like a ragged curtain of death. Elsewhere not a tuft, not even the largest rock sticking up through layer on layer of stone-hard ice. Everything turned to ice that winter. Everything! Even my heart felt as if it were frozen in my breast.

Often Amor Jonsson visited me; I could almost say he visited me in season and out. At last his visits and his ambiguous conversation began to get on my nerves. One evening when just the two of us were in my room I could control myself no longer: "What do you want with me, anyhow?" I burst out. "You're old—I'm young. Why do you keep looking me up?"

"I wonder if you don't really know why?" he asked, without being the least moved by my vehemence.

I felt the blood rush to my face but I answered determinedly, "No."

Amor Jonsson sat a moment bent forward, sat looking down obliquely before him. Then he straightened himself suddenly and said quietly—and for once very soberly, "Then it really is time for you to find out . . ."

I had got up from my chair at the table. He took my place at once, tried my quill on his fingernail, smoothed a piece of paper thoughtfully the way you do with a parchment, carefully wrote some lines, and said casually, "You have your brother and the boys here on the place? . . ."

He said it without looking up. And when I did not deny it, he went on writing.

When he finally handed me the sheet of paper and I had read what was on it, I had to laugh. It said that Amor Jonsson had sold me two farms—the names of which I hardly even knew by hearsay—the one of forty hundreds, the other of twenty; sold them for considerations mutually agreed upon. Maybe the man had gone crazy.

"What are the considerations?" I asked coldly.

"That you be a good husband to my niece," he said calmly, looking me firmly in the eye.

"This is supposed to be a gift then?"

"It's the price for the girl, my boy. Whether I give you the farms and you hand them on to Young Olof, or whether she inherits them from me—it's all the same thing. Now, as far as any gift here, it's not the farms I'm giving you, but Young Olof. The only question is whether you'll take her."

"Yes, or whether I'll take her from you."

"Exactly."

I gripped his hand . . . Amor Jonsson said, "I bought these farms so recently that neither Monsieur Jon nor my sister Olof knows that they are, or ever have been, in my possession. Now call the men in so that they can witness the transfer."

The reading of the deed before the necessary witnesses, as well as their signing, took place without a remark of any kind—except for my brother Pall saying, "Sixty hundreds. It's the size of a dowry!"

"Yes," I answered looking him in the eye. "Are you riding with me tomorrow to Keflavig? For the betrothal?"

He turned pale, and then he turned red. And tried to take my hand. I turned my back on him in a fury.

Amor Jonsson had been standing and watching us fixedly, but with no particular astonishment.

"Well—well," he said when Pall had closed the door behind him—and there was approval in his voice.

Then my anger turned on him. I looked around for the newly written deed and shouted, "The hell with your farms!"

"I agree with you," he answered quietly, and put the document carefully into his pocket.

And so, the next day the three of us rode to Keflavig. Amor Jonsson, myself, and my brother Pall.

The sharp spikes of the horseshoes bit the ice hard and

cruelly. It did my heart good. We rode in silence . . . I will never forget the uneasiness in my brother Pall's eyes.

I asked permission to speak with Monsieur Jon Palsson, Madame Olof, and Young Olof. We gathered in the living room—the four men and the two women. Without any preamble I said to Monsieur Jon, "I have come to ask for your daughter's hand."

When I had said that, there was nothing said for a long time. But there were eyes exchanging glances.

Monsieur Jon held his powerful head upright. It was impossible to tell what he was thinking. Nor was it when he asked, "For whom?"

"For me, myself," I said, and with an act of will avoided Young Olof's eyes, which were unwaveringly fixed upon me, and only on me.

Whereas from time to time I returned my brother Pall's glance both bitter and fearful.

"You don't have a family—eh?" Monsieur Jon Palsson asked. "You've come alone?"

"My brother Pall, you know him, and my friend Amor Jonsson are my witnesses and spokesmen."

"And as the bride price I suppose you intend to give us a title to your tithes and taxes," Madame Olof put in, smiling.

I bowed to her. "I might possibly expect your forgiveness, Madame Olof, if I did let myself be tempted to pay your daughter's bridal price with God's good money," I answered, "But I'm afraid that she will have to content herself with mere earthly goods."

"I suppose you have talked with my daughter?" Monsieur Jon asked

"No."

"Did you think that I could give her away without her consent?"

"No."

"Well, what do you say, daughter?"

Finally I too looked at Young Olof—met her black eyes

suddenly filling with tears. She was very pale. And her lips were trembling so badly that she was unable to talk. She stood without moving her arms, and fought against a sob welling up in her breast.

"Now, now," said Madame Olof, rising imposingly. "If the girl's finally met a man, in God's name, let him take her." She put her hands in mine.

"May you be very happy, my children."

After which she went to her brother. "And you, Amor . . . Though you aren't by mother's child you're the son of our father. You've always been welcome at Keflavig, but never as much as today."

But now Monsieur Jon Palsson stood up. "That's all well and good, but what are you giving my daughter?"

I mentioned the two farms that Amor Jonsson had made over to me the evening before. "They are hers—in any case," I added

"Then let's write out the bridal agreement," said Monsieur Jon, and went over to his desk. "Keflavig is too dear to match sixty hundreds and I have no intention of splitting the place up. But there are other farms . . ."

Then Young Olof said her first word in the conversation, she said, "If Keflavig is too good a bridal price for me, then I'm not worth marrying, Father."

"Now you're acting more like yourself," he snapped. I'll give you a hundred and twenty hundreds, not including Keflavig. What do you say to that?"

"That you can give your dog what you don't want to keep yourself."

"Now, now," said Madame Olof soothingly. "Of course the girl will get Keflavig. That's a piece of property I ought to have something to say about. It's only yours by marriage, my dear husband."

"Yes, and only yours by birth, my dear wife."

Possibly it really was Monsieur Jon Palsson's intention to withhold Keflavig from his daughter's dowry—possibly. In any event, she got it; the deed of conveyance was made out and then signed by her parents, Amor Jonsson, my brother Pall, and the eldest of Monsieur Jon's servants on the farm. Madame Olof produced an appropriate bridal supper, after which my affianced bride and I, according to old custom, were led to the same bed.

We did not talk to each other that night. We still had not talked to each other alone, never had talked together alone with the single exception of the day when, side by side, we waded home up the muddy shore. There never seemed to be any words possible between us. And in spite of my youthful desire that night my heart was dark, dark and heavy.

In the morning we lay there feeling each other's warmth, but still not talking. Until Young Olof raised up on her elbows, looked gravely into my eyes and said . . . No, what she said I won't say, but the evil band that had wrung my heart split at her words. Because from them I understood that not only was she pure and innocent, but that she loved me.

As we got up and dressed afterwards she was gloomy and thoughtful. She was trying to say something. And finally it came.

"You know, Eiulv, I kissed Pall—you know, on the ice—lots of times . . . What are you going to say about that?"

"What the devil does it matter to me when and where and how often you've licked that pup's muzzle," I answered in a rage, stamping my foot.

For a moment she looked at me in fright. Then she threw her arms around me and kissed me. I could not see that that was any reason for kissing, and I freed myself from her. Which she patiently submitted to.

That is the way Olof's and my marriage began.

But when later in the day I rode back home to Baer together with my brother Pall . . .

Never will I forget the look in his eyes . . .

A month later Young Olof and I were married in Baer church by our good Dean, the Reverend Jon Ormsson. That was the fifth Sunday in Lent, and the text was: God sendeth the angel Gabriel.

And to us, too, young people now starting out together on life's long journey, the Reverend Jon spoke in the day's text. "Open your ears, young man and young woman, that you may always hear the voice of the Lord proclaiming," he said. "Only thus can one find the way to God. And man is only himself, is only man, in his search for God. Perhaps you will believe, if one day God grants you a son, that it was he whom the angel prophesied. But I say to you: Put not your trust in the light of the rolling wheel of the sun and let not your hearts cling to mortal flesh. He who dwells in his own heart will die with that heart . . ." Thus spoke the Reverend Jon, the Sinner.

But piety and childish faith are one thing; something quite different is the icy blast of lonely death. Lonely death? . . . Well, death and horror.

My brother Pall had not taken his eyes from me the whole day. Only in the evening—at Keflavig—when my bride and I were alone, did he step up to me.

"I have a wedding gift for you, brother," he said lightly.

I had known it. How long? I do not know. But the tension which rose furiously to my heart—it was not born at that moment. It was older. Young Olof placed herself close to my side; then we stood, silent, and looked at Pall. And waited.

But Pall said nothing. Whether intentionally or to find words, I do not know. Finally, it came:

"Jon Thorgrimsson—fell . . ."

"The poor devil . . . Today?"

"No—it happened last Thursday."

"Why haven't I heard about it?"

"Well—the people at Syvendeaa haven't been in any hurry to spread the news . . ."

"Was he hurt?"

"Hurt? . . . That's certainly the least you could say."

"Who's taking care of him "

"God—presumably."

"Was he killed?"

"Don't you understand what I'm saying, brother? . . . Jon Thorgrimsson at Syvendeaa fell last Thursday out at Skor Cliffs. He's dead. He's gone."

"The death wasn't reported at the church today. That's curious."

"There's so much that's curious, brother. There are so many kinds of slippery slopes. And many kinds of death . . . Jon Thorgrimsson fell out on Skor Cliffs. Nobody saw how it happened. No one has seen him since. Maybe the sea will bring him back to us. Maybe not. And there are others whose fall nobody has seen . . ."

I could not think of an answer, my thoughts and feelings were in such a whirl. And Young Olof freed me from the burden. With steady hands she lifted the bridal wreath from her head, putting it on the table, and turned caustically to Pall: "Good night, Gabriel. You go . . . Another time when you have a message maybe you can choose a more appropriate time."

As soon as we were alone I fell into a chair and wept. Young Olof stood at my side, stroking my hair from time to time. Softly she asked me. "What is the matter, my friend . . .? Is it so bad?"

"God only knows," I said, and got up.

And that night, certainly, I obliterated my fear and

pain in her arms. But my sleep was heavy, and I woke the next morning to great unrest and much vague pain.

The wedding days that followed now—it is good that I will never live through them again. I would rather have ridden home with my young wife immediately, on Monday. But Monsieur Jon Palsson was not a man to dissolve a wedding party for no better reason than that a farmer on a back country farm had disappeared. And I did not want to be the man who made Jon Thorgrimsson's disappearance into an event of unusual significance.

And maybe . . . maybe I was thinking of Bjarni. And his farmers. And of the grave he dug that spring day.

VII

Easter fell on April eighteenth that year; Young Olof and
I had been married the fourth.

On Good Friday I spoke in Baer church, spoke for the
first time in my church of the torment and death of our
Saviour. As I talked I could see, down among the men,
Bjarni of Syvendeaa and, down among the women, Steinun, Jon Thorgrimsson's widow. Gudrun Egilsdottir, on the
other hand, I could not see, nor Bjarni's brother Jon, nor
the hired girl Malfrith. Did Bjarni and Steinun have any
notion of what was being said about them? Or were they
defying the gossip?

They were remarkably sober; other than that, there was
nothing to be read in their faces. On them both lay the
healthy man's sometimes terrifying calm, as if death did
not wait at every turn.

As I forgot my written text and began to speak simply
from my fearful heart, I could not avoid noticing that
Bjarni and Steinun really were the only ones among my
auditors who were perfectly calm. And my auditors were
many that day, as many as the little church could hold.
But everybody else's eyes were uneasy, fluttered nervously; sought me out, sought out one another, sought out
particularly, even if furtively and hastily, Bjarni and
Steinun.

I spoke of the blinded men who had murdered the Son
of God Himself. I said, "We are all like these poor pathetic people. Each and every one of us becomes, sooner or
later, willingly or unwillingly, a tormenter and a crucifier.

We all murder the Son of God. In ourselves or in our neighbor. Our desire and our torment in the flesh leads us astray so that we plunge ourselves, and plunge others, into the abyss of darkness, die and kill. But just as we humans build markers of stone on the heath to guide the wayfarers, so did God set the cross on our path and gave us His own Son to kill and hang upon it, so that we might observe and verify that the body's life is not the true life and the body's death not true death. For our life is the way of death. But our death the gateway to life."

When afterwards, confused and feeling ill, I stepped out of the church, there was nobody around Bjarni and Steinun in the ice-covered churchyard—and nobody around me.

I looked about me helplessly. Gray and cold the heavens hung, once more heavy with snow; and the sea out there, gray and cold, seemed to rise up to them. It was as though all life was to drown in the icy gray and cold. An eddy of wind swept up some granules of ice and spun them around Bjarni and Steinun. When it died down there was a golden sparkle to Bjarni's yellow beard.

"I was extremely sorry to hear the terrible way you lost your husband," I heard myself say to Steinun—I had taken her hand and was holding it as I talked. "I would have prayed for you and your five fatherless children in church today, if it had not seemed to me that one should not speak of the death of a poor sinful human in the same breath with our Saviour's death. But I will ask the Reverend Jon to do it the day after Easter. Is there anything else I can do for you?"

"No—nothing," Steinun answered quietly.

Only those two words: "No—nothing."

Did I realize the abyss of truth these two words opened for me? I don't think that I did realize, not completely. And still I turned hastily to Bjarni, pressed his hand silently, and went—without saying any more. Hid myself in my study.

. . . The second day of Easter at the church I saw Gudrun Egilsdottir and Bjarni's brother Jon.

Something about the young man was so light and cheerful that I hurried over to him to talk to him a little, although I really had nothing to say to him. As soon as he saw me, his blue eyes darkened and his weak features turned stiff and at the same time faded.

"You've come equipped with new shoes and provisions, Jon Bjarnason," I said jestingly and put my hand on his knapsack.

His features lightened at once and he answered cheerfully, "Yes, I'm on my way to the spring fishing."

He hesitated a moment—and then added quickly, 'And after that I've promised to go to Arni's at Laginup."

"So your parish will be Sauthlauksdal then?"

"Yes."

"And I suppose you won't be back at all to Syvendeaa?"

"No."

His boyish glance rested on me shyly a moment. I took his hand.

"Good luck, wherever you go, Jon Bjarnason . . ."

Gudrun Egilsdottir was standing nearby, standing and coughing. It looked very much as though she did want to talk to me but didn't quite have nerve enough to come over. How can I excuse my not going over to her? . . . But I did not. I did not do it . . .

Still—when after the service she was standing talking with the Reverend Jon Ormsson, I did go up to her.

"So, you're still having trouble with your chest, Gudrun," the Reverend Jon called out, and clapped her on the back. "Poor Gudrun—poor Gudrun."

"Oh, it's bad, it's as bad as it can be, my dear Dean . . . Yes, and with my chest, too . . ."

There were tears in Jon Ormsson's eyes. "Poor Gudrun," he went on, "You've really bothered me today, you really have. But how can I possibly reproach you for that? Your cough—that's certainly not the normal church cough, no.

And to forbid you God's house—we really don't have the heart to do that, eh, Curate? But the others, you know, Gudrun, the others cough along with you. And don't have any shawls to muffle it in. Poor old man that I am, I have to shout till I don't have another breath in my body—and start to cough myself. And so all of you sit there and cough, and I stand there and cough, to the glory of God at Eastertide . . . No matter how I shout—nobody can hear me; nobody hears me . . . "

"And yet my poor ears told me that the Dean was praying for the fatherless children—and for *Steinun.*"

"Yes—oh yes . . . Tell her that, Gudrun—as a poor consolation."

"I will . . . And for us others the Dean didn't pray?"

"What others, my dear Gudrun? What others?"

"For poor dead Jon Thorgrimsson, I mean—and for me."

"Jon Thorgrimsson—is that possible? Did I really forget to pray for poor dead Jon Thorgrimsson? Well, well, and now it's too late. You're going to have to do that the Sunday after Easter, Eiulv. Remember that now. If it is you, my friend . . . Yes, yes, Gudrun—It's been a hard winter at Syvendeaa I guess. Like everybody else, like everywhere else, yes."

"Oh yes. This winter's really been a hard one at Syvendeaa."

"Really's been a hard one at Syvendeaa, eh? You have your cough; I have my game leg, my game leg, Gudrun."

"You talk about my cough. Only God knows the real cross I bear. But for me you don't pray, Dean."

"Not for you in particular, no; but I do for all who suffer and are heavily laden. Coughing, Gudrun, and pains in the chest—I don't know whether the bishop would allow prayers for something like that in the church. I don't know. God has given you this cross, my good woman . . . "

"My cross—about that you don't know . . . "

"Poor Gudrun—no. We don't know each other's crosses

. . . Oh my, no. How true, how true. But we must bear our cross, every one his own cross, Gudrun. As we must die our deaths, alone."

"Death—Dean . . . Can all death be destined?"

"He sees the sparrow's fall—you know that, my good woman . . . Eiulv, my brother in the Lord, have mercy on this poor woman and have your wife warm a little milk for her. Good bye, Gudrun, poor Gudrun . . ."

And he spoke thus, my Dean, "Have mercy on this poor woman."

And I went in with Gudrun Egilsdottir and had some milk warmed for her.

While we were going the short distance from the church home to my place, I kept thinking how different the conversation between her and my Dean could have gone. And in fact, should have gone. But to me Gudrun said nothing, nor did I say anything to her.

. . . Once again Bjarni and Steinun came to church to-gether—and alone. It was the second Sunday after Easter. It was just as though they were trying to challenge village gossip and the people's enmity. Because, was not the reason for it that one of them could not stay home when the other left? How could you know? You could not see it on the two of them, or notice anything at all—not anything.

And still something had happened . . . something had happened.

Never will I forget that strange day.

It had snowed through the night, on into the morning. Piles of snow had fallen in white silence. And then all of a sudden the warmth pulsing in from the sea, as if the fjord had begun to boil—first like a capricious breeze, and then like a hot storm that shook the church so that the congregation was looking nervously about, and listening more to the blast of the wind than to my words.

But when we were standing out in the churchyard afterwards, the sky was swept clean in a twinkling of the stacks of spring clouds. The heavens spread pale and icy over us. The storm was over. Quite suddenly it was so cold that you could watch the ice freezing over the little puddles that had formed between the graves.

Bjarni and Steinun were standing alone today, too. But there were people standing around them. People asking questions.

The rumors were that on Thursday evening Gudrun Egilsdottir had got sick. Very sick.

She was supposed to have had such attacks of powerful and painful vomiting that she had been unconscious for a while. Had thought she was going to die, was what they said. But then she had managed to come to anyway . . .

Bjarni and Steinun were able to report that she had no particular aftereffects. She was just a little weak . . . No wonder, was the general opinion.

"Funny sicknesses these days," remarked Ingibjorg Egilsdottir from Krokshus, Gudrun's sister.

Her husband Rognvald sought out her eyes nervously . . . She said no more.

But Olaf Sigurdsson, our parish clerk, muttered bitterly, "Funny she got better, would be more like it."

I was standing a little outside the circle, standing talking to Amor Jonsson. I was willing to listen, but not to become involved. Certainly Amor Jonsson wanted to hear what they were saying, too, and what it was they were answering. A peculiar worried attentiveness shone from his yellow eyes.

Margret from Lambavatn, Monsieur Olaf's wife, was asking in detail what Gudrun had eaten that day, and whether somebody else on the farm who had eaten the same food had showed any ill effects. She spoke quietly, as though to smooth over the obvious bitterness of her husband. And she closed—friendly and benevolently— with, "So you really shouldn't think that it could have been poison."

"Hahaha," Monsieur Olaf laughed, "Hahaha."

Then there was some conversation about the dead Jon Thorgrimsson—that he still had not been recovered from the sea. And that as a rule you could still find anybody if he fell in the ocean, that near to land. But that there still were strong currents in and around Bredefjord, strong currents . . .

"Isn't there a current in toward shore from out there in the fjord, Bjarni?" Monsieur Sigmund, our county sheriff, asked, while his eyelids slowly fell to hide his large gray eyes, and just as slowly raised again.

People fell silent, and they turned their eyes on the tall man with the long face.

"We got a flounder the other day," Bjarni answered simply, turning readily toward Sigmund.

"A flounder . . . uhhuh . . . "

Monsieur Sigmund smiled with one side of his face. "Was it edible?"

"It got eaten."

Amor Jonsson stuck the handle of his whip under my arm.

"Let's go, son."

I went with him. He said, "They say that that Bjarni is on the hotheaded side. And dumb."

I said nothing.

"Dumb," my friend answered himself. "Maybe . . . maybe. Hotheaded, though, I know he is—as wild fire."

. . . So it was half a month later that all three of them came to church from Syvendeaa: Bjarni, his wife—and Steinun. And all three took communion.

The Reverend Jon was there, in spite of his bad leg, and spoke on the mission of the Holy Ghost. And so it was he who gave them the bread and wine.

I had already had terrible premonitions and a hard battle with myself, and I gave thanks to my God when the Reverend Jon came. Without understanding that my Dean's coming probably just increased my responsibility.

. . . Three weeks later was Pentecost.

That day nobody came from Syvendeaa.

VIII

The Friday after Whitsunday Bjarni Bjarnason was standing again with a coffin on Baer churchyard; this time he
had his wife in the coffin.

I had seen him come, for my brother Pall had come in
to me in my study and had reported: "We've got a visitor
from Syvendeaa."

In spite of the tone and the smile which introduced the
words, I pretended not to notice anything and followed
him out.

In the middle of the broad moor, with a shining mirror
surface of water on both sides of him I saw a man coming,
a man with two horses and something black balanced on
planks between the horses—it looked like a coffin.

You could not see either the man or the horse distinctly, the way the water shimmered in the sunlight. You
could see only the coffin. But still I recognized the man
too, knew at once that it was Bjarni. Who else would be
likely to be on the road alone with a corpse?

It was spring again—almost summer. The air lay soft and
gentle against the skin; the sun shone brightly with a
powerful beam; the stones radiated heat, and the new
grass reached up in dazed bliss—as though with closed
eyes. I tried to imagine how it had been in winter, when
the ice lay over everything. It was impossible.

Then Bjarni was here . . .

My brother Pall went to meet him. I went meanwhile
to my study, got the church key.

When I came back out Bjarni and Pall were standing

outside the church door. I nodded to Bjarni and put the key in the lock.

"It's Gudrun who's dead," Pall informed me, meaningfully, "dead from the pains in her breast."

Bjarni said nothing at all. Nor did I say anything.

While they took the coffin in, I remained standing outside listening to the hum of the flies. There were a lot of flies humming . . . I saw that Bjarni and Pall were putting the coffin on the women's side—between the door and the pews. I let them alone.

When they came out the church door it struck me how Pall had grown in that year. He was getting to be a full-grown man! While I was locking the door, Bjarni went over to his horses standing tied to the churchyard gate and returned with a shovel and a spade. This time he was equipped . . . Pall had got the pick in the church when they had been inside with the coffin.

My brother Pall eyed me accusingly. "Would you like me to help Bjarni dig the grave?" he asked ingenuously.

"If you don't have anything else to do," I answered indifferently, went ahead around the south side of the church, and pointed out to Bjarni with a glance the grave plot alongside the farmers.

Bjarni sighed; then he began to hack out the turf in squares which he stacked in a pile. He did it with great calm and deliberation. But he did not lift his head one single time. Only when I greeted him had I caught a glimpse of his eyes.

Pall had stepped away. When he had seen my choice of burial plot his eyes suddenly showed uncertainty. A little after that he had gone.

For a moment I stood there silently. Then I said: "It's been two years, Bjarni . . ."

"Yes—and they've been two long years," Bjarni answered quietly—without looking up.

Again we were silent.

Then Bjarni wiped the sweat from his forehead,

straightened up, and I saw again his blue, oddly sparkling eyes. "Do you remember last summer at the bird cliffs?" he asked—and a kind of smile curled in his yellow beard—"the time the cliff split off and I was hanging in the air with one hand? . . . I thought then it was going to be me that would be lying here, alongside my farmers."

Bjarni dug some more, hacked the frozen earth loose, and shoveled it away in ice-larded clumps. "But that wasn't how it was meant to be . . ."

I remembered with great clarity the day Bjarni had spoken of . . . A sheer, ocean-sprayed mountain wall that looked from a rocking boat below like something growing into the sky. A storm of shrieking birds—a white-shining, black-sparkling cloud of sea birds which, like a continuation of the breakers, swirled up at the black cliffs, and disappeared in the mists of the mountain. When as a child I saw that sight for the first time, I did not have a moment's doubt that it was the angry sea itself capriciously spraying winged fish from its belly. Even last year it gave me a chill to come up against the cliffs' fantastic, relentless, ineradicable life—that storm of life where, amidst noise and stink and filth, existence triumphs, life renews itself, springing young and fresh and blood-warm from the sterile rocks. Every summer.

Yes—I still remembered the day. Remembered Bjarni, too, and the other bird trappers crawling like flies up and down along the cliffs. Remembered the splash of the falling rock fragment; remembered Bjarni hanging on by one hand . . .

And so that moment he had thought about his farmers? Of course he had thought about his farmers.

"Have you heard about the black bird that's been seen over the town?" I asked him.

"I don't believe that kind of stuff," he answered calmly. "I've heard so much of that ever since I was a kid. People scare so easy."

"Are you never afraid?"

"What am I supposed to be afraid of?"

"Weren't you afraid that day on the bird cliffs?"

"Afraid? . . . No-o, I don't think so. I began to think about Christmas in the old days—when I was a boy. I saw a kind of warm, red light. Bjarni and Egil—you know, down there, they . . . all of a sudden so near to me. I was . . . I was pretty near to letting go . . ."

He gave a faint laugh at the thought. A melancholy laugh.

I said, "Come in and have something to eat when you've finished."

Then I went away, and left him alone with his two graves.

But he did not come in to see me afterwards. And when I went out to look for him he was gone.

IX

The Reverend Jon came very early the next Sunday; no doubt Monsieur Olaf of Lambavatn had asked him to. Everybody came very early that day.

It was hardly past nine o'clock when my brother Pall came in to me in my study, to get the church keys:

"They want to see the coffin, they do."

"Who wants to see the coffin?" I asked him.

"Well—the people in the parish."

A little later I went out; there was a whole crowd standing bunched around the Reverend Jon out in the churchyard.

While I was still uncertain whether I should go over or not Amor Jonsson rode up beside me, jumped from his horse, and calling to Pall, threw him the reins, taking me by the arm and urging me inside ahead of him.

"You, do you know anything?" he asked when we were standing in my study.

"Nothing."

He stood swinging his whip. "You didn't . . . You didn't take the lid off the casket, of course?"

"I sat out here the whole night . . . I sat out there both nights . . . Only my wife knows that."

"What does Young Olof say to all this?"

"We haven't talked about it. Up to now I've—said nothing."

"Good; you don't have to answer for something you didn't say . . . Monsieur Jon's right on my heels; we passed Sigmund, and Olaf had Margret stay home today. I noticed, before, that he'd already got his hands on the Reverend Jon. Let the others do now what they think is necessary and proper."

Monsieur Jon came stamping in to us, out of breath from his fast ride, and dropped himself into a chair—nodding to Amor: "Keep an eye out for eavesdroppers."

To me he said, whispering, "We have nothing to do with what happens here, Eiulv. Do you agree with me? As to what has happened, only God knows. And for what God alone knows no man can be judged. Monsieur Olaf is shooting off his mouth, but he doesn't know anything. Nobody knows anything. Sigmund is sniffing . . . But it's one thing to smell a fox and another to start him from his lair. The whole story's a mess from the beginning. And for that we have first and foremost the Reverend Jon to thank. Already last winter—already before Jon Thorgrimsson disappeared—Monsieur Olaf and Monsieur Thorberg Illugason got together with him, wanted to take him with them out to Syvendeaa. He made excuses with his bad leg and the state of the roads. He wanted them to go there without him. But his clerks begged off . . . Well, as I said, son-in-law, let them be the ones to open the coffin; but let us be quiet and watch, temporarily . . ."

I sat at my desk, troubled and fearful. I could not speak and my thoughts wavered. Without words. Without resolution.

Be quiet and watch . . . Yes, what else was there to do?

It was only later that I realized that for the whole of that terrible day I had had Jon Palsson on one side of me, and Amor Jonsson on the other.

. . . The Reverend Jon reminded his parishioners insistently that the day was Holy Trinity: the Son had gone home to the Father and the Holy Ghost; He was sitting now at the Father's right side.

I closed my eyes . . . It was so easy, when the Reverend Jon spoke, to see the Trinity before you—in cloaks of heavenly blue and crowned with suns. In the Reverend Jon's world there was no real sin. Human beings were children—at the worst full of bad habits. In the Reverend Jon's world the Devil existed, but he was a cheerful, hairy Devil, horned and with a tongue of fire.

I had to hide my face in my hands; my tears streamed down. I felt sick—from lack of sleep, probably.

And then suddenly the Reverend Jon was finished with his sermon. They sang, and the church emptied. It actually did—people left. In a little, then, some men would come, pick up Gudrun's coffin—take it out to the grave.

Beside me Amor Jonsson was still sitting; he got up with me.

Bjarni and Steinun were standing at the door, close to the foot of the coffin, standing and waiting. They stood there with bowed heads motionless. When I saw them standing there that way everything went black.

Amor Jonsson laid his hand on my shoulder firmly. But I went resolutely forward between the pews.

But before I reached them the bell rang. Called.

We stopped, my friend and I, so unexpectedly did it happen. And Bjarni and Steinun lifted their heads with a jerk. And looked around. Looked around like frightened birds. Looked at each other. And then stood motionless again.

Suddenly people crowded in through the church doors. But there was no force to their entry. Only slowly did the space around the coffin fill up: first there was one row close against the walls, then two rows. Then there were more. More and more.

My friend and I stood by ourselves—inside the circle.

And now a loud-voiced group approached the door from the outside. Only when they crossed the threshold did the force of their voices dwindle; the quarrel died away.

Silently they stepped to the coffin—the Reverend Jon, my father-in-law, Olaf from Lambavatn, Sigmund from Stakk, and Thorberg Illugason. Together with my brother Pall, equipped with tools.

The Reverend Jon placed himself at the head of the

coffin and spoke—quietly—although he had great difficulty controlling his voice:

"My friends . . . Evil rumors in the parish have brought to my ears that the departed Gudrun Egilsdottir is not supposed to have died a natural death. I have, therefore, given permission to disturb her last rest and have the coffin opened. When I refused I was reproached on many sides with wishing to hold a protecting hand over the evil-doer. Now my friends—look for yourselves. Should you, which I hope and believe, see before you nothing but a poor human gone to her eternal rest in the Lord, let it be an admonition to you to root out the poisonous weeds of suspicion from your minds and not persecute a sorely smitten brother and sister with horrible accusations. You, Monsieur Jon, and you, Monsieur Sigmund, I appoint to view the departed . . . Who will raise the lid?"

"I ask to be excused, my dear Dean," answered Jon Palsson judiciously—my brother Pall had already begun to loosen the nails—"Monsieur Olaf is nearest."

Olaf from Lambavatn was already standing alongside Sigmund, willing enough.

White, stiff linen enclosed the poor stinking cadaver, lying stretched out before us on rough shavings heaped up snugly along the sides of the coffin—lying there in the shame of death, exposed to the sullying view of the living.

Monsieur Sigmund approached with a sheepish and desperate, yet greedy expression on his long face. He lifted the cloth from the face of the corpse, which became visible for a moment—so distant in its pale immobility, with the blind glance of the closed eyes fixed on empty space. Then he laid the cloth awkwardly back in place. The face showed nothing out of the ordinary.

Although there was nothing said, all of a sudden the people who had been the most eager to see the coffin opened had lost their eagerness. What they had expected to see is not easy to say. Certainly something more horrible than their thoughts could express. Possibly a purple,

44

swollen face. Possibly a bloody, hacked body. But it was only poor Gudrun Egilsdottir just lying there dead.

Sigmund's hands were shaking, and his heavy eyelids drooped over the pupils as he bared the breast and belly of the corpse. The large hands on the lean arms that had been crossed stood out dark and rough against the pale skin. The breasts hung like empty sacks at each side. The belly curved out, blue-veined, greatly bloated. From the collarbone a blue shadow fell on the right breast. Sigmund felt of the place, again and again. When he lifted the left arm from the breast in order to get at the place better, the hand hung down a little.

Finally he bared the legs. The thigh bones were clearly outlined in the loose flesh. Sigmund felt the legs, moved the toes. Then he moved quickly back and made way for Monsieur Olaf who, with sweat pearling on his broad, weather-beaten forehead and with a nervous look in his dull, stone-gray eyes, approached unwillingly. All the eagerness had gone out of him.

He, like Sigmund, felt the purple spot near the collarbone, lifted the arms, moved the toes. And withdrew with spread fingers, apparently not knowing what to do with his hands.

Nobody said anything. Until the Reverend Jon after a long time asked, "Well—Brethren?"

Sigmund stammered tonelessly: "There is a purple spot there at the collarbone—I don't know . . . The flesh doesn't feel any different there than anywhere else, and it isn't swollen. The left arm's not completely stiff; the toes aren't either. That certainly doesn't have anything to do with poison. But how should I know? This is really the first time I've seen a corpse. And then the belly . . . Was the woman pregnant?"

"My good man," the Reverend Jon answered in a fatherly tone, "whether the woman was pregnant or not, it's not considered a matter of murder to get one's wife pregnant in any case. And now as to the purple spot . . . Since you are so unfamiliar with the appearance of the fleshly shell emptied of the spirit, you probably don't know that where there has been protracted pain underneath, the flesh turns purple frequently, in and after death.

"No, I didn't know that," Sigmund answered tamely.

"I've seen two cases of it with my own eyes," Olaf offered with relief, drying his forehead.

"And now, brothers and sisters," said the Reverend Jon propitiatingly, "you wanted to see the deceased Gudrun— you got to see her. Here at her bared shell I enjoin you: If you know something, tell the truth, here and now. And say it plainly and freely. If you know nothing, then be silent . . . Here at her bared shell I ask you all, each and every one of you: Is there anyone among you who knows —or even has a reasonable suspicion—that the deceased Gudrun Egilsdottir did not die a natural death?"

There were some isolated no's. For the most part there was silence.

During all this I had watched Bjarni and Steinun carefully.

They continued to stand motionless, side by side. Whether their calm demonstrated fear, or inner security, I did not know. And could not know. They had said nothing; they had hardly even moved their eyes. From the glances that swept over them you could see that some persons thought they were behaving as though they were guilty; but others seemed to think that their behavior showed they were innocent.

I for my part was conscious only of the poor carrion that was the departed Gudrun, lying there so pathetically in her coffin. Finally I could stand it no more. I went over to her, made the sign of the cross above her, covered her up, and said to my brother Pall, "Fasten down the lid, carpenter."

Somebody at the same moment touched my shoulder. When I lifted my head I saw people were crossing themselves and praying. Wordlessly the Reverend Jon put his cassock on me and with his own hands fastened the collar about my neck.

There were other helping hands, and singing we carried the coffin to the grave south of the church. Bjarni walked beside the coffin—walked and wept. Steinun I could no longer see.

The singing died away, and there was the coffin before me—black, black. Black as myself.

But at this grave I could not speak. I only said, "Here you can rest in peace, Gudrun Egilsdottir."

And then I consecrated her with the usual words of death and resurrection.

X

Gone is the summer—so sings my bird—gone is the summer, gone is the summer—and soon it is Yule . . .

It was Young Olof singing—my wife. Almost every day she went around singing her little song, her song of summer and of Christmas. Her lips were so fresh and delicious to stop with a kiss. God blessed us with much joy in each other.

Once she whispered in my ear, "Thanks for you, Eiulv."

And I said to her, "There is another kind of happiness than ours, Olof. There's the happiness of sin—and of darkness."

"Sin is only for servants," laughed Olof and went—by which I was cut off from reproaching her for her unchristian thoughts.

That was the only time I even hinted to her at the unrest and inner conflict that soured my summer's happiness. Probably she understood that she helped me most by not letting me put anything into words. Possibly she was also afraid to see me worried and undecided. Or afraid that afterwards I would not be able to endure her having seen me that way. But perhaps it was only her distaste for the somber and the gloomy, her passionate sense of purity, that made it possible for her to keep firmly at a distance not only from the town gossip, but from any actual knowledge of these things at all.

She sang her song. And without her I do not know how I would have made out.

. . . Along in the summer I began to notice that Monsieur Jon Palsson came to church every time there was a service. And that he was troubled in his mind. He said not a word to me, nor did I talk to him.

But when one day Bjarni and Steinun were also at the service, and when he, as soon as he caught sight of the two, made for them, it immediately became clear to me why my father-in-law had recently been so conscientious a churchgoer.

I could not possibly have done anything else but follow him. I have never in my life been so nervous. I trembled in every fiber as you tremble before a wrestling match with a strong opponent. The quiet Monsieur Jon, whom I had come to know not the least from the few months' marriage with Young Olof, was the man I last of all wanted to contend with. If Bjarni were really guilty—he had every reason now to be careful.

Bjarni started, too, when he saw Jon Palsson coming— that was plain enough. The flickers in his blue eyes were gathered together in a dark sparkling point. Steinun watched him a moment in astonishment; then she stood there, as quietly as before—with the single difference that she was frowning. Monsieur Jon neither said a word in greeting to the two nor gave his hand. He only measured Steinun with a sharp glance and then turned to Bjarni. He said, "People insist with increasing definiteness that the departed Gudrun, your wife, is supposed to have been poisoned by that woman there, Steinun Sveinsdottir."

Bjarni smiled. But the smile failed him. He said—and said awkwardly—"And I suppose the general opinion is that I'm an accessory."

"My good man, this is a serious matter . . . There seems to be a good deal of probability that the departed Gudrun died of poisoned soup that Steinun is supposed to have given her in a ladle."

"She didn't die that way; she recovered."

"All right. But was there poison in the soup?"

Here Bjarni lost his head suddenly. He was wordless for

a moment, and then he shouted, "Who says there was any poison in the soup? . . . Who can prove that?"

Steinun looked from Monsieur Jon to Bjarni, turned her back on us, left. Her behavior could have been right, I felt —under other circumstances.

Monsieur Jon said, "Take it easy, Bjarni . . . There was poison in the soup, then?"

Bjarni could hardly speak for anger, but he managed finally, "No . . . But vicious tongues have poisoned it since then. As they've poisoned our whole life at Syvendeaa."

Monsieur Jon looked at him a moment doubtfully, then he said, "Now you're twisting away from me, Bjarni. But I can see that you're afraid, man. And now I realize that you've got reason to be. Now I know you."

With these words he took me by the arm. And we left.

But after Mass he went over to them again; he even followed them over across the yard, for they were already on their way home. But he went very slowly, so slowly that they finally chose to stop and wait, although by hurrying a little they could easily have avoided him. An astonished glance from Bjarni's eyes caught me—I was again in Monsieur Jon's train. A glance that pained and disturbed me. Which I understood—and did not understand.

Monsieur Jon went up close to Bjarni and Steinun, took hold of them, was silent a moment, and then said very softly, "The truth I will leave to God to reveal. But the fornication at Syvendeaa, that's got to come to an end."

He released them suddenly. And we went back to the farm. When I looked back over my shoulder a moment later, Bjarni and Steinun were still standing there turned toward one another—as though they were standing at a grave.

XI

Monsieur Palsson did not discuss his plans with me other than to say, "Actually it's the business of the Dean, rather more than that of the sheriff, to clean up the parish—but what can you expect from the Reverend Jon?"

A few days later they rode past, in the middle of the bright night, without stopping in Baer—Monsieur Jon and Monsieur Sigmund, with four men and some horses. They took the road to Syvendeaa.

Young Olof said—for we were out that night and saw them ride past—said without looking at me so that it could as easily count as not having been said, "She's a bold woman, Steinun. Her I have to thank for seeing my father riding now, with five men, against a woman."

She laughed briefly and unhappily. And left me alone.

I made my way down to the shore; sat and threw stones into the water.

Already in the course of the day it was said in Baer that things had been cleaned up at Syvendeaa: Steinun and her brood had been forced to move east across the mountains. To her own parish.

"So now she's nearer the judge," my brother Pall remarked. "There'll be more on that road from Syvendeaa."

Time passed. Several dismally forboding weeks slipped by.

And then it was the twenty-sixth of September—the fifth Sunday after Trinity—that Deacon Thorberg Illugason, our neighbor, together with his hired man Gudmund Einarsson, on their way home from church found a man's

body washed ashore on a point that juts out at one place—
Bjarni's Point—and came back to report it.

Thorberg Illugason, that pious man, was very troubled
—his report he closed with the words, "You never have
any trouble finding what you don't want to find."

"And you didn't recognize the man?" I asked, and
looked from him to Gudmund Einarsson, who was standing there staring down in front of him, his downy young
face all red.

Thorberg was quiet a moment. Then he sighed, "Well,
maybe . . ."

Bjorn Palsson from Krok and Bjorn Halldorsson from
Sker had had something to discuss with me and had
therefore not ridden home. I asked them to wait and look
at the body together with the rest of us. In fact, they
might just as well go along with us, so that we could all
five see it while it was still untouched and give evidence
about its condition.

My brother Pall had come up. I told him, "See if you
can put together a stretcher and follow us with some
horses—we're going to get a body down at the shore."

"Maybe a new visitor from Syvendeaa?" he asked.

"A new chance for you to show your skill as a carpenter,
anyway," I answered him. Whereupon I together with my
unhappy neighbors and the two Bjorns set out for Bjarni's
Point—to greet my guest from the sea.

Bjarni's Point! When my neighbors had told me about
finding the body they had both neglected to mention by
name the place where the body had been washed ashore;
they had called it "the point over there—the other side of
the muddy pool." So "Bjarni's Point?" I asked. At which
Thorberg had nodded, while Gudmund had blushed and
cast down his eyes.

There was no talking on the way over. Nor was there
any talking as we stood beside the departed Jon Thorgrimsson. For it was he all right.

He lay there in the sand; the skull was bare and white;
there was neither skin nor flesh above his jaws. He lay

half on his side, staring with empty eye-sockets over toward Baer—the road he had yet to go. His mouth was wide open as though frozen in a scream, a scream without lips or tongue. Underneath there was still some flesh hanging from the jaws—some pale, ragged flesh—but just above the neck of the shirt there was skin visible. In the lacerated tissues of the neck was a hole in one place that slanted over toward the breast. Bjorn Halldorsson stuck his finger in it and said, "There's where he stabbed him, the bastard."

He broke off—in his confusion he was on the verge of putting his finger in his mouth—and mumbled prayerfully, "God save my tongue."

The other four of us were unanimous in not listening to him. A little later he said thoughtfully—he was the only one of us that had known Jon from a long time ago— "Uhhuh, the body and the arms and legs I recognize, even with the fingers and toes missing. You others must at least recognize the clothes?"

"Yes," said Bjorn Palsson with so much inner gravity that he could hardly form the words, "it's Jon Thorgrimsson, all right, that's easy to see. But the Jon Thorgrimsson lying here, he didn't fall from Skor Cliffs, that much is sure. That's what I say if they cut my tongue out of my mouth for it. Otherwise he wouldn't be lying here, all in one piece."

Something like that probably several had thought. Now it was said.

Bjorn Halldorsson rinsed his fingers in the water, smelled of them, rinsed them again. Then he found a stick, dried it off, tested carefully how deep it would go into the hole in the corpse's neck. He got it in four or five inches; then he pulled it out and showed to the rest of us, wordlessly, how deep it had gone. Nobody said anything.

Pall was there then with the horses and the litter. The body was put on it, the litter loaded on planks between the horses, and we got under way toward home.

"He had to crawl most of the way to the churchyard

himself," remarked my brother Pall—to the horses or the corpse or anybody who would listen. "Funny he didn't wash right in over the churchyard wall."

We put him in the church at the altar, and then went in to my study to make a deposition on the finding of the body.

I wrote out the deposition without consulting the others. I described my dismal guest exactly. I mentioned the hole in the neck that you could stick your finger in; mentioned that it had been tested with a peg and had proved to be four or five inches deep. And I added that we considered it to be most likely that the hole had been caused by a stab; was the work of some man's hand. I mentioned all the dead man's clothes, underclothing and outer clothes, and ended by saying that, aside from the clothes, we could determine from the limbs and teeth that the dead man was Jon Thorgrimsson, farmer at Syvendeaa, of whom it had been said in the winter that he fell from Skor Cliffs.

This deposition I then read to the others. They sat during the reading with bowed heads. Nor did they afterwards look either at me or at each other, and they said nothing. But they signed. After which they slunk out of the room, one by one, silently, without a word or a goodbye.

So I sat there—with my deposition.

As long as I was not alone I had been so certain that it was only in this way that I could answer to God for it; just the way it was and no other way. Not until the others had gone did I fully realize that we five men had sat here and written—a judgment on Bjarni.

And now there was no turning back.

Olof, my wife, came into my study and sat a while. I showed her the paper, the deposition. She read it and laid it silently aside. She sat a little longer. Then she went. And I was alone again.

Was I a judge? Was I an executioner? Once more I

read the deposition through—"was the work of some man's hand . . . of whom it had been said." And the deposition had to go to the authorities. Would probably have to be laid before the judge . . .

When the day dawned I was stiff and lame. I had sat and slept with my arms on the table and my head resting on my arms. And I had dreamed. Dreams whose terror and alarm were still in me but which I had forgotten.

I got up, shook the cold and stiffness from me, took the church key, and went out to the dead man. I lifted the covering from his naked skull to pull myself together by the sight of him.

"Am I the one you're looking for, Jon?" I asked him.

There was a peculiarly cruel and ruthless ferocity on those teeth from which all flesh was stripped. There on the blunt, naked nose bone lay the scorn of death itself. Death's own devouring scorn. This man who had been so weak and pathetic in life—now he lay here stronger than all of the rest of us together. Lay here dominating us, simply by virtue of having died. Having died a suspicious death.

There was something in me that revolted at serving him. Who knows—perhaps he took his life himself, I tried to tell myself.

But he was lying there so humble suddenly. So humble. So humble and mistreated and helpless.

I replaced the cloth on his poor stinking skull, whereupon I sat down on a pew beside his litter and wept and prayed.

Then I got saddle and bridle from the shed, put a piece of dried fish in my pocket to chew on, and went out to look for my bay, which together with our other horses was standing up under the cliffs waiting for the dew to dry.

Even as I put the saddle on him I did not know where I was going to go. Monsieur Jon Palsson and Monsieur Sigmund, and Olaf from Lambavatn—they were the authorities, the nearest authorities. So I rode north to Sauthlauksdal—possibly because I knew that all the others were home, but that it was virtually impossible that the Reverend Jon Ormsson could have returned yet from his circuit visits.

I took the bay by the reins and we zigzagged up the slopes; clambered up the steep slopes along a twisting path whose loose stones slipped away under the horse's feet, rolled and rolled, endlessly in the still morning.

The cliffs back of our farms are almost as high as the strip of sand down below is wide, and in these cliffs the water has been able to cut a gully in only two places. It was up through one of these gullies that the bay and I were going. Finally we reached the mountain ridge.

We stood a little and took a breather. The bay pricked up her ears and looked down, sent a whinny after our other horses, waved her ears unsatisfied at having got no answer.

Down below lay my little church parish, Rodesand— eleven visible farms, and Keflavig besides, lying in a dale by itself out toward the west, and Syvendeaa hidden on a lonely shelf in the mountains far over toward Skor Cliffs . . . Down below stood my little church, whose thin bell tones had grown so familiar and dear to me—almost as though they were my own inner tones. It had rung hollow, hollow melancholy in me—the whole summer. How was it going to sound in case the departed Jon Thorgrimsson was buried without anything being done? I didn't dare think about that. And so I was riding here.

I was in no hurry to get northward over the short heath. I took my time, sat and chewed my dried fish, let the bay pick her own way. But even if it only goes a foot at a time—every road has an end. It was not even ten o'clock when my bay and I reached the bottom of the narrow, deep Patreks Fjord, stood listening and waiting in the yard in front of Sauthlauksdal, and for a second time hammered on the door.

The Reverend Jon had not returned home—Madame

Ragnheid seemed astonished that I, who certainly knew better, should ask for him. She went with me into the parlor, said that I must certainly have some particular reason. You could see it in my face, by the way, she said. I admitted that the reason was this: I had some important, some extremely important, business. Madame Ragnheid asked; I answered. At last she asked to be allowed to see the deposition that I wanted to lay before the Reverend Jon. I showed it to her, hesitatingly, for actually it was an official document and ought not, perhaps, be shown to just anybody. She read it; she read it twice. Then she said, "No, thank God, my husband the Reverend Jon is not home. And fortunately this is a matter that won't stand for any delay."

She opened a desk cover and pulled forward a chair. "Here are pen and ink and paper, curate," she said quietly and authoritatively. "Sit down here and write to Scheving. The letter will be taken there right today."

When I did not sit down immediately, not so much because I hesitated as because my duty suddenly overwhelmed me—my unavoidable duty—Madame Ragnheid added threateningly, "If Jon Thorgrimsson is put under ground without Judge Scheving having seen him, then they are going to need a new administration in Rodesand, spiritual as well as temporal."

I sat down and tried the pen, for this probably was the moment I had really been waiting for. Without doubt it was to sit here that I had taken the road to Sauthlauksdal when I rode from home this morning.

I wrote as follows—I can remember every single word still: "Yesterday after services in Saurbaer there was found at Bjarni's Point at Baer by parishioners on their way home from church the corpse of a man washed ashore, which I had examined and brought immediately to the church. From the clothes, etc., the dead man was recognized as the departed Jon Thorgrimsson of Syvendeaa. This information I did not wish, in the Dean's absence, to delay imparting to your honor, if you would be so good as to occupy yourself with the rumors which were circulating this summer. We, who examined the corpse, were astonished that a man who is supposed to have fallen from the top of the cliffs should not have a broken bone in his body."

This is what I wrote and to it I signed my name.

Then I hurried to seal the letter so that I would not have to show it to Madame Ragnheid, and I wrote on the outside: "To Judge Gudmund Scheving, Haga, Bardestrand."

When I brought the letter to Madame Ragnheid she was startled. "Finished and sealed? Well I must say! You write a fast hand, curate . . ."

Then she balanced the letter in her hand and added, smiling, "Ah well, the letter is your business—the messenger mine."

XII

What I went through in those days that now followed, it would be impossible for me to tell. I was in such a pitiful state that I passed the day humming, could not do anything—could not even stay in one place. I did not once try to think—to consider intelligently what I had done, and what I was going to do and going to have to do. Quite the contrary, I fled before my thoughts, hid myself in an inner fog of wretched confusion and misery.

When on Thursday it turned to sharp, windy snow, I breathed more easily, I don't know why. For a long time I stood in the doorway and enjoyed with a kind of satisfaction the tremendous snow storm out there, the snow dance; took pleasure in the storm's roaring blast.

Out of the snowfall appeared unexpectedly my neighbor, Thorberg Illugason, lashed by the storm, icicles dangling from his beard and hair.

"I've got an appointment here," he explained to me briefly, and brushed the snow from himself—and pulled at the clinging ice. "Gudmund is coming later."

"Which Gudmund?"

"Gudmund Einarsson, who else?"

"An appointment here, what does that mean?" I asked, and I noticed suddenly that I was freezing.

"I don't know, my good man," Thorberg answered reluctantly. "Got a message from the sheriff . . . We're supposed to look at the deceased Jon—once more, as I understood it."

He was not disposed to conversation and neither was I. I asked him to go into the kitchen and get warm, I myself sat down in my study. Now it's coming, I thought. And I sat there and drummed my fingers on the table. Now it's coming...

It was the judge that I had expected to see. But it was my father-in-law and Monsieur Sigmund who a moment later came in to me in my room.

Monsieur Jon pressed my hand warmly. "Now look at that, son-in-law . . Well, the weather couldn't be much worse. But the occasion couldn't be better."

"That isn't the kind of flotsam I like to collect from the shallows at Baer," I answered, troubled and perhaps a little warily.

Jon Palsson tried to read my face. "Exactly. Exactly for that reason."

"We ought to examine the man, as long as there's daylight," said Monsieur Sigmund, annoyed; he wanted to get it over with. "It's getting to be the regular custom here in the parish for the dead to be examined in the church."

"The man has been examined," I protested. "Examined well enough. There's a deposition been made of it, sworn to by four good men, and myself as the fifth."

"Nonetheless the judge asks—in a letter to me which Monsieur Jon has seen—that the corpse be examined again," Sigmund said with authority.

"So—the judge has only written."

"The judge has ordered Monsieur Sigmund and me to hold another examination of the body," Jon Palsson inserted placatingly, "and he has likewise ordered us if necessary to arrest Bjarni of Syvendeaa and bring him over to Haga. You understand? Monsieur Sigmund agreed that we should approve the same men who examined the body before. But since the judge asks in his letter that the body be viewed by six men, I thought that you five could make a certification of your doubtless correct and exact initial deposition and then the Reverend Jon Ormsson could endorse the addition. He ought to be here any moment."

"He's taking the matter lightly—Judge Scheving . . ."

"Not at all, son-in-law. But his grandfather has a case that could run into money in Reykjavik—he has to go there."

"Oh well, if it's a matter of money for Gudmund—then it's a matter of life and death."

"Didn't you know, then, that for prosecutor—with authority to summon whom he pleases and set the day for the trial himself—he's appointed Monsieur Einar Jonsson in Kollsvig, to whom we therefore have to send our report of inspection and to direct all further documents in the case?"

"So that's the way it is. Then there'll be something done. That man will summon the living and the dead."

"In any case he'll summon all of us."

Monsieur Sigmund dropped his eyelids. "Just let him do it. You can certainly say that with that man as prosecutor, Bjarni and Steinun still have a chance to get off, even if they should be guilty."

Monsieur Jon smiled. "To make up for it the Reverend Jon can't possibly get off. The Sinner's going to be judged."

Speak of an angel and you hear its wings, as they say. There was the Reverend Jon, and he was angry.

"By what right and authority do you order me to be here, sheriff?"

"Not by God's authority," Jon Palsson tried to calm him jestingly, "since it's on the orders of Gudmund Scheving."

"May I see the letter? . . . But here it says only 'the minister.' The Reverend Eiulv is a minister, too. The Reverend Eiulv is the only minister in this case . . . Einar Jonsson, counsel for the prosecution, uh huh . . . uh huh . . . I'm clear on what I have done or left undone up til now, I should think . . ."

"Likely enough, hm," murmured Monsieur Sigmund.

The Reverend Jon pulled himself together. "Well, in the name of God and the forty knights . . . Reverend Eiulv—do you realize what you've set in motion?"

"I have no intention of trying to escape any part of my responsibility—God help me," I answered.

Then suddenly he put one arm around my shoulders. "Eiulv—my friend . . ."

And my old Dean wept; actually wept, so that the rest of us, embarrassed, had to drop our eyes.

Together with the approved earlier examiners we went out to the church, wading forward through the biting current of freezing, turbulent water. The poor corpse, lying there so abandoned on its litter, had begun to decay very badly now that the salt water was no longer preserving it. Jon Thorgrimsson seemed to be hurrying toward his dissolution. But not until now—six months after his death.

Jon Palsson exclaimed softly, "Well now, my friends. Has that body been lying for months in the ocean? And lasted until now? As hot as the summer has been? I'd think that he'd had at the most a three-months trip in the ocean. And he's supposed to have been under way six . . . Not likely. But where has he been then?"

Nobody answered him.

The hole in the neck, it appeared, was not as open as before.

At the Reverend Jon Ormsson's urgent suggestion, we five inspectors agreed to add to our previous deposition that it no longer seemed as evident that the hole had been caused by an act of violence. Since I hardly wanted to have conferences in my church, either about this or anything else, and since, moreover, I thought we ought to let the departed Jon rest in peace, I asked the Reverend Jon and the sheriff to go with me to my study where we could discuss the matter. The men I asked to wait for us.

The Reverend Jon refused, in the meantime, to take any part in it. "I'll stay here the night, Eiulv," he said, putting one hand on my shoulder. "I can write on your deposition in the morning. But I don't want to know or to have any part in what happens. Do what you think right. And God help you . . ."

There was silence after he was gone. Finally Monsieur Jon said, "And what do the three of us have to talk about, anyway? That man Bjarni's to be arrested, to be put face to face with his housemate and interrogated about his possible participation in his death—those are the judge's plain orders. It's too late today. But it has to be done tomorrow."

He was silent a little and then he added, "That the man has to be put in temporary custody whether he answers one way or another—on that we're hardly in disagreement."

He rose quickly and concluded, "I'm going in to see my daughter. I haven't said hello to her yet. You're hiding her well, Eiulv."

So the two of us were left sitting alone, Monsieur Sigmund and I. Sitting silent together. Until Sigmund said, uncertainly, "I'd really like to get some sleep . . ."

"But we haven't had supper," I objected.

"I'd just like to get some sleep," he excused himself.

So I showed him to a bed and wished him good night.

XIII

The next day the weather was clear and fine, though somewhat gusty. A lot of snow had fallen, but the sun thawed it and the wind packed it hard.

We were at Syvendeaa a little before noon—the two sheriffs, both Bjorns, and I. I was really superfluous, nor had anyone asked me to ride along. But I had my own business and I was not unwelcome in the little group—quite the contrary. That the others were not here of their own free will—that was plain to be seen on all four. Even Monsieur Jon was uncomfortable with his errand and he made no secret of it.

I could not resist digging at him a little. "You rode over here faster last summer," I remarked.

"It's one thing to clean out a den of foxes, and another to go get a man for the block," he shot back.

Whether Bjarni had seen us come I don't know; at any rate, we did not see him until we had dismounted in the farm yard and he stepped suddenly out of the door.

"Friends on a visit," he said jestingly. That's nice, although maybe not just friends . . ."

"You probably know what we've come for," said Jon Palsson sharply.

"Your business at Syvendeaa has got to be so various that a man just can't keep track of it, Monsieur Jon," Bjarni answered. "Maybe the cattle have done some damage and will have to be taken away—that's possible. But otherwise, you look to me this time as though you had the idea of taking away the rest of the people in the house that you left here in the summer."

"Not a bad guess. Get ready to come along."

Bjarni stiffened—he was plainly surprised. He opened his mouth. But he stopped at asking any questions.

The horses in the meantime stood snorting and rubbing against each other and against us, the riders. They found the weather too cold for standing there and holding a long conversation, and they made no secret of it.

Sigmund from Staak said, "You must have heard, Bjarni, that poor Jon was finally washed up on shore?"

"No," Bjarni said softly—and cleared his throat. "You're the first to tell me about it. It was sure high time."

"Yeah, he's lying back there in the church at Baer and he'd like to say hello to an old housemate."

"Monsieur Sigmund," I said sternly—and I intended it at the same time for my father-in-law—"we're not here on our own business but on the authorities'. The thing is, Bjarni, we have orders to show you the departed Jon Thorgrimsson's corpse, so that you can say whether you recognize it and possibly tell us something more about his death. To make a show of force or even of harsh words here, gentlemen, I think is an impropriety . . . I'm sure you're willing to go along, Bjarni."

"Of course I'll go along, if that's the way it is," Bjarni said amenably. "The kids are big enough for me to leave them alone—for that little while."

"The children we can take home to my place," I answered. "That's the reason I'm here, Bjarni. That way we can avoid troubling the authorities with them—for however long the case lasts.

"The children you can handle better when there are two of you, Eiulv," Monsieur Jon objected, dissatisfied.

"For however long the case lasts," Bjarni repeated awkwardly. "What case?"

I said amicably, "If you're innocent, Bjarni, you can't have any more earnest wish than that the rumors about your and Steinun's guilt in the deaths of your wife and her husband get taken up and thoroughly investigated. And discredited . . ."

"Do people think that Jon was murdered?"

"There's a hole in his throat—like a stab wound."

"I didn't stab Jon Thorgrimsson—I can give my oath on that," Bjarni answered firmly—and with relief.

After which he got his saddle, took a bridle in his hand, and went after his horses grazing near the farm.

The boy Gisli we found down along the shore. He was a slight boy with bright, timid eyes. When he understood that something unusual was afoot he fastened himself to Bjarni's legs—would not let go of him. The two little girls, his dolls, we had to get from the indoors. They did not move from the bed where they were sitting, hand in hand, when we asked them to come along. Even when their father called they moved only the barest bit. But at any rate, they made no resistance when we carried them out, Bjorn Palsson and I. Silently they let themselves be wrapped in shawls and set up ahead of us on the pommels; their rigid glances never wavered a moment from our faces.

Bjarni closed the door, locked it, and looked around. Looked out over the fall-gray fjord, looked up over the snow-streaked mountains. Sunk in thought, he mounted his horse and rode with us.

XIV

Young Olof was out when we rode into the yard at Baer, was outside and took the children. It was as if she had expected them, although I had not by any word intimated my intentions to her before I rode from home.

I saw her say hello to Bjarni for the first time, with a timid little nod—as though finally something had happened which had turned him into a fellow human being. Then she went away with the little girls, who stuck tight to each other, and with the resisting Gisli.

Bjarni followed his children with his eyes until they had vanished through the door; then he stood for a moment gazing at the door steadily. After that he turned to me and said, trying at the same time to smile, "So now you have them all, Reverend Eiulv. First you got the two dead ones, and now you take the three—living ones."

His glance was even more troubled than it had been that day he had brought me his farmers.

I was in a very awkward situation . . . It was unbearable for me to think that Bjarni should be confronted with Jon Thorgrimsson in my church, but particularly that he should—as had been ordered—be questioned at the bier about his possible implication in the death. There in God's holy house. If he spoke the truth, it did not matter so much . . . If he lied—would his sin not be multiplied thereby?

But precisely because of this situation—that being in a church could possibly influence him to speak the truth, where otherwise his poor blood and the natal frailty of the flesh could tempt him to lie—I let it go on, although troubled in my mind.

Again we stood around the departed Jon's bier, we five coroners, our Dean, the two sheriffs. And then Bjarni.

As we stood there—during which time I did not take my eyes from Bjarni—I got the impression that this was not the first time he had seen Jon's corpse. What it was that gave me this impression I am not able to say. And immediately I hesitated, was seized by the opposite impression. For when the Reverend Jon now made the sign of the cross over the body and after that lifted the cloth from the naked skull, there was something in Bjarni's eyes and features that convinced me that it really was the first time; that convinced me for a while.

Monsieur Sigmund, to whom the judge had sent his letter, fluttered his eyelids. Ponderously and significantly he asked, "Do you recognize this man here, Bjarni?"

Bjarni, who was standing staring at the naked skull, whispered very low, "No . . ."

There it was. I was uncertain again. Yes, he had seen him. Otherwise he would not have lied. For he had to recognize him.

"Let him see the whole body—without fingers and toes," burst out Bjorn Palsson, quivering, his hands shaking as he dragged the cover from the bier, letting it fall to the floor and kicking it away.

It was so fantastically inappropriate to see Jon Thorgrimsson lying there without hands projecting from his sleeves that it almost made him seem alive. From the arm stumps there radiated an oddly ferocious threat, as though the dead man in an uncontrollable rage had worked the toes and fingers off, worn the flesh from his jaws, screamed the tongue clear out of his mouth for some purpose. A purpose which he had still not forgotten. Yes, as though in a blind determination he were staring at it—with both his empty, threatening, weirdly visionary eye-sockets.

68

Bjarni must have felt something similar. At any rate, I noticed that in spite of the icy cold of the church, moisture collected on his forehead. Bjorn Palsson groaned. He said, somberly triumphant, "Well, now do you recognize him?"

Bjarni was silent at that. Sigmund asked, "Are you going to claim you don't recognize Jon Thorgrimsson, lying right here?"

"The clothes seem to be Jon Thorgrimsson's, that's true enough," Bjarni answered—as though in a trance.

"Do you see that hole in the neck?" Sigmund asked.

"No, where?"

Sigmund pulled him closer; showed it to him. Tried to get him to touch it. Then suddenly Bjarni changed his mind. "Yes," he answered almost eagerly. "Yes, I see it all right."

"Do you dare deny that that hole is your work, Bjarni?"

"Yes, I do," Bjarni answered, relieved, and dried his forehead, "as God and the saints are my witnesses. I'm ready to stake my eternal soul on it now or any other time."

That the man was telling the truth—for me that was beyond a doubt. I stood there in confusion; I could make neither head nor tail of it. Joy and relief were lurking in my heart but could not find expression.

The others were also uncertain, that was obvious. Became uncertain and confused. Even Bjorn Palsson was standing with stiff, uncertain eyes, believing and not believing. He had lost his bearings completely.

"And you can't think of anybody else who could have given him this death blow?" Monsieur Sigmund asked subdued. "His wife Steinun, perhaps?"

"It doesn't look very much like a woman's work," Bjarni answered, suddenly confident. "The man could have stabbed himself."

Monsieur Jon looked around to see if anybody else wanted to speak. Then he said, very gently, "In that case there'd have to have been blood visible on the snow—there where you said that he'd fallen."

"Yes, there would," Bjarni said, all too willingly.

"Yes, but, " Bjorn Palsson stammered, "yes but, you forget that . . ." Then he stopped suddenly. Uncertain again.

Monsieur Jon Palsson, who was the one among us suffering the most from the stink of the body, said determinedly, "Nothing's going to come of this, Sigmund. Let's carry out the judge's orders and turn him over to Eiulv."

"First the man has to be arrested," Sigmund objected, taking some comfort in remembering all at once his official duty.

"Well," answered Jon Palsson, and turned to Bjarni, saying with restraint: "In the name of the King and of the law I herewith arrest you, Bjarni Bjarnason, on suspicion of murder of your wife, the deceased Gudrun Egilsdottir, and of the deceased Jon Thorgrimsson lying here. I haven't the heart to put you in irons. Give me your word of honor that you'll not try to escape. Then you can go without irons until you come to Haga."

Bjarni put out his hand. Jon Palsson did not take it. "Give Monsieur Sigmund your hand on it," he said and left.

I was confused and astonished that Monsieur Jon could continue to be convinced of Bjarni's guilt. And he was—there was no mistaking that. We still had not seen what effect it had on Bjarni to be faced with—it. What Bjorn Palsson had been on the verge of blurting out at the wrong time. Besides, it was incomprehensible to me that Monsieur Sigmund had stuck to the hole in the throat and had not then or later by any word touched on the real evidence. Leniency it could not be. More likely, forgetfulness. But Sigmund had not been along the day that Jon was found. So he could not know what it was, then, that had made the strongest impression on us.

As far as Jon Palsson was concerned I was not in a moment's doubt. He was keeping quiet deliberately.

He thought that the first interrogation was botched anyway, and was going to leave it to me to straighten it out.

"You come along with me, Bjarni," I said, and took his arm. "Not as a prisoner, because you're not mine, but the sheriff's, prisoner. I am your minister, not your warden. And until morning you're my guest. For the first time, to be sure."

"For the first time and the last, Eiulv," Bjarni answered, trying to smile. He walked heavily, as though he had difficulty in moving his legs.

"That's something neither you nor I know," I answered, troubled.

Since the others came along even after we were out of the church, I said to them, "Now, you can stay around, brothers . . ."

Then I went in with Bjarni, my parishioner. Truth to tell, I felt at that moment as though he were my only parishioner. Yes, as though he were the man for whom I had the most responsibility with God.

XV

When we were seated in my room and while I was still considering how I should proceed, Bjarni said—with that smile that was no smile—"I'm not afraid of men . . . And I'm not afraid of God either . . . And the Devil least of all. But *you* I'm afraid of, Eiulv."

"If that's the truth, that's bad, as bad as can be," I answered him, "since it's certainly I who has been appointed by God to help you in your need, poor devil."

"Men can't help each other," Bjarni answered with suppressed fury. "Men only kill each other."

I was silent. I was determined not to use any improper methods. Truth would conquer by its own strength.

"There are so many ways of killing, Eiulv," Bjarni went on, trying as well as he could to control his agitation. "You kill and are killed. Even the dead return . . . and kill . . ."

"A man who has sinned against his fellowmen and against God has to take his punishment, Bjarni," I answered, troubled.

"Don't you believe that I have been punished as hard as I can possibly be?" he whispered hoarsely.

"No, Bjarni, you haven't," I answered. "If you had been, you'd be at peace. Your suffering comes from your not having been punished, not yet. Man's fear of punishment is nothing but the horror of his own actions. After you're punished, everything can be all right again; not before. You must have learned, man, that the way you're living, man can't live."

"No, that's true . . . a man can't live like this."

"And you are a man, Bjarni. Trust in God. And trust in yourself."

"I've always trusted in myself . . . God—it seems to me I knew him once. But that was a long time ago. He was probably only something I imagined—like everything else . . ."

"Without God there is nothing," I said quietly.

"Then he has a terrible responsibility," Bjarni sighed.

We were silent a long time.

"It was a strange thing to discover that I was alone in the world," Bjarni offered after a long time.

"When did you feel that?"

"The first time, the morning that my farmers went. The next time . . . No, there wasn't any next time. You know—they were gone one morning. Without my having any inkling of it . . . As though the night had taken them."

He groaned. But then he added, "I don't want to think about it . . . It doesn't help anyhow."

We were silent again. Then I said, "You know very well, Bjarni, that no power on earth can keep you from telling the truth ultimately. The whole truth. Why not now?"

"You're leading me on, I see," Bjarni answered—bitter all of a sudden. "I was your guest, you said before. And still you keep on poking. What is it you want to know?"

"I want to know the truth about how Gudrun Egilsdottir and Jon Thorgrimsson died."

"Haven't you ever seen anybody die?"

"Yes."

"All right then. You've seen it. But do you know from that how death comes? And where from? . . . I've seen it too. But I don't know."

"Now watch yourself, Bjarni," and I felt an evil anger welling up in me against my will. "I won't stand for that tone. Either you stop it, or else I'll show you no mercy."

"If I needed your mercy or anybody else's—then I'd have had it."

"Why do you say that?"

"Because it's the truth, Eiulv. You're determined to ruin me with every devil's trick . . . You'd like to take my head off my shoulders."

"God forgive you, man, for naming the devil in this hour."

"If He'll forgive me the rest, He'll forgive me that too."

A fury of doubt ate itself deeper and deeper into me without my being able to put a stop to it. Fury against Bjarni, fury against myself. Fury and impotence. I was determined, if possible, to keep my calm and reason. But I knew that I would not be able to do it for very long if we went on this way. So I asked him—straight out: "Was it you that murdered the departed Jon Thorgrimsson?"

"Out there in the church before—*then* you believed me," Bjarni answered, a shade scornfully.

"Yes—because you didn't do the stabbing."

"And still you're asking?"

"Yes . . . For either it was you that stabbed him—and you didn't. Or else he didn't die of that stab—and he didn't either."

"How did he die then?"

"I'm the one that's asking . . . How did he die?"

"I already told you what I know about the whole thing."

"No you didn't . . . And now you're going to talk."

"Well then—it was the morning he went over to Skor . . . When it got later and he didn't come back, Gudrun and Steinun began to get worried. Steinun asked me to go look for him. So I did. I could follow his tracks in past the first cliff and to the middle of the second, in the middle of Rodeskred—if you know where that is. And then they disappeared . . . And that's all I know. But down below I thought I could see some confused marks, as if somebody had dragged a dirty sack over the ice. I decided from that that the man had fallen and killed himself."

"Yes—I know that's the way you always explain the dead Jon's disappearance."

Bjarni had been lost in thought; his eyes grew attentive. "That's all I know."

"You're lying, man."

Bjarni started. For the first time I saw him change color. "Then you know more about it than I do," he answered drily.

"Yes, this much I know myself, Bjarni: that a man who falls out over Rodeskred doesn't get by without any bones broken."

"Rodeskred," Bjarni mumbled in confusion. "Did I say Rodeskred? I made a mistake then."

"Yes, and you did it every time you told about Jon's death."

"You can just as well say Rodeskred. But it was before you really get up to the top. It was alongside the cliff, you know. I didn't think about it before, that it could be misunderstood."

"Jon couldn't have dropped without breaking something, not even from that kind of fall. You're lying as hard as you can. But the truth will come out some day . . . Is that all you're willing to tell me?"

"What am I supposed to tell you? . . ."

"No—if that's the way you want it . . . So that's what I'll write to the prosecutor."

"What'll you write to the prosecutor?"

"That you continue to deny having any part in the death of the departed Jon Thorgrimsson. But that you were vague in your explanation when I called your attention to the fact that Jon couldn't have taken a fall from Rodeskred without some broken bones, and altered your statement about the place he's supposed to have fallen from. Together with the fact that I noticed, in spite of your denial, that you seemed to have something on your mind. That's all I know. That's what I'll write."

"Well," Bjarni said, half objecting, half consenting. "Well, all right."

XVI

Early the next morning I went to Bjarni; my uneasiness drove me to it. I wanted to talk with him again. But he was sleeping. Or was pretending to sleep.

I did not see him until he, together with the others, was standing ready to ride east over the mountains.

Rognvald, his brother-in-law, had been sent for, and he was standing, humble and nervous, taking orders from him about the care of the farm.

"Yes—but," he objected, and his eyes flitted back and forth. "Yes, but . . . yes, but . . . I don't want to be at Syvendeaa at all . . . not one night."

"That's nothing to me," Bjarni answered quietly. "You're responsible for taking care of what's mine while I'm away. I'd hate to be in your shoes if everything's not in order when I come back."

Rognvald tried to say something, but he could not get it out. He stood there with tears rolling down his cheeks.

The men standing around them were amused. Even Bjarni laughed. For the rest he looked fiercely at everybody—at me too.

I took him aside and said, quietly, so that the others would not hear, "Well, Bjarni . . . God be with you, whether your road leads to acquittal and life or to condemnation and death. I did my best to help you."

"Oh, I understand that," Bjarni said scornfully.

"Yes, ridicule me," I went on. "I've deserved that, as miserably as I mismanaged things. What you've done I don't know. But that you're off the track, that much I do know. Think it over when you're alone. And if you have any use for me, just let me know. I won't look you up again myself."

Immediately after that Bjarni left, led and guarded by Monsieur Sigmund, the two Bjorns, and Gudmund Einarsson.

Later in the day I saw Rognvald with two men, herding his sheep, driving his cows, and riding his horses out past Baer. Rognvald had got permission from Sigmund to let Syvendeaa stand empty if he took all the livestock home with him to Krokshus. It gave me a peculiar sensation to see the cows moving there in the cold and snow, and there was something transitory and doleful about the ambling sheep, as though the last bit of home and hope was trailing away from Bjarni and from Syvendeaa with them. I, standing there and merely watching—did I not have an essential part in bringing this about? And what was still worse, could I absolve myself of the guilt for the dark and unknown events which had caused Bjarni's cattle to be driven past me in one direction, while he himself as a prisoner was taken away in the other? I felt impelled to go into my church and seek clarity in a prayer to God. But— Jon Thorgrimsson was lying there.

I called for my brother Pall and ordered him curtly to put a coffin together.

Pall was certainly the only man who was not unhappy these days. He asked, "Are you keeping an account of all your services for the Syvendeaa farmers? The horses the other day, and bringing back the corpse, whether it's to be paid for by Jon's estate or the departed Bjarni's—oops, I mean the deceased Jon's estate or Bjarni's? He's still alive. And besides him, three children to be fed and taken care of; and now a coffin."

Pall clearly intended with this chatter to make me angry. He only aroused my pity.

That same evening Amor Jonsson came for a visit.

"Where have you been all this time?" I asked him. "But I must say I didn't miss you. I forgot about you."

"A good sign—and a bad one," Amor Jonsson answered and smiled somberly.

I took him in to my study. "My friend," I began, "I have so many things to talk to you about . . . The only thing is, I don't know if I can."

"Don't do it," Amor Jonsson answered. "Let it alone. Every bird has to fly on its own wings. But I can believe that you're getting dizzy—in the midst of the dark birds."

Shortly after that he resumed. "I've been keeping myself away, my friend, while this was going on. My dreams are enough for me. Not for anything will I get mixed up in the Syvendeaa saga . . . I've seen too much, man," he added and rubbed his eyes tiredly.

We went in to my wife, sat a while and talked. My friend got up very soon and said, "You need to get some sleep, Eiulv. And so does Young Olof. You both have your burdens to bear," he concluded, with a smiling glance at my wife's straight but now thickening figure. And stroking her cheek lightly with his fingertips he left us alone.

"You're so pale, Olof," I burst out, for I noticed it suddenly and I thought my heart would give way in fear and overwhelming pain. "Why are you so pale?"

"It's nothing," she replied with shining eyes, and kissed me. "Nothing at all. I'm all right, Eiulv . . ."

I could not sleep. Once when I heard that she was awake I asked her, "The children . . . How are the children?"

She was silent so long that I began to believe that she was asleep. But finally her answer came: "They are difficult children, those three."

My heart beat; it seemed to me that it must fill the room with its beating. Young Olof whispered, "I've never known children like them before. Don't you think you ought to try to talk to them, Eiulv . . . I'll do what I can," she finished and curled up against me.

I tried to talk to Bjarni's children, but I could not manage to get their confidence. They did not hear a thing I said to them, just followed my expression with hostile eyes and watched my movements fearfully. There was some possibility with Gisli, particularly after he had discovered that there was a shore, here too, where he could rummage around. With the girls, however, there was nothing whatsoever to be done, other than to wait. It was not possible for me to coax even the tiniest utterance from them. I heard during their stay at Baer only two words from the mouth of one, five from the other.

This happened one day when I had sat and talked to them, talked to them and told them stories. Gradually I had come to a standstill. Silent and bewildered I walked back and forth, undecided, but without paying any particular attention to them any more sitting there on the edge of the bed, hand in hand as always.

Then suddenly one of them said, softly and quickly, "Bad man."

And the other repeated in the same tone, "You're a bad man."

There was burning fear in their glances as I, dumb and appalled, turned toward them. But they were quiet. As quiet as before. The children's words hit me hard. I sat down and wept. Everything collapsed for me. It was as though God had spoken to me—through the mouth of these innocents. When I had got hold of myself again, I looked at them carefully. Who could understand them? They sat as immovable as before. And as unmoved. When I left, their eyes followed me to the door.

I could not understand at all why the children had this attitude toward me and what they thought about me.

One day when I met Gisli outside in the yard and stood a while talking to him without his answering, he asked me with a peculiarly childish and sorrowful threat in his voice, "What did you do with my daddy?"

It came so abruptly and touched me so unpleasantly that I could not find an answer for him immediately.

"The girls say that you took him and did something to him," he went on.

"No, I didn't, Gisli," I answered.

"Is he home at Syvendeaa?" he asked incredulously.

I shook my head hopelessly.

"The girls and I want to go home anyhow," he finished —and suddenly took to his heels, flew down toward the shore without once turning his head, as though he expected to be followed and punished.

I took that for sheer childish nonsense, what he had said. Except that now I understood that the children thought I was responsible for their father's disappearance. And wasn't I?

Then one morning, in biting winter weather, the three children were gone. They were gone.

They must have sneaked from their beds in the midst of our sleeping household. It was hard to believe; nobody had heard a thing. How had they hidden themselves?

They were found on the ice, Gisli drowned in a hole in the ice, the girls lying hand in hand, frozen to death alongside it.

There was no perceptible difference between the girls, dead and alive. It was as though fate, which had caught up with them here, had already lain in ambush for them from birth in their frozen hearts, and in their poor bodies so stiff with fright and desperate courage.

These children, whom I had such good intentions of helping—that is how it went for me with them. I began to be afraid that I brought misery with me; that I brought crime and cruel death.

I was on the point of going over east to see Bjarni. But then I couldn't do it.

. . . A little past the middle of the month Einar Jonsson in Kollsvig, the appointed prosecutor, had summoned a number of people from Rodesand for the trial, which was to be held in Sauthlauksdal on November 8 and the following days; from my place, only my brother Pall and me. Monsieur Jon Palsson and Monsieur Sigmund were among the summoned. And, of course, also the Reverend Jon Ormsson, the Sinner. His name was even mentioned twice in the summons, whose longest passage, a passage of several parts, had to do with what he alone was responsible for.

XVII

Monday, November the eighth, I was up before break of day. Long before dawn. It was important for me to be there early.

My brother Pall got ready too. I asked him, "Why were you summoned as a witness, anyhow, Pall?"

"Oh, I might have a couple of things to say."

"You stay home," I ordered him.

It is so strange to go along, alone, between the mountains, in the frozen light of the moon and the stars. There was wind-polished snow lying on the lowlands, and the slopes were smooth and icy. I was on foot. When I got to the slopes I tied on my ice shoes and went up the trail at my own pace. At every step the spikes bit into the ice with a hard crunch that rang evilly in the still of the foreboding night. Now and then they struck sparks from the stones, so that you could feel in the nose the fire that lurks in all things. As I went along, my life became for me so peculiar and strange that I hardly knew anymore who I really was or where I was going. If only it was all nothing but a dream, I wished. Maybe you are still a boy and are just walking along here on some errand or other for your father. That I had inherited property, had become a minister, had married, and was now walking here—on such a mission—did that make any sense? Could it be anything else but fantasy? But if it really was that way—if I was really walking along here and was not dreaming at all but was really living this, and the night was the night, the moon the moon—did I really want my life changed?

Would I rather be walking along here as a boy, merely a boy, lost in one of the manifold dreams of my childhood? What about Olof, my wife, Young Olof? Would she be a dream too? Was it possible for me to bargain with God so that Bjarni and Steinun, and the two who were dead—oh, all those dead—were just a product of my imagination? And to bargain for *that* price? . . . No, it was not possible for me. Anything but that.

I stopped and caught my breath. The sea down below was black, with sparks of gold. Where I stood was a steep, glistening slope, dizzyingly high but still with cliffs towering over me. Suddenly a feeling of joy, of dark, hot joy rose in me. God had put me in a difficult post. I would not betray Him. Intoxicated with the cliffs, the freezing cold, and the night-dark sea I went on. But now with God at my side.

He can be so near to you at night, the invisible and omnipresent Being.

When I was nearly halfway over the Sand Mountains the blue of the night was beginning to fade, the shadows dissolved, and the heavens' blue light gave way to a bright, demanding day, which nothing could prevent from spreading its cold power over the earth.

The first person I talked with in Sauthlauksdal was the judge's clerk. I talked a little with him privately. He had just got up . . . No one had seen him . . . When we parted he had his right hand in a sling, was, in other words, not capable of performing his office.

I had been able to learn some things from him, too. I had learned that Judge Scheving had come in the evening ahead of time with the prisoners and the appointed defense counsel, Monsieur Gudmund Sigmundsson from Bathall; that the prosecutor had also come, that he had sat and talked with the Judge far into the night; together with the fact the Reverend Jon Ormsson had hardly said hello to his guests and had not been seen since. Madame Ragnheid, on the other hand, was treating people as though it was a wedding—or a funeral—was how my informant, the brisk young clerk, closed his account.

I went at once to find Judge Scheving.

Gudmund Scheving had just got up. He stood there, small and erect, rocking on his toes, looking out of the window and whistling.

"Who are you?" he asked me cheerfully.

I told him my name.

He took his hands out of his pockets to shake mine and said, "Well . . . I hope you are more amenable than your superior. He looks marvelous—a veritable apostle. But you can't go by appearances. He seems to be quite offended, this man of God, that the children of his parish aren't allowed to murder one another in peace and quiet without a rebuke from the authorities. He's relying on God and the bishop, he says."

"Your honor . . ."

"That's what he told me, would you believe it, the old buck!" Judge Scheving laughed. "You know, you're a pretty lively bunch over here in the west, I have to give you that. God only knows whether you are all as hot and bothered in love and other forms of bloodshed. I have my doubts. You hear a few things. I get the urge now and then to throttle an enemy myself, if only it wasn't so damnably irregular. With muscles like Bjarni's it mustn't be so easy to hold yourself in. I give you my word, he wears my best irons like mere toys. Almost like jewelry. He could smash them, and all of us with them, any time he wanted to—that's for sure. Dead sure. What I don't understand is why he doesn't do it. And you know I must say, his taste . . . there's nothing wrong with that. Well, you know that woman yourself. It's enough to make a man cry if a couple of people like that have really lost their heads, my dear Reverend."

"I'd like very much to have permission to have a few words with Bjarni," I interrupted.

"That can't be done. Not until such time as we've got by the worst of this. You've been summoned as a witness, if I remember correctly."

"No, only as a coroner."

"Only as a coroner—uh huh . . ."

He looked at his papers. "Oh yes, that's right . . . Well . . . in your capacity as minister . . . All right. What do you want to talk about with him, by the way?"

"I only want to tell him that the three children he left behind—are dead."

"Praise the Lord. Now, don't misunderstand me; but there couldn't a better thing have happened to them, Reverend. Excellent . . . supposing, that is, that they died a natural death, of course. And that seems to be a hard thing for you to do, here in the west. Go right on in to him, my good man. That might just crack his hard heart and save the rest of us a good deal of trouble."

"These children that died, I was the one taking care of them," I went on. "One of them drowned, the other two froze to death, while running away back to Syvendeaa."

This information finally stopped the flow of words from the judge. He wavered.

"They wanted to go back," he said hesitatingly.

"Yes, they wanted to go back. Children are funny, your Honor. I thought that it would be best, now that you're here, if you'd investigate to what extent neglect on my or my household's part can be said to have been responsible for the poor children's misfortune."

"I wonder if we shouldn't wait until some other complainant turns up, my dear Reverend," he smiled. "Right at the moment I have more than enough hanging over my head. Don't you think so? Two hard-boiled criminals. Dumb witnesses by the dozens besides. Lord, yes."

He bent his arms up and stretched, so that he creaked in every joint. I took that for permission to go.

Way up under the peak of a hayloft, where there was so

little room that you had to creep in on all fours, I found Bjarni together with his guards, all buried in hay until only their arms and heads were visible.

There seemed to have been a conversation going on between the guards, but as soon as I showed up they raised up on their elbows, all four, and let me know, all of them talking at once, that I had no business here, none at all. But there was one of them who knew me. All the same they grumbled when I sat down in the hay alongside Bjarni, instead of going off about my business.

Bjarni was noticeably changed. His hair and beard were tangled and dirty, his features were both slack and tense. He was so distrait that he hardly noticed me.

I took hold of his right hand right at the irons, which I had expected to feel cold but which felt warm to my hand —with a kind of menacing and loathsome friendliness. I said, "I have something awful to tell you, Bjarni."

When I finally got control of myself and told him that his children were gone—those are the words I used— all three of them, he answered dully, "They've been gone a long time, Eiulv. For me everything's gone, everything . . ."

The guards had stopped grumbling. They lay silent and withdrawn, each in his hole, chewing on long straws that they had found in the hay. I tried to tell how it had gone with Gisli and the girls. But Bjarni interrupted me with a sigh, "Don't you think I have something else to think about now, Eiulv? . . ."

I fell silent. The four guards scowled at him. He went on almost apologetically, "It isn't something you can remember easily, how it all happened—now that it's so long ago . . ."

The oldest of the guards cleared his throat and said politely, "This is what you can't talk about with the prisoner."

"You'd better go now, Eiulv," Bjarni said tiredly. "I've

got so many things to think about. Just one little thing I don't remember—it can finish me, you know. Since we talked, you got me to doubting what I said about Rodeskred—you know, the place where I said poor Jon fell. I might have to pay a lot for that. Why didn't I keep quiet about it anyhow? What do I know about where Jon fell? I didn't see the man fall. I can swear to that. Listen, Eiulv . . . No, why don't you go. Let me think about it . . ."

He turned over on his side, away from the rest of us.

I crawled out again through the square opening in the turf gable end. Bitterly confused and dejected I staggered on weak legs across the yard. The witnesses had come, they said. There was a lot of confusion at the farm. Gudmund Scheving was talking loudly and angrily. "How can you just go and sprain your hand like that, you bungling idiot," he complained. "Did you ever hear anything like it? I suppose you were too busy grabbing at the girls—is that it? And here I am with two criminals, judges and witnesses, supposed to hold court. Without a court reporter. Are you out of your mind, man? You can hold a pen, at least, damn it. Let me see that paw."

"Your Honor," I intruded, "I'm not a particularly experienced reporter . . ."

"But you have a summons, man. You're to be questioned."

"But only as a coroner."

"Where's Monsieur Einar gone to? Monsieur Einar! My dear friend, listen a minute . . . Will you go along with letting one of the witnesses act as reporter?"

Monsieur Einar Jonsson of Kollsvig came up, short and fat, looked at me gloomily, after which he turned toward the judge. "The spiritual responsibility in the parish is the Dean's, you know; the Reverend Eiulv is only his curate," he explained circumstantially—with his underlip thrust out. "For that reason I only summoned the Reverend Eiulv as coroner. Besides the Reverend Eiulv has been active in the matter, I think you could say, at least since the departed Jon was washed ashore; but you know all about all this, Scheving. In this case, as an emergency . . ."

"In this case, as an emergency. All right. You always know how to put it into words, my friend. And now enough chatter—my fellow judges are already sitting in there."

He led the way into the parlor of the house, a capacious room where the four assessors and the defense sat in a silent row behind a long table. For the court reporter there was a little table prepared at one of the windows. I sat down and tested my pen. I was very ill at ease and dissatisfied with myself. Why was I sitting here? What was I trying to do here? I was no judge, not a witness either, hardly involved in the affair, in fact. I was on the verge of getting to my feet and calling out that there was nothing in the least wrong with the court reporter. That it was only that I had imposed myself on something that was none of my business.

Judge Scheving took his seat in the middle of the long table with the prosecutor at his right; the defender he had at his left.

The assessors were Jon Thorberg, a foreman from the market town across the fjord—a pale sleepy man, taciturn and a trencherman, well disposed toward high and low; our conciliator, a good, honest, and upright farmer; and two more farmers, the prosecutor's friend and brother-in-law, Olaf Bjarnason, together with his friend and neighbor, Arni from Laginup. That was very like Monseiur Einar to have assured himself in advance of a majority among the assessors.

It was ice cold in the room. The stove, which was used very seldom, smoked instead of heating. There was so much coughing and hawking and spitting that I could hardly follow the judge's dictation to the effect that the court was convened, and that so and so had been appointed as witness and as assessor, and so on. Jon Thorberg circulated a good-sized pocket flask, took, as the last one, a proprietary swallow, and huddled up in his fur coat.

"For the time being you can just go ahead and sleep," whispered Judge Scheving jestingly, "if you'll only not snore. Otherwise I'll fine you for contempt of court, you understand? A fine of ten bottles of brandy."

While the smoke grew thick in the room and my fingers stiffened in the cold, the case went its laborious way.

Monsieur Einar Jonsson's appointment as prosecutor was read and marked as Exhibit A. Then he presented the document with which he had called the accused as well as the witnesses, with appropriate indications as to where and when each one had been summoned. After that the men were brought personally before the court to determine which of the witnesses summoned had appeared in court. There were five missing, among them my brother Pall. None of the five absent had a legal excuse.

"Why didn't your brother appear?" asked Monsieur Einar gruffly.

"If you come to have any reason to think that clearing up the case is going to depend on his evidence, you can demand, and probably get, the judge's ruling to have him brought by force," I answered drily.

Judge Scheving, occupied with his papers, smiled cheerfully but said nothing. Only when Monsieur Gudmund Sigmundsson had presented his appointment as defender did he emerge from his papers, rub his hands to get a little warmth in them, and ask animatedly, "Well, Monsieur Einar, how did you have in mind to proceed, my friend?"

Monsieur Einar made a circumstantial statement—and asked that it be made a part of the record—that first of all, now, Bjarni and Steinun should be interrogated, individually, of course. After that the witnesses called should be administered a joint oath and then questioned, individually, of course.

"Excellent," Judge Scheving concurred. "Do you have that, Reverend? You don't mind my tone with you? As my court reporter. Listen, foreman, don't you have a drop on you? . . . Ahh, that's more like it."

He turned toward the guard at the door. "Have Bjarni brought. But listen, take off the irons before you bring him in. We don't use torture here. The accused is to be questioned as a free man. 'Free and unfettered' it says in the law, Reverend."

Then he turned to the others. "And now there'll be no joking in this court, gentlemen."

He was suddenly sitting straight, grim, his eyes riveted on the table. Just a boy, to look at him. But a dangerous boy.

Bjarni was brought in. He was suddenly standing there in the middle of the room, red in the face—and rubbing his wrists, apparently without realizing it.

Judge Scheving looked at him grimly, stared at him as though there was something that he had to see before words and emotions could distort it.

"Well, Bjarni," he said, then, with a gentle threat in his voice, "finally we've got this far . . . Good morning, man."

Bjarni tried to answer something or other; it came out as nothing more than a soundless movement of the lips.

"Now . . . But gentlemen of the court," Judge Scheving interrupted irritably, "we still are lacking various documents which ought to be presented first . . . Take the prisoner out in the meantime."

Bjarni was led out. He didn't seem to be happy about the delay he got this way. He clutched at the door frame as he went, as if he were on the verge of collapse.

I suspected that Judge Scheving had probably not forgotten the documents whose reading now followed.

Monsieur Einar fumbled with his papers, not a little confused. But the judge steered the case with easy authority. First my letter of the twenty-seventh of September was read. Then his own letter to the sheriff at Rodesand, in which he ordered him to have a coroner's jury view the body again and at the same time arrest Bjarni. Then a letter from the sheriff to the judge, a deposition about the viewing of the body and Bjarni's arrest. And finally a short deposition about my conversation with Bjarni that evening.

"Do you confirm this deposition?" Judge Scheving asked me.

"Yes," I answered.

"Have you anything further to add?"

"No . . ."

Judge Scheving looked at me carefully. Sat there a moment thoughtfully . . . drummed his fingers on the table.

Monsieur Einar let a broad smile play visibly on his thick underlip. "I wouldn't like this deposition underemphasized," he said finally, with his eye on the judge, "now that it has actually been presented. Even if it is really primarily concerned with the feelings which the examiner presumed in the examinee . . . The Reverend Eiulv seems to consider the axe and the block useful for a great many things, among others as a cure for heavy thoughts."

The judge asked mildly, "Does the prosecutor wish to have that made a part of the record?"

"No, no," answered Monsieur Einar confused.

"Bring in the prisoner."

XVIII

Judge Scheving did not notice Bjarni this time; he was annoyed. "Now we've forgotten to have the prosecutor and the defending counsel sworn in."

Whereupon the prosecutor took his oath that he had no prejudice toward the accused, while the defending counsel took his oath that he had not proceeded and would not proceed so as to conspire with the defendant in any way prejudicial to the truth, or at variance with the law of the land.

Bjarni stood staring at the floor during this. He was obviously paying no attention to what was going on around him. A change had taken place in him from the first time he had been in, but it was a change that was hardly to the advantage of the examining judge: he stood there defiant and lethargic, sunk in his own thoughts. It struck me that although the handcuffs were off he was still bound.

"Bjarni Bjarnason," Judge Scheving called out suddenly, and Bjarni started but stood motionless immediately again, attentive and composed. "You stand here today before this court charged with having brought about the death of your fellow householder Jon Thorgrimsson and of your wife Gudrun. Do you plead guilty?"

Bjarni peered somberly at the men around the table. "No," he said deliberately.

"You're supposed to tell the truth, man," Judge Scheving rapped on the table. "But since you want to make the case as difficult for us as possible—why, talk! How did they die? But tell it exactly; you're not to leave out the slightest detail. Write it down, Eiulv . . . All right, begin."

Bjarni sighed heavily. Me he had avoided looking at up till now, acted as though he did not know that I was there.

"The last Thursday in March . . ." he began, his voice suddenly a little hoarse.

But the judge interrupted him. "What date?"

I nodded to the judge that I knew the date. But there was an interruption in the court procedures from a girl coming in to tend the stove.

"You there, Goldilocks," Gudmund Scheving burst out and clucked his tongue at her. "Why don't you take your little black friend out with you if you can't persuade him to be a little more fiery? Can't you talk, chesty? Huh, sunshine? You ought at least to answer your judge. I wouldn't mind being smothered in your hair, but not in this damned smoke."

The girl was outside, and the judge himself again.

"Go on, man."

Bjarni wiped his forehead and started over. "The last Thursday in March—just before noon—poor Jon and I were going—down to our sheepfold. We let the sheep out and drove them down to the shore . . ."

"So, you know it by heart, eh?" Judge Scheving interrupted him angrily. "Fine, go on."

"Then we went back to the pens . . . There we left each other. I—went home. The departed Jon set off across the valley—the path that leads to Skor Cliffs. Jon told me that he wanted to see if it was possible to get through. He didn't have any more hay at all at the place. In Skor, though, we both had some hay left that we hadn't brought back yet because of the poor roads. You know how the roads were last year. Nothing but ice and snow . . . I'd loaned him my staff—it was an aspen staff—because his wasn't any good. His—it was just one of those spruce branches, you know, not one you could depend on. I took it back with me, back to the pens I mean . . ."

Monsieur Einar cleared his throat and asked, "How was the departed Jon Thorgrimsson dressed when you left each other?"

Bjarni looked at him startled—apparently because he had been interrupted in his story. He knotted his brows, reflected.

"He had a blue knitted cap on his head—I remember that," he went on—at the same time darting a look at the prosecutor and weighing his words carefully as if he sensed a trap. "What else did he have on? . . . He had a knitted sweater on—that was blue, too. And a vest knitted of multicolored yarn. That's right. What the buttons were like I can't remember . . . And then he had a pair of weather-beaten leather pants on—old and patched. The color of his stockings—no, I wouldn't try to say what that was."

"That's fine," Judge Scheving cut him off short. "It's a little more to the point for you to remember exactly what happened to the man than what he was wearing."

"What became of him?" Bjarni repeated suspiciously. "Well, look—he didn't come back by the time his wife Steinun and I expected him . . ."

"He didn't?" Scheving put in. "So you'd talked about expecting him back—at some definite time?"

"No, not like that," Bjarni answered uncertainly, as though he were on thin ice. "When I got back to the sheep pens I went on in to the living room; I didn't talk to Steinun at all, not until she came herself and asked me what had happened to her Jon. That was the first I thought that he should have been home long ago. I told her the truth, that I couldn't figure out, either, what had happened to him. She asked me to go look for him, and I did. Now I'm just sorry that I didn't leave it alone, that I didn't stay home, or at least take my brother Jon along.

Because then I'd have had a witness. But what's done is done. So I went, like I said, alone . . . I could just make out where Jon had walked; I followed his tracks over the valley—across the snow drift that's always there, along Landbrot, you know, where the cliffs begin. And then I went on past the first cliff to the Sandcliffs there—Rodeskred. There the footprints stopped, as far as I could see. And it was there I noticed that you could see something down there on the snow and ice sheet. Or at least I thought I could see that the ice was not clear, but spotted —as if somebody had dragged a dirty sack across it. And that was the reason I thought that it was there Jon must have fallen. But as anybody knows, it just wasn't possible with the roads the way they were to get down to the shore, either from up there or in from the valley, so good reasons kept us from looking for him there. Besides, he must have fallen in the water when it was flood tide, or anyhow the high tide must have got him later . . . Well, when I saw that, I went away scared and worried back to Syvendeaa. I got home just before sunset, and right away I told my wife that there wasn't any doubt that Jon had fallen over at Rodeskred. It was my wife that told Steinun."

As busy as I was writing down Bjarni's testimony I had little opportunity to watch him. The way he told the events sounded reasonable; that Jon could have fallen straight down into the water at high tide, and that it was the reason that he had fallen from the cliff with his arms and legs unbroken, I had not thought of before.

"Is that all?" Judge Scheving asked drily.

Bjarni was silent; there was a defiant gleam in his blue eyes.

Monsieur Einar sat and stared at Bjarni maliciously. Finally he asked mildly, "And you have never seen either the departed Jon or anything he had with him that day again?"

"No," Bjarni answered stubbornly, "not if I don't count the corpse in Baer church that they claimed was his—the day they arrested me."

"But I heard that his leather pants were washed up on shore," the prosecutor growled. "Isn't that true then?"

"Yeah, I guess that's right," Bjarni answered indifferently.

"Maybe you didn't see them?"

"Whether I saw them or whether I heard about them—I don't remember exactly."

Judge Scheving brought his heavy fist down on the table. "Your account must be honest and without reservation, Bjarni," he reminded him sternly, "This is a pretty serious matter we're investigating, isn't it? Not the least for you. That you can't remember everything that in any degree touches on this unusual event—That I simply refuse to believe. It's only six months since it happened, man. Did you see the trousers or didn't you?"

"Sure, I saw them," Bjarni answered slowly. "Since you're making so much out of those old, ragged trousers."

The judge clapped Einar Jonsson on the shoulder. "Now you, Mr. Prosecutor."

"In what condition were the trousers?" the prosecutor asked—with a grim smile that was in odd contrast to the casual question.

"One leg was ripped, I remember that."

"Right side out?"

"I don't remember. Wait—let me see . . . one leg was wrong side out it seems to me. They were all plastered with seaweed. I don't remember any more."

"You can remember all right who found them."

Bjarni shrank—had to clear his throat. "It was Gisli, my son, and Steinun's son, Svein."

"How old are the boys?"

"Eight. They were the same age."

"When were the trousers found?"

"I don't remember that. I'm sure it was some time around the beginning of summer."

"Think again," Judge Scheving interrupted. "Was it nearer the first or the fifth week of summer?"

"Sometime in between, I think."

Judge Scheving shook his busy head in annoyance. The prosecutor continued. "Where were they found?"

"At the edge of the shore down below the farm."

Judge Scheving broke in. "Now listen, Bjarni. Why are you so afraid to tell the whole truth about those trousers? You are spoiling an already bad case with your vague answers, you ought to know that. I'm asking you for definite answers. Where did you see the trousers for the first time?"

"On the kitchen wall—up in a crevice by the roof."

"All right. When did you see them there?"

"The day after they washed up on shore. The day they washed ashore I was out with the sheep—the whole day. In the evening, in the kitchen, was when I first heard about the trousers—that they'd found them. And who found them. The next morning I took a look at them— there where they were. I didn't touch them with so much as a finger. And then I went right out to my sheep. I was pretty busy. I was the only man at the farm."

"Uh huh, we know that . . . What did you do with the trousers once you'd seen them and recognized them?"

"I left 'em alone, that's what I told you."

"What became of them?"

"I don't know, I haven't seen them since. But I think Steinun took care of them as soon as they were dry."

"Dry? Were they hung up to dry? Who dried them?"

"Steinun. Of course."

"Well, so what became of them?"

Bjarni shook his head wearily. "How should I know? Steinun did say something about wanting to make them over for Svein. Or use them for patching. That's all I know."

"Even about the departed Jon's death?" Judge Scheving asked, in the midst of this conversation about the trousers.

"Yes," Bjarni answered tiredly. "I've told everything I know. Every bit."

"You've told us what was convenient for you to tell us— neither more nor less," said Judge Scheving angrily. "Well, we'll track the truth down—you can rely on that. Not only is your testimony inadequate, it's misleading besides. And it can't be substantiated. Jon Thorgrimsson can't have fallen out at Rodeskred without having suffered some wounds on his body. Even if there had been water down below, he'd have had to have been battered on the way down."

"Yes but—I didn't say that he fell out at Rodeskred," Bjarni interposed angrily. "I said I thought he did. I didn't see the man fall, there or anyplace else. And you can't punish a man for having an opinion about a case. Even if the opinion's all wrong."

"Let's take it easy now," Judge Scheving hushed him. "What is punishable we'll find out in good time. Now, let's try talking a little about your wife's death . . . Just tell us what you know about that. But tell it in detail and in good order."

Bjarni was silent. You could see he was already tired. He looked around for something to lean on. When he found nothing, he stretched his arms up and supported himself by a beam above him.

The pause that Bjarni's silence produced was used by the court to cough and clear their throats. The smoke was no longer nearly as painfully thick, nor was the cold so bitingly sharp, but their throats had got dry. Jon Thorberg would have liked to, but didn't dare, bring out the bottle again—without a sign from Judge Scheving. And he got no such sign, however much he watched for it.

Since Bjarni continued to say nothing, the judge got him started again. "She's supposed to have got very sick once in the winter—so I understand."

"Yes. Oh I know all right that she and others both made a lot of fuss about her throwing up a little."

"When did she do—this throwing up?"

"Some time before she died."

"Some time—How long a time, man?"

"About three weeks—I think that was it."

"You think that was it? You don't remember it?"

"Not exactly, no. But she got sick one evening suddenly —and began to throw up. Somebody throws up—that's happened before. But it looks as though we can't do that at Syvendeaa."

"Were you in bed that time?"

"Not yet."

"What was the reason for her throwing up?"

"I don't know any special reason. The next day she was already well again. And after that there was nothing unusual about her—right up to the day she died."

"How did she die?"

"That day she was kind of poorly—could hardly keep on her feet. But even though she felt sick, she wanted to go with Steinun down to the pens where they were going to milk the ewes. But when she came down to the pens where I was standing waiting for them she got sick suddenly—just toppled over, so to speak."

"What did she say? What words did she use to describe her indisposition?"

"What did she say? I don't think she said anything. She seemed to have lost her voice. I didn't hear her say anything."

"Most extraordinary . . . Give the man a chair."

Bjarni sank down on the chair which the guard at the door put before him, and he sat there a little out of breath, smiling awkwardly and pitifully around. "It must be the smoke," he muttered, stroking his forehead over and over. "And it's so warm here—isn't it?"

"Go on," said Judge Scheving quietly.

Bjarni pulled himself together and continued. "Yeah,

where was it I quit now? . . . Steinun—she'd already started milking—ran home when she saw Gudrun fall and got her something to drink. Some water in a bowl. That is —she didn't manage to get it drunk. We tried to pour it into her; what else were we supposed to do? The time she threw up, water had helped her a lot. But this time we really didn't get very many drops down her. No we didn't . . . Well after that we carried her home to bed—more dead than alive . . . Right after that she gave up the ghost."

When Bjarni stopped talking nobody said anything. He sat a moment there himself, quiet and thoughtful. Then he seemed to wake up suddenly—and got restless. He looked around, taken aback by the silence around him. He ended by adding desperately, "Well—that's the whole story . . ."

Judge Scheving sat with his head in his hands almost as though he were asleep. Monsieur Einar peered at him time after time. Then he began, slowly, "Where were you —the time the deceased Gudrun got sick and toppled over?"

"I was standing in the entrance of the pens," Bjarni answered readily. It seemed suddenly important to him to get everything clear now.

"Uh huh. And what was it you were doing while Steinun was away—getting water for Gudrun?"

"When I saw her fall I yelled to Steinun that my wife had got sick, and I asked her to hurry up and get some water. I rushed over to Gudrun myself, moved her over a little, and sat down beside her. There's where I sat until Steinun came back."

"Where were you and what were you doing, before and while Steinun and Gudrun were going together down to the pens?"

"I was out after the milkers, had been out since morning getting them together back to the pens. I was standing there by the pens when Steinun came, and right after that my wife came too. I wasn't anyplace else and I didn't do anything else that morning."

"How did you carry Gudrun home?"

"Steinun went home first for a blanket. That was when she'd got the water. We took her home in the blanket."

"Tell me once more. What did you do and what did Steinun do that night when Gudrun got sick in the winter?"

"I went down and got her something to drink and stayed up with her afterwards; but not for very long, because she got better fast. Steinun came in to see her a little bit while I was down after the water, and while she was drinking it, too. Then afterwards she went back to her place."

Judge Scheving stepped in. "Did you sleep in the same bed with Gudrun—the last part of the night?"

Bjarni was confused—answered uncertainly, "Yes—the last part of the night."

Judge Scheving sank back again into his thoughts.

Monsieur Einar interrogated Bjarni for more details concerning Gudrun's death. But Bjarni knew nothing more to tell.

"Wasn't there anyone else at all present?"

"Sure. The children—after we had brought her home."

"But only the two of you saw her die . . . Isn't there anyone else at all that saw her home at Syvendeaa—after she was dead?"

"Sure. Bjorg from Skog. I went and got her three days later so that she could help us put the body in the coffin. She was living at Melanes then."

"You, in other words, do not admit that you brought about the death of the departed Gudrun."

"That kind of talk is just vicious gossip."

"And that vomiting—you didn't bring that about either?"

"No."

Monsieur Einar could not think of anything else, but he

seemed to think that he had to go on with the questioning. "Can you take your oath that you did not stab Jon Thorgimsson to death or push him over Skor Cliffs?" he asked in confusion.

"Yes."

"Can you also take your oath that you did not kill your wife, Gudrun Egilsdottir, with poison?"

Bjarni got up relieved and went up close to the table. "I would like to take my oath to that right now," he said insistently, "on both."

Judge Scheving, who had sat and watched Bjarni carefully, answered drily, "That's enough of that . . . Take the prisoner away."

As soon as Bjarni was out the door the judge jumped up from his chair, stretched, clapped Jon Thorberg on the shoulder and said with relief, "Ahh, let me get a swallow of honest brandy on top of that damned brew of lies."

He drank—three long swallows. And then sent the bottle around.

"If you were to ask me if Bjarni's a scoundrel, I wouldn't be able to say," he said, and took a quick turn around the room.

"He's lying, the fool," he babbled on, "although he isn't any good at it. So probably he did the killing—even if he isn't any good at killing. There's no real scoundrel's blood in him, the slob."

"Wouldn't you call a murderer a scoundrel?" the prosecutor burst out, shocked.

"God forbid. I'll get him on the block yet, whether he's a scoundrel or not, if he's just guilty . . . and if you, prosecutor, can prove that he's guilty."

Judge Scheving broke off, and added, "Do you think that's going to be easy?"

Monsieur Einar answered slowly, "Well, let's see. I should think we've plenty of evidence."

Gudmund Scheving was irritated again. "There's circumstantial evidence enough, friend Einar . . . plenty of witnesses who haven't seen anything . . . and conflicting statements and self-contradictions. And all the rest. But when we don't have any proof—it would be nice if we had a little confession. So that the law can be properly satisfied. Can you get me that?"

"We'll see."

"Oh yes, we'll see something or other. But Bjarni's head rolling on circumstantial evidence alone, that you're not going to see . . . All right, let's have the woman."

XIX

Captivity did not seem to have had the slightest effect on
Steinun. I had never seen her so erect and calm, as she
stepped across the floor, taking a view of me and the
court, her brows knitted slightly. A black wool bodice
with velvet cuffs and velvet edging fit tightly on her well-
shaped arms and her proud bosom. Her scarf was carefully tied and fastened with a brooch; her skirt hung in folds,
unwrinkled. It was only by some straws clinging to her
shoe that you could see that, like Bjarni, she came from a
haymow.

Judge Scheving regarded her with unconcealed admiration. Even Foreman Thorberg shot her a thoughtful look
from out of his fur collar. On the other hand the farmers,
all of them, kept their eyes under control.

"Well, my dear Steinun," Judge Scheving began softly.
"Now Bjarni has gone and told us the whole truth. I hope
you're not going to make any secret of your part either.
There wouldn't be any point in it. The best thing would
be for you to confess openly."

"What is it you want me to confess?" Steinun asked
coolly, meeting his eyes steadily.

There was a peculiar light in her eye, a kind of bright
firmness. A sudden flush spread over her dark skin.

Judge Scheving said nothing, said nothing and looked
at her.

Monsieur Einar waited a moment; then he said grimly
without raising his eyes from his papers: "You are accused, Steinun Sveinsdottir, of knowledge and complicity

in the murder of your husband, Jon Thorgrimsson, and of Bjarni's wife, Gudrun Egilsdottir. Tell us the truth and in detail every single thing you know about the death of these people."

"That's easy enough," Steinun answered, turning her head somewhat toward him without moving her body. "My Jon I saw the last time the day he disappeared. That was in the morning right after the stock had been fed. He said he was going to go over to Skor and he asked me to fix some shoes for him. I made him a pair of shoes out of lumpsucker skin, and after that he left. He was holding the shoes in his hand when he went out of the house. Bjarni had just gone into his kitchen—to eat, I think. A little while later he left too."

"How long after?" Judge Scheving asked quietly.

"Oh, as long as it takes to eat breakfast," Steinun answered at once. "When he went, he said he was going to have to hurry up—Jon was waiting for him, he said. They always drove the sheep together down to the shore. The paths had got slippery and there wasn't any more pasture, just seaweed . . . A little while later Bjarni came back and said that Jon had gone. And I knew, I told you that, where he was going."

"Was that all he said?" the prosecutor asked.

"He didn't say any more than that to me."

"Where did he go for the rest of the day?"

"He went to sew leather in the house."

Steinun stopped as though expecting further questions. Judge Scheving muttered, "Go on."

She continued. "Well . . . when I began to think that Jon had been away too long, I went out several times to look for him, but he just didn't show up. And I said to Gudrun Egilsdottir, 'What's happened to my husband?' and she said, 'Yes, that's funny. Let's ask Bjarni to go over and look for him. He could have got himself stuck some place out there on the slippery paths.' So we both asked Bjarni to go out, and he did right away. It wasn't till sundown that he was back home again. I could see him coming from inside, and I saw he was alone. So I went around a corner of the house when Gudrun went out to meet him. 'Didn't you find Jon at all?' I heard her ask him. And I heard him sigh and say, 'No, I didn't see Jon, but I saw where he fell.' I didn't hear anymore. Because when I heard him say that, I ran away so I could be alone. But a little later Gudrun found me anyhow, where I was hiding, and she was the one who told me that Bjarni had seen the marks where Jon had fallen out on Skor Cliffs. We all knew what that meant . . ."

"You have never seen Jon Thorgrimsson since?" Judge Scheving asked.

"No I haven't."

"And you haven't seen anything that he had with him either?"

Steinun hesitated an instant—maybe you could hardly call it hesitation. "Nothing but his leather trousers," she answered softly.

"When and where and how were they found?"

"The boys, Svein and Gisli, found them on the shore and hauled them home."

Somebody shoved violently at the door; the guard turned the key—looked to see who it was, and there, suddenly, was Jon Ormsson. His leg seemed to be even worse than usual, but he limped determinedly up to the judge and asked in a quaking voice, "I just wanted to ask, your honor, if you really find it proper to interrogate my parishioners like criminals on my own farm and in my own home without my permission, without their minister's and pastor's permission. It's possible that that's legal. It's possible. But I would just like to say that I don't find that very humane. Not very humane at all."

Judge Scheving smiled caustically and answered without standing up or offering him his hand. "Finally I have the honor of saying hello to you by daylight, Reverend. If you will just let me go on sitting here and wait a little before I can express my thanks for all the hospitality you have shown. The fact is, you are interrupting me in a court session, in a secret examination."

"Nothing is hidden from God," the Reverend Jon Ormsson answered solemnly. "And certainly I am His most insignificant servant . . . But I'm not going to let myself be pushed around in my own house."

He sat down heavily and exhaled. His troubled eyes passed over Steinun and remained fixed on her—with affection and apprehension.

"Can the prosecutor permit the Reverend Jon Ormsson to stay and be present for the rest of the hearing?" Judge Scheving asked, directing his question before him to the thin air—amusement in his voice.

"Since the Reverend Jon Ormsson has been summoned as a witness and thus may be said to have a part in the proceedings, it cannot be permitted," Monsieur Einar answered sharply.

"You can hear it yourself, Reverend Jon, you'll have to go. You're part of the proceedings."

"All the more reason for me to stay," Jon Ormsson answered calmly—not taking his eyes from Steinun.

"You can't remain without the permission of the law, man," announced Judge Scheving. He found his snuff box and took a pinch. "The law permits you to remain . . ."

Then he turned conciliatingly toward his irritated friend and asked amicably, "Is the prosecutor finished with the accused?"

"Finished before we began," mumbled Monsieur Einar, and turned abruptly toward Steinun. "How was the departed Jon dressed and what did he have with him the day he made his way over to Skor—and died?"

Steinun wrinkled her brow in thought. Then she listed what he had worn. She listed it somewhat more exactly than Bjarni had done, said that his jersey had had bone buttons, the vest a red border, and that Jon had had a blue woolen muffler wound around his neck. Besides that he had had a pair of mittens along, the two pairs of lump-sucker-skin shoes, and his staff.

When she had finished, the prosecutor asked, "Wasn't there anybody but you who knew that Jon intended to go over to Skor?"

"I don't think he talked about it to anybody else, except the brothers, Bjarni and Jon."

"Wasn't that a funny idea of Jon's to make his way alone over to Skor—with the roads the way they were?"

"I don't see why. At home we only had hay for barely a week, but in Skor we had hay stored that we had to get home."

"Bjarni had hay in Skor too?"

"Yes, he did. But Bjarni was better off at home. He didn't need hay."

"The shoes you say you sewed for Jon—Is there anyone who saw you sew the shoes?"

"I really don't know."

"You don't know?"

"Bjarni and Jon saw me, I suppose. I wouldn't be able to say for sure."

"When were the leather trousers found?"

"Sometime toward the holy season."

"What makes you remember that?" Judge Scheving interposed quickly.

"Why, the fields had begun to turn green."

When the Judge did not question any further, Monsieur Einar resumed. "Did you see those trousers at any time?"

"Yes."

"Where did you see them?"

"On the kitchen wall, where they were."

"Were they in good condition?"

"No, they were ripped, especially along the seams."

"Turned right side out?"

"Yes."

"Both legs?"

"Yes, but the seat was wrongside out."

"How were they otherwise?"

"How were they? . . . They were wet and plastered with seaweed."

The Reverend Jon Ormsson, who had sat for a while sunk in his own thoughts—he had been sitting looking at something he was holding in his hand—thrust his hand suddenly out toward Steinun and asked mildly, "Do you recognize this button?"

Steinun started, but collected herself and answered quietly, "Yes, I can describe it exactly without examining it, because Jon made it himself. That button—it was my first present to him. That is—the silver. It's made from the only silver coin I ever owned. I gave it to him, gave it to him the day he took me from my home. I was so happy that day. And he was so good to me . . . He melted down the silver himself and drew it out into wire—and gilded it. The fastening and the inside he made of copper, and then he covered the copper button with silver wire . . . oh yes, it was only afterwards that he gilded it. I know that button all right. He always had it in his shirt collar."

The Reverend Jon rose and said gently, "Here, take it, dear sister; with this button in your hand you will not be able to speak falsely."

"The button isn't mine and never was," Steinun answered, refusing to reach for it. "What do I have to do with it?"

The Reverend Jon limped, troubled, to his chair.

"The button isn't yours either, Reverend Jon," the prosecutor burst out sharply. "How did you come into possession of it?"

"I found it on the church floor the day the departed Jon's body was inspected the second time."

"And you put it in your pocket, with the idea of keeping it perhaps? Judge, I must ask you to take note of this circumstance, this peculiar situation. Why didn't you hand it over to me?"

"I didn't know then that you were the master of recovered property in Rodesand," the Reverend Jon answered, shaking with anger.

"Well, all right," Judge Scheving said conciliatingly. "This button turned up at the right moment. Another bit of luck—for the judges. And we've got the case on an even keel. You have our thanks, Reverend Jon, you were the very man we wanted. Let's go on with the case now, prosecutor."

Monsieur Einar turned sourly toward Steinun. "What became of the leather trousers?"

Judge Scheving sighed sadly. "The leather trousers . . . Good Lord, now our friend Einar wants the trousers too."

"They went on lying where they were without anybody paying any attention to them," Steinun answered indifferently.

"They did? How long?"

"Till just before they took me away from Syvendeaa. One day they were just suddenly gone."

"Did you have anybody look for the departed Jon?"

"No."

Judge Scheving asked, with emphasis on each word, "How can it be possible that you made no attempt to have your husband's body found? People usually do something when somebody disappears like that. Even animals that disappear, people usually go and look for."

"I didn't have any doubt at all," Steinun answered, having recovered her composure. "I was sure Bjarni had told the truth. Along the shore at that time you couldn't possibly go anywhere. Besides, the ocean would have taken him already long before. That's what I thought. Which is the way it turned out to be."

"What?"

"That the ocean took him."

"Shall we say it *got* him? . . . What the devil! . . . Monsieur Einar, you go on."

Monsieur Einar had grown irritated at the Judge's tone and at the continual interruptions and he made no secret of it. He said slowly, "Possibly we ought to talk a little about the departed Gudrun . . . There was one time she got pretty sick, isn't that right?"

"That's right."

"How did it happen?"

"It wasn't my fault," Steinun answered resentfully.

"Just wait a little," Judge Scheving cut off a new question from the prosecutor. "Reverend Eiulv, you're recording accurately everything as it takes place?"

"When did it happen?" the prosecutor continued.

"One of the first days of summer . . . in the evening, along toward bed time."

"What did you do about it? And what did Bjarni do?"

"As soon as I found out that Gudrun had got sick I went in to see her and sat down with her. When I'd sat there a while she had to go out, and I went with her and helped her. When that was over Bjarni came up to us and brought her some water to drink. Then we went in again —all three. And after that she got better. The vomiting wasn't so bad any more and the pain was going away. When they didn't have any more use for me I went to bed."

"Was Bjarni already in bed when Gudrun got sick?" asked Judge Scheving.

"He was, but he got up right away."

"Where had he gone to bed?"

"With his wife, I assume."

"You know that he'd gone to bed, but not where?"

"I could tell that he had gone to bed by the way he was dressed," Steinun answered icily.

"What a hell of a woman," Judge Scheving muttered, shaking his head. "You ought to be put in front of a judge of your own sex . . . Don't you know any reason for Gudrun's sudden and remarkable sickness?"

"No. Not unless it was the chest pains that always bothered her."

"Right. Chest pains . . . What about the soup you gave her that evening?"

"Oh—that little bit of soup."

"That little bit of soup, uh huh. We know that you mixed something or other in it."

"I did not."

"Who then?"

Steinun had got suddenly to the end of her endurance. She reeled and was on the point of collapsing. The Reverend Ormsson stood up, gave her his chair, had her sit down, and put his hand on her head. "Tell only what you know, sister. If you have committed a sin whose consequences God has absolved you from by its failure, you must not let a lie poison your heart by concealing it. To want to kill is not yet to have killed—remember that. Whatever you have done, my sister, keep to the truth and to God."

Judge Scheving stood up, stole on tiptoe around the table and brought the Reverend Jon gently and considerately, but firmly enough, to a seat. Then just as quietly he went back to his place.

It was silent in the courtroom. For a long, long time it was silent . . . The weather must have changed. Although my back was toward the window I could tell from the changing light in the room that there was a broken blue sky with driving clouds.

I had almost forgotten Steinun, perhaps because I could not bear to look at her anymore or to remember that she was there, when she began to speak with an altered voice—dead and broken. "The evening before—before she got sick in the night—I was in my pantry, busy serving up the soup for my children . . . Some of that soup —I put in a ladle—so that Gudrun could have a taste of it. Right then Bjarni came in and asked who the soup was for in the ladle. I said it was for his wife, Gudrun. Then he took a paper out of his pocket and sprinkled something, I don't know what it was, on the soup in the ladle. I thought it was some kind of joke. Just then we heard Gudrun out in the hall, she was on her way to the barn to milk. So I handed her the ladle—and she ate the soup— and gave me back the ladle."

"What was it that Bjarni sprinkled in the soup?" Judge Scheving asked cautiously.

"I don't know."

"What did it look like?"

"It was some kind of fine powder—yellowish."

"A color like that on that tile stove?"

"Yes, something like that."

"Like powdered alabaster?"

"Yes, pretty much like powdered alabaster."

"Did you know that it was poisonous?"

"No, certainly not."

"Didn't Bjarni tell you what it was? You must have asked him about it."

"No—neither one."

"Hadn't Bjarni told you what he had in mind?"

"No."

"That's impossible."

Steinun hesitated. She muttered something or other which none of us heard. But then she said, "No—he didn't."

Judge Scheving was silent. He sat and regarded Steinun, who had straightened herself again and sat proud and gloomy. He may have forgotten to go on. But it was also possible that he was deliberately leaving it to the prosecutor to go into detail about Gudrun's death—that early spring day at the pens. Steinun's evidence about this agreed generally with Bjarni's. Except that she said that Gudrun had fallen and remained lying there before she reached the pens.

"About halfway?" the prosecutor asked.

"Yes—about that."

"And she just lay there, is that right? Possibly she didn't get down to the pens at all?"

"She was certainly more than halfway," Steinun interrupted uneasily, "but you could hardly say she was clear down to the pens. I don't really know. I was so confused."

It had begun to grow dark. Judge Scheving collected himself finally—straightened up in his chair. "The sun is going down," he said casually. "This isn't supposed to be a witches' Sabbath. And you don't seem to have anything special to tell us today, Steinun . . . Well, another day you'll be more communicative. When you finally realize that it's not a vain tissue of lies we are out after, but the solid cloth of truth."

Steinun got up from her chair and looked around uncertainly.

"Just wait a little," Judge Scheving said sharply. "Are you in a hurry to get out to the hay?"

Only when she had heard and acknowledged the record of her testimony was she taken away and turned over to the custody of her guards.

When she was out of the door Judge Scheving yawned and stretched carelessly.

"A hell of a business, this . . . Bjarni's gone back to his first explanation of where Jon's supposed to have fallen—Rodeskred. He wants to float away on the flood tide. Well, you can't make pants out of that leather. Apropos! Nobody really got those trousers by the legs. They weren't expecting us to know all about them. And where Gudrun fell they don't seem to be able to get together on. And that stuff Bjarni put in the soup—he kept that quiet . . . They weren't smart enough to have people look for Jon either, if only for the sake of appearances, and that's an unfortunate circumstance. So I don't see any way out, since we don't have any corpus delecti, aren't even in possession of the victim's members, and since the possibility of any eye-witness at all appearing seems to be excluded. We'll have to get ourselves a confession . . . Does the prosecutor think he can produce one?"

Monsieur Einar grunted.

"I for my part don't believe I can," Judge Scheving went on. "I'll still manage to tangle them up in their own yarn. But if I got a confession out of this business—I'd be mighty astonished. And I dare say I could risk a spring lamb that you won't manage to do it either, friend Einar."

Judge Scheving broke off, and drummed his fingers on the table.

"What does the court think about asking the Reverend Eiulv to talk with the accused?" he asked offhandedly.

Monsieur Einar projected his lower lip in disagreement. The others agreed.

"I have to have time to consider whether I dare to or want to take that on," I answered reluctantly.

Judge Scheving rose abruptly and announced briskly— chanted, "The court is adjourned. We convene at dawn."

XX

When we came out of the courtroom there was a crowd of people outside the doors and along the paths. Everybody wanted to know what the accused had said and whether they had confessed. When they heard that we were not allowed to let out anything at all of what had taken place in the court they began to produce their own versions.

"The murderer Bjarni was plenty pale around the gills," one of them said with a laugh.

"That criminal Steinun wasn't any better," said a woman's voice, breathless with excitement.

"Did you see how she was dolled up? Like she was going to church."

"You'd better say, like for a wedding."

"Wedding—they've already had that. Plenty of times, too."

Everywhere there was a throbbing current of blood-heated air through hairy nostrils, bearded masculine mouths, and tender feminine lips.

I stood leaning on the farmhouse doorframe, staring blindly at the graying evening.

"It's a wonder their blood brotherhood didn't show," whispered someone, not without some admiration—"a couple like that."

"Oh, it'll be obvious enough, all right," an old toothless man was baying, "but only on the chopping-block—haha-ha, only on the block."

A messenger came to tell me that the Reverend Jon

wanted to talk with me. In his room I found, besides him, my father-in-law; the table was set for three. The Reverend Jon talked on and on, with an old man's melancholy. "They didn't do it, Monsieur Jon, I am convinced of it—God be merciful to me a sinner. They can't possibly have done it—can't you see that? They may have wanted to be rid of Gudrun, once Jon was gone. Maybe they even tried to get rid of her. But God saw that it failed—can't you see that? Whatever they did manage to give her, there wasn't much harm it did her. She just threw up a little and recovered from it. They are sinners, terrible sinners, that I can see now. God have mercy on them. That God wants to punish them by not freeing them immediately from the suspicion that they have brought upon themselves with their sinful lives—that I can see too. But you don't give somebody poison a second time. You just don't do that. Besides that, anybody who has once been given poison will keep his eyes open from then on . . . And how are they supposed to have killed her otherwise, can you tell me that? There wasn't any wound to be seen on her body —you saw that yourselves. And now the departed Jon . . . The hole in his neck wasn't anything else but a split in the rotting flesh. It's possible that an eel ate into him in the ocean. You know yourselves how many kinds of predators there are in the ocean—known and unknown. No, no, those two didn't do any killing. They sinned all right, they sinned terribly. But they didn't murder, they didn't murder."

Monsieur Jon didn't listen, just sat there and chewed. Sat and looked at me. When the Reverend Jon finally stopped, we went on eating in silence, all three of us.

There was a candle burning in the middle of the table, a long, slender bloom of flame on a heavy, golden stalk. I refused to think any longer about alabaster. Jon's wife Ragnheid came in and reported that Judge Scheving was asking for me.

She went with me out of the room and showed me that

she, in spite of the crowd of guests, had put me in a little room by myself. She was extremely friendly toward me, friendlier than she had ever been before. Friendly and motherly.

I found Judge Scheving alone in his room. Before he shut the door behind me, he called some name or other out into the darkness of the corridor. I realized that he was making use of his door guard, here, too. He was showing his liquor a little. The first thing he did was to mix a couple of drinks. Then he offered me a pinch of snuff. Finally he came to the point.

"Have you thought, Reverend Eiulv, about whether you'll talk with the prisoners?" he asked cheerfully. "The night is favorable—to many things."

"The last time Bjarni and I talked together, I told him that I wouldn't visit him any more unless he sent for me," I admitted frankly.

"Well, so that's it . . . What do you know!"

Judge Scheving reflected and then he asked softly, "What do you think about this whole business, my dear Reverend?"

"I haven't been summoned as a witness."

"You can be."

"Besides, I don't know anything."

"You don't . . . But you have your own ideas."

"Here at this place everybody has his own ideas. Only the ideas are more or less different. And I wonder if most of them aren't way off the truth."

"It isn't in my capacity as judge that I sent for you—you mustn't think that." And then, his manner altering, "But then, I don't ask you to believe me, think what you want to; but I'm sorry for the two of them—that they've got themselves in such a mess. Actually I'd like to let the two of them go—if only they could clear things up a little. But I'm not going to risk anything myself. They don't mean that much to me. And they don't deserve that either; they really messed up their affairs miserably. But I can understand them, in a way. And certainly you do, too? Who was going to help them get rid of those two nuisances—besides themselves? It's a stupid way to think, but perfectly natural; they forgot that the law is the law—and it goes beyond just the law. You believe you can do something, and you do it. And then afterwards you discover all the same that you couldn't do it. It's like getting up your nerve to jump a crevice, jumping, getting a good grip on the other side of the cliff, and hanging there—until you fall. Because you do fall—sooner or later."

Judge Scheving was silent. So was I.

"You're not talking," he began again. "Well, of course you're a minister . . . Maybe I'm completely on the wrong track. Maybe you're just as naively unsuspicious as your superior. But look here, what I wanted to ask you about was, whether you think there would be any point, shall we say, in not pushing them too hard so that the two bunglers—hm—get themselves off?"

Judge Scheving walked back and forth. He went on. "You don't have anything to say? . . . Look, it's not by any means impossible that we simply won't be able to convict them of—murder. But granted that we possibly could—but didn't try to. Or in any case didn't try too hard. What would you think about that?"

Judge Scheving picked up the bottle.

"Have a drink, man. You've got way behind . . . Since you're a minister I proceed on the assumption that you're convinced that all guilt should be taken care of on the other side . . . so that earthly punishment is, and can only be, a secondary matter. Am I wrong in thinking that some such thought has—flitted through your mind? Well . . . to make it short and sweet, do you believe that Bjarni and Steinun—after this—under any circumstances at all, will be in a position to lead lives—that won't simply destroy them?"

"How can I know that? . . . But I—hardly think so."

"You hardly think so? I'm glad to hear that! In a way . . . From the first I've had difficulty believing that Bjarni was simply a scoundrel. Steinun, on the other hand, is not so easy to figure out, she's more—complicated. Anyhow, I don't understand women. They're not in my book. But if we're agreed that we can't benefit the two poor devils any more than by helping them off with their lives in a legal, decent manner, why I think that we, for everybody's sake, have to have a confession. And that you can get us. And only you, sir."

"Are you saying that it's my duty?"

"What?"

"To get them to—tell the truth?"

"Certainly not. No, don't claim that's what I said . . . Because obviously it is in the general opinion, and for that reason, your duty. But just between us, my friend, if you have the slightest hesitation about mixing in the affair, then—don't do it. I'll go further and say that unless you are fully convinced of benefiting these two unfortunate people by it, you haven't a speck of right to mix yourself in their quarrel with earthly justice. Let me manage this damned affair, as well as I can."

"Have you any objection to my being with the witnesses when they are brought in in the morning?" I asked. "Even if the reporter's hand should have got better?"

"Not in the least. The way things are . . . Now that hand, that can hardly have got much more usable in the course of the day. He got a little too much punishment in the snow for that . . . Well, I'm supposed to talk to him."

"I think it's with me you'll have to talk."

"Hahaha," laughed Judge Scheving. "Don't you think I worked that out long ago? You really are naive. Oh well . . . Good night, Reverend Eiulv . . . My position is damnable enough. But still, I'd like even less to be in your place."

XXI

I don't want to talk about that horrible night. If I managed to drop off for a short time, terrible dreams deepened the darkness around me. The darkness and the solitude. And yet what I dreamed was nothing more than that I heard heavy steps approaching along dark corridors —Bjarni's steps. They would sound louder and louder until they stopped at my bed; and I would wake up with him leaning over me, and clutch at the dark. And when I did he was not there.

Of course not. He was sleeping out there in the barn, among his four guards. And anyway, what did he have to do with me? No, what did I have to do with him? Young Olof and the child she was carrying—they were my people . . . I commended myself to God and fell asleep . . .

There was also a dream with ice and dark holes in the ice, and with wandering children in a blizzard. And then Bjarni's footsteps sounded again—until he stood leaning over me.

The night passed like that.

Now and then when I came up out of my dreams I could hear far away singing and shouting, and the thundering laughter of many voices. Endless laughter. That had to be some of the witnesses indemnifying themselves for the time they were wasting.

When the pitch darkness little by little began to be thinned by the day and I rose from my bed beaten to a pulp, it seemed to me that these last days had been longer than all the rest of my life put together.

The court was convened very early and the twelve witnesses called and sworn in. They were a motley crew. Some were barely awake, some of them seemed flatly not to realize, or be able to work out, where they were.

Judge Scheving was furious. His voice was shaking as he read the oath. It was a hard job to get the crew to repeat the words without a mistake.

"What are you so worked up for, old pal?" Gisli from Skapadal asked thickly, leaning happily over the table and trying to embrace his superior. "Let's be friends. Let's—be —friends."

When the oaths had finally been administered, the witnesses, except for Jon Bjarnason, were sent out again. Gisli and a few others in the meanwhile seemed rather disinclined to leave such distinguished society abruptly.

"Now that I'm sworn," Gisli insisted, "let me get at it. I'll tell you all about it. Every bit. Every word. Everything that happened. Amen."

"Take that drunken pig out and tie him up so he can sleep it off," ordered Judge Scheving, his face bright red.

"He's going to tie me up, the devil?" Gisli asked, taken aback and looking stupidly around. "Tie me up? Tie up Gisli from Skapadal? . . . Now I've heard everything."

As soon as the room was cleared the prosecutor began questioning Jon Bjarnason, Bjarni's brother. His glasses far down on his nose, he read his main questions carefully off a piece of paper. The first was:

"What knowledge did you, Jon Bjarnason, have about the quarrels at Syvendeaa the previous winter, between the married couple, Jon, deceased, and Steinun, and between Bjarni and Gudrun, deceased, and likewise between the two farmers, your brother Bjarni and Jon, deceased?"

Jon Bjarnason stood there, his young face dead white, his blue eyes hidden behind heavy lashes, and could find no answer to such a long and difficult question.

"Did they have differences, the Syvendeaa people?" Judge Scheving said, to get him started.

"Uh huh—they had some, particularly the men—and then Jon and Steinun."

"How was that?"

"Oh, they were always at it, all the time," Jon Bjarnason mumbled and suddenly flushed deep red. "Or else they went around sore and not talking."

"Why were they at each other?"

"Poor Jon used to complain almost every day to Steinun that she followed Bjarni wherever he went, followed at his heels like a dog, he said. And that she didn't even notice him, and he was her husband. He was full of complaints; he made trouble whenever he could."

"How did Steinun take that?"

"She answered him the same way, or maybe even worse."

"How about Bjarni?"

"He always had to mix in their quarrels. Every time he heard them fighting he took Steinun's side. That wasn't about to make things any better. And so then he got to wrangling with Jon . . . It got so you couldn't stand it at Syvendeaa, the last year."

"Did you ever hear Jon and Bjarni threaten each other?"

"No, I never heard that."

"Did they ever fight?"

"Not that I know of."

"You didn't hear any threats at all?"

"Not any threats, no; but lots of mean and angry words."

"And you didn't ever see them fight?"

There was a scornful twist at one corner of Jon Bjarnason's mouth.

"No." . . .

"How was Bjarni with his wife?"

"He'd always been good to poor Gudrun—up till then. During the winter, though, it got worse and worse. It ended up with husband and wife sleeping apart."

123

"Are you sure about that?"

"Yes."

"Gudrun—how did she take that?"

"Poor Gudrun didn't mix much in the others' quarrels. She kept herself out of it as much as she could. But I guess she complained once in a while to Bjarni about his relationship with Steinun. At least she talked a lot to me about it being Steinun's fault that Bjarni wasn't as good to her as before. Steinun was ruining their marriage, she said."

"What more do you want to ask, Monsieur Einar?" Judge Scheving asked.

"Did any quarrels take place between the men or between the couple, Jon and Steinun, the day that the departed Jon died?" the prosecutor read from his paper.

Jon Bjarnason was silent. Judge Scheving again had to intercede. He said gently, "Tell us a little about that morning, Jon Bjarnason."

Jon Bjarnason paused and then began. "That morning when I was finished in the stalls I hurried up into the kitchen. I hadn't eaten my breakfast yet . . . "

"Whom did you meet in the kitchen?"

"The kids and Malfrith; there wasn't anybody else."

"Go on," murmured Judge Scheving—with apparent indifference.

"I sat down to eat," Jon Bjarnason continued, always very softly and with lowered eyelids. "In a little bit I heard poor Jon and Steinun jawing at each other some place or other; they seemed to be standing in the doorway and quarreling. What they were quarreling about I don't know. All that I heard was Jon saying, 'You pushed me,' or maybe, 'What're you pushing me for?' And Steinun said, 'What are you lying for, you? What do you mean I pushed you?' That's all I heard."

"You didn't see them?"

"How was I supposed to see them? I was sitting up in

the kitchen; they'd gone on down. I didn't even look toward the stairway. We were used enough to that."

Judge Scheving set Monsieur Einar in motion again; he asked, after having looked at his papers, "Did any offensive incidents take place between Bjarni and Steinun?"

"The way they acted offended me," Jon Bjarnason answered mildly. "You couldn't help being a witness to how they got together alone in nooks and corners—here and there. Or out around . . ."

"At what time of day did they seek each other out particularly?"

"Particularly in the evening. When the rest of us were in the kitchen or were dozing off at dusk."

"Why did they seek each other out so persistently?"

"How would I know?"

"Well, not to quarrel, eh?"

"Those two were the only people on the farm that didn't quarrel and were always cheerful with each other."

"Only with each other?"

"Yeah, they talked a lot more cheerfully with each other than either of them talked to the rest of us."

Judge Scheving cleared his throat—asked uncertainly, "Did they have sexual intercourse with each other?"

Jon Bjarnason blushed right up the roots of his blond hair, but he answered firmly, "Not that I know of."

"Did they sleep together?"

"I didn't see them."

The prosecutor asked, "About when did you see the departed Jon for the last time?"

"The morning he disappeared; I met him at the stalls. He was feeding the cattle."

"What did you talk about?" asked Judge Scheving.

"I don't think we talked about anything in particular, or else maybe I've forgotten. All I remember is his complaining that he had to go down to the shore and get water for the cows—at the mouth of the creek. There wasn't any water in the river up by the farm. I told him he'd live through it all right. The rest of us were used to it and didn't particularly mind it. The water ran out pretty often after a lot of snow or frost. But I didn't offer to do it for him. He was always so crabby."

"You don't remember any more of what he said?"

"Yeah. He said, 'One thing's about like another here at Syvendeaa . . .' And then I finished and went on about my business."

"And after that you didn't see him?"

Jon Bjarnason shook his head.

"Did you hear him mention going over to Skor?"

"No, and it wouldn't have been possible either—with the roads in that condition. You could try it all right, if you were dumb. But the slopes were sheet ice; everything was iced over, every stick and stone. To try to bull your way through would have been certain death."

"Did you hear anybody else talking about Jon having to go to Skor?"

"Nobody but Bjarni."

"When did you hear him talking about that?"

"The same day—after Jon had gone."

"How long after?"

"Oh—a good while. We ran into each other at the door; he was coming from outside. I remember that, because he talked friendlier than usual and went with me to the yard. He said Jon was going—the pighead, I remember he said. And he said something about that Jon didn't know his way around Skor Cliffs and that he'd never make it. 'He can be thankful if he comes out of it alive,' he said, and put his hand over his eyes. And then he said, 'Look there —he's already up to the drift; and he's keeping right on . . .' But I couldn't see anything."

"You couldn't see anything? What was the weather like?"

"The weather wasn't bad. But it was over against the sun."

"Was the departed Jon a daredevil? I mean, was he eager or inclined to expose himself to danger?"

Once again there was a twist at the corner of Jon's mouth.

"Jon Thorgrimsson didn't amount to much—in any way."

Judge Scheving let Monsieur Einar break in here. "Didn't Jon ever talk to you about being worried or afraid of what Bjarni might think of doing to him?"

"No, never. I don't think he was afraid of Bjarni that way. But he was mighty unhappy about the way Bjarni and Steinun were behaving; and he didn't make any secret of that. Not in front of me, either, although I didn't want to know anything about it and never answered him . . . But he was a slob."

The prosecutor asked Jon Bjarnason after that if he had not known, or at least had not had a suspicion, that Bjarni had disposed of Jon, which the young man denied with conviction. He also denied having seen the departed Jon, living or dead, after the day he disappeared. To a question about how far Bjarni had been out looking for Jon the day he disappeared he answered, "I heard from the others that Bjarni had gone to look for Jon. But I didn't know any more than that, until he came back and told me and the rest of them that Jon had gone that morning over to Skor, and that he'd been out to see what happened to him but couldn't find him. On the other hand, he had seen signs that he had fallen out by Rodeskred. And that seemed to make sense."

"Was there much talk at Syvendeaa about Jon's disappearance?" the prosecutor went on.

"As far as I heard neither Bjarni nor Steinun mentioned his name—after that day. Poor Gudrun, though, and Malfrith, talked quite a lot about his death."

Judge Scheving interrupted the prosecutor here. "Those shoes that Steinun sewed for Jon—did you see her sew them? Or did you hear Jon ask her for shoes?"

"I didn't see her sewing any shoes and I didn't hear him ask her either."

"Tell me—could you really escape having at least some suspicion that Bjarni had murdered the departed Jon?" the Judge asked gently.

"That never occurred to me at all," Jon Bjarnason answered, subdued and paling a little.

"That really didn't occur to you?"

"The idea never came into my mind until I heard them whispering about it once in the summer."

"Who do you think started the gossip going?"

"That I don't know."

"Did you believe, when you heard it, that the rumor was true?"

"I didn't believe it, no. But it was already bad enough that people were saying it."

Judge Scheving leaned back in his chair disappointedly and asked the prosecutor to continue. Monsieur Einar read from his papers a question about the deceased Gudrun—if she had been sick every day, and what the connection was with the vomiting she had had just before she died.

Jon Bjarnason answered wearily, "She wasn't particularly sick—except from her cough. Although she was always complaining about the pains in her chest. I pretty much took that to be whining. But then one evening around Holyrood she began all of a sudden to throw up, and she kept on and kept on; it just didn't stop."

"How did that happen?"

"I don't know anything about that. Except for what she told me herself, the morning after, when she asked me to get some water for her to drink . . . She said, 'I think the idea was to finish me off last evening—with the soup Steinun gave me; there was something wrong with the soup, there was something in the bottom of the ladle that felt like sand.' That was all she said. And I didn't spread it around either."

"Did she get over it?" the prosecutor went on.

"Yes, she did. Because when I came in again in the afternoon she was up, and looked as though she was doing fine."

Both the prosecutor and Judge Scheving tried to involve Jon in contradictions with respect to what he knew about the soup under discussion, which Gudrun had thought had been poisoned. But that was unsuccessful. The young man was so frank and was so obviously acting in good faith that he did not even become aware of the snares they set for his feet; and so he escaped them without being disconcerted for so much as a moment. When they finally came out with it and asked in a straightforward way if he did not have knowledge that Bjarni and Steinun had murdered Gudrun, he lifted his heavy lashes for the first time in the long examination, looked from one to the other with his sad, blue, youthful eyes, and said with relief, "I don't know anything about that—anything at all. Because at the time that the departed Gudrun died, I had been out for the spring fishing a long time. Since then I haven't set foot in Syvendeaa."

Judge Scheving wrinkled his nose. "Now tell me—where did Steinun stay after Jon had gone that day?"

Jon Bjarnason knitted his brows in thought. "Right after I'd heard them in the door, Steinun came into the kitchen and sat down to card and spin. She was still sitting there when I left."

"She wasn't downstairs in the meantime?"

"No, she was sitting working with her wool."

"What did you do?"

"I had my work to do in the stalls and the barn."

"Are you certain that that's all you know? Remember your oath."

"I remember it."

"That wasn't much," sighed Judge Scheving when Jon Bjarnason was out the door. "Is that really all?"

Monsieur Einar pushed out his underlip doubtfully.

When the others said nothing, Arni Tordarson said pointedly, "Jon Bjarnason has been working as a hired man for me since the spring fishing. And besides that, I know him from before. A thoroughly reliable young man. His evidence is truthful down to the last detail—I will stake my life on that."

"Let's not get so excited, Arni," Judge Scheving silenced him smiling. "Obviously the young man is telling the truth. Just the same—it's unfortunate, insofar as he's told the truth. And it's a strong and understandable reason not —to know too much, that your brother's neck is in danger."

The next witness was Malfrith, formerly a hired girl at Syvendeaa with Bjarni and Gudrun.

Malfrith came swaying in, blushing and casting quick glances everywhere—a little bit bewildered, but still in good form. Maybe for the first time in her life. The prosecutor presented her with the same questions, more or less, which he had given to Jon Bjarnason—as far as he could. For it was not easy to keep a check on her stream of words.

"Oh yes, oh yes, they led quite a life at Syvendeaa— you can say that again," she started off. "I'll answer to God for my words, any time at all. And to you, Scheving. They all fought—and that was the least of it. But they fought— all of 'em, except me and good old Jon Bjarnason. The two of us never said a word. Never a word. Except pleasant ones. There were enough of them wrangling, I can tell you that. And there was always something new. Always. Bjarni got himself another bed to sleep in besides his wife's. And Steinun wouldn't sleep any longer in the same bed with her husband, either. The beds were too narrow, they said. And so they put asunder in frivolity what God had joined together. But the quarreling didn't stop for that. Or the wrangling. Reasons you ask, Judge? Yes, let them ask who have the wit to understand, I almost said. What other reason could there be anyway than that Bjar-

130

ni and Steinun couldn't stay away from each other? And that Bjarni always took Steinun's side, always, in the quarrels with her husband . . . That wasn't to be put up with, either by Jon or Gudrun, if you want my opinion. Just try to put yourself in their place. No, Judge. Jon and Gudrun were unhappy about it—what could you expect? Aren't you supposed to stay in your lawful marriage bed, I ask you, Scheving? Well now—you can see yourself . . . No, you know what, Einar Jonsson? You're a fine one! A fight he asks. Between Jon Thorgrimsson and Bjarni? Listen to that! Bjarni, who could have taken him by the heels, the way you'd take a fish by the tail, and knocked his head against a rock—if he'd wanted to. I'm not saying he did. Threats—you say? . . . What you'd call it I don't know, but once I heard Bjarni say to Jon, 'Steinun isn't going to have to put up with your bad temper for much longer.' Those were his exact words. I heard it with my very own ears. What did Jon answer? . . . He answered that he guessed he wasn't going to live through another winter like this one. That was what he answered, poor devil. And I guess you could say that he wasn't far off, either."

Malfrith in her excitement had completely forgotten to keep hold of her shawl. It slid quietly to the floor and it took some time to gather it up and arrange it properly around her shoulders. The prosecutor exploited the occasion to introduce the question of whether a quarrel had not taken place between the men or the couples the same day that Jon disappeared.

"Quarrels—well I guess!" Malfrith replied and was off again. "They stood there and quarreled in the door, Jon and Steinun. That's all I know. You hardly bothered to listen to their eternal wrangling. I was sitting inside in the kitchen along with the kids and poor Gudrun; I was sitting and minding my own business. An offensive situation, ts, ts! They were in love with each other—you couldn't miss that. You could see that with both eyes shut, I can tell you that . . . Every time Bjarni went down in the evening—wouldn't you believe it, Steinun was running right after him. And him after her. Or do you think they just sat around twiddling their thumbs? Not by a long shot. Not at Syvendeaa! And you can just bet that it was a long while before they'd show themselves again. All that—that was on the daily menu at Syvendeaa. Ts, ts, I should guess it was. Yeah sure . . . If you went by a dark corner, a whispering and a buzzing . . . to put it as decently as possible. The good Lord hush my mouth . . . But you only needed to look at Jon—or Gudrun . . . It was a pity. When did I see poor Jon the last time? The day he disappeared—I should say so. I've got eyes in my head. He was up earlier than usual that morning. And when he'd been out a while he came back in and said, 'Good morning . . . .'"

Judge Scheving, who had sat there amused, said suddenly and impatiently, "Now listen here! Be quiet for a minute!"

"Well—I suppose I was brought here just to be quiet," Malfrith burst out, offended.

"You're here to answer what you're asked."

"Well—well I never . . . Answer, all right."

After that she answered only in monosyllables. The prosecutor would ask her to tell about something; she would ask him to question her. She would answer his questions all right. But to every question she answered yes or no. Until Monsieur Einar asked whether she had ever seen the departed Jon after he had died, to which she answered, "Sure—as a ghost."

Judge Scheving took a hand in the interrogation, talked with her comfortably and got her calmed down. But she was cautious, maintained that she didn't know. Which was probably true enough. She had not seen Steinun sew any shoes for Jon, nor had she heard Jon say anything about intending to go to Skor—not that day. But there had been a lot of talk about the hay there which they couldn't get home. When Judge Scheving asked whether Jon's disappearance had caused any sorrow at Syvendeaa, she answered, "Sorrow, well I should hope so . . . poor Gudrun came crying in to me where I was sitting in the house—it was just right around dusk. I asked, 'Now what?' 'There's one less of us,' she said."

"Bjarni and Steinun—were they unhappy."

"Steinun was pretty quiet . . ."

"Wasn't there any talk at all that evening about what happened?"

"Mighty little . . ."

About the departed Gudrun's sickness she had nothing to report: at the time Gudrun was sick she had been away from Syvendeaa.

Judge Scheving asked the farmers if it was correct that the witness had changed jobs at the time stated. Which they confirmed. But that was too much for Malfrith.

"If you don't trust me, then I won't say anything," she sighed, unappreciated.

The prosecutor asked her some further questions, to which she contented herself with shaking her head.

Judge Scheving bent forward over the table and said with friendly emphasis, "Be a good girl, Malfrith, and answer me just one little thing: didn't you have any suspicion at all that Bjarni had murdered the departed Jon?"

Malfrith shook her head and answered firmly, "No. I was certain sure that he'd fallen over at Rodeskred."

When she was out the door Judge Scheving sighed resignedly, "Those were our principal witnesses . . . What do you think, gentlemen?"

Foreman Thorberg circulated the pocket flask—he was an easygoing man and knew from experience that a man who answers in liquor gets off easy. Monsieur Einar thrust out his underlip, the others contented themselves with silence.

Gisli from Skapadal was let in. He had obviously been sleeping, and he didn't relish being wakened up. He was a long way from being as cooperative as before. To the prosecutor's question about the differences at Syvendeaa, he answered sleepily and irritatedly, "Ask me something I know about. Or else quit asking me questions."

"What do you know about the departed Jon's death?"

"Nothing! Except that Bjarni told me he had fallen at Rodeskred when he was going to get some hay in from Skor."

"What facts or evidence can you present in support of the charge that Jon is supposed to have been murdered by Bjarni?"

"None. I just know it."

"Previously you were more communicative about the matter."

"I only said what everybody's been saying, that Jon must have good bones to have fallen over at Rodeskred and come away with nothing broken. And I'll stick by that. I know the shore down there."

"And what if it happened at high tide?"

"The high water mark at Rodeskred anybody can see with his own eyes."

"What do you know about the death of the departed Gudrun?"

"Nothing."

"Haven't you ever heard that Bjarni and Steinun are supposed to have murdered her?"

"You hear a lot."

"Of course; but you did believe it?"

"I still do."

"You talked to Jon last winter—isn't that right?"

"Yeah —a good week before he died."

"Where did you see him?" Judge Scheving let fall carelessly.

"At Syvendeaa. I was in to say hello a minute. We were old neighbors, as your honor probably knows."

"Can you remember anything of what he said to you?"

"He didn't say much."

"Was he in a good humor?"

"He was grouchy, the way he usually was. First he said

something about that he sure wished he'd never moved away from Skapadal. He didn't seem to be very satisfied with things at Syvendeaa. I told him that he'd been eager enough to change my company for Bjarni's. Then he said something about Bjarni not being much worse than Steinun. I wasn't about to believe that there could be anything wrong with Steinun. At Skapadal she'd always gone around so quietly. But then all of a sudden he didn't want to talk any more."

"What was the departed Jon like to live alongside of?"

"He was an old slob . . . Not to mention that you could never get a drop from him."

"Did you talk with the departed Gudrun too?"

"No, not that day. But I met her on the ice down below Maberg one day that winter—it was the first Sunday in summer, I guess. She was on the way home from church; I was going to the boat. I said, 'What a winter, Gudrun. Our sheep are dropping like flies from starvation. It's going to end up with us all dead.' She said I shouldn't talk like that, and she said that it was a sin to get drunk on a holy day. We stood there a little and chatted. And then she said, 'Well, I'd better not stay here too long or I'll run out of time, and I've got orders to come home by evening.' 'You get orders from your husband?' I asked. 'Not only from him,' she said. 'At Syvendeaa I've got two bosses—and the worst of them is Steinun.' I asked if she'd turned into a hired girl. 'You'd think so,' she said. 'But I guess I wouldn't complain if I weren't any worse off than a hired girl,' she said. And when she'd said that she went. Since then I've never seen her—not alive."

"Didn't you talk with her at Syvendeaa?"

"No, the few times I came there I only talked with Jon. But I could see all right that she wasn't happy. I saw her cry, too."

"Is that all you know about these matters?"

"Whatever else I know I only heard. But it'll do."

"All right," said Judge Scheving in dismissal, "We'll

save that for another time."

The fourth witness called was Gisli's wife, Jartruth, a tall woman, somewhat intimidated, with a sharp eye and no little perserverance—once she got going. Questioned about the notorious quarreling and fighting she answered shortly that she hadn't seen anything of it.

"What do you know about Jon Thorgrimsson's death," the prosecutor went on.

"Nothing but that he's supposed to have fallen over at the cliff by Skor."

"Is it known to you that Gudrun was poisoned?"

"Nothing besides what she told me herself."

"Let's hear it," Judge Scheving intruded, in a temper.

Jartruth shot a nervous glance at him, shuffled her feet nervously, and got going. "I'd promised Gudrun some knitting, and I brought it to her myself—that must have been the second Sunday in summer. She was home alone with the kids because Jon Bjarnason and Malfrith were out, and Bjarni and Steinun were at the church at Baer that day. I gave her the knitting and she looked at it and said, 'Thank God for your hands. Jartruth. You can see in every stitch who knitted it.' That's what she said. And she gave me some more wool then, but she sighed and said, 'Well, it shouldn't make any difference to me now how Bjarni's dressed.' After that she didn't say anything for a long time and then she said, 'Thursday evening it was pretty near up with me, Jartruth, my dear . . .' 'How was that?' I asked. I was scared. She said, 'Oh, I got to throwing up so that I thought I was going to lose my insides.' 'What had you eaten?' I asked—without any suspicion. 'I don't dare tell you,' she said. 'Bjarni and Steinun can turn up any minute—and might hear us.' I said, 'Let's step out to the door, and then we can keep an eye on whether they are on their way.' So we did that. Then Gudrun told me, whispering so that the children wouldn't get to hear it, that Steinun that evening had given her a ladle of soup to eat. 'I thought there was some kind of sediment at the bottom,' she said, 'a lot like sand by the feel, but shiny to look at; it tasted bitter when I swallowed it—it burned and smarted in my throat. When I told that to Steinun she said that it must come from the pot the soup was cooked in—"I still haven't got it really cleaned since I cooked the flounder that was washed up the other day," she said, and I didn't think any more about it after that.' That's what Gudrun said. I asked her, 'Tell me, Gudrun—do you really think that the soup was poisoned?' She said that in the night when she'd suddenly felt deathly sick that she'd got suspicious. She said, 'I hadn't any sooner finished the soup in the ladle than I felt the pains in my chest.' Yes, that's what she said—that's the pure truth."

"Go on," said Judge Scheving in a low voice.

"There isn't any more," Jartruth answered, darting her sharp eyes around the room. "We didn't manage to get any more said to each other, because right away we saw Bjarni and Steinun coming out on the ice. So I wanted to get going. Gudrun wanted to get shut of me too, I could tell."

At the prosecutor's question, whether she hadn't talked with Jon Thorgrimsson, she answered that she had not, because she didn't know him.

"You didn't know him?" Judge Scheving asked incredulously. "But hadn't he been your neighbor in Skapadal?"

"That was before my time," answered Jartruth, and red showed in the whites of her eyes—and not anywhere else.

"Before your time? How is that?"

"I've only lived in Skapadal a year and a half."

"Are you that newly married?" Judge Scheving laughed.

"We were married in the summer," Jartruth answered, and dropped her eyes.

"Let the bride go," Judge Scheving ordered cheerfully. "Out to the bridegroom with her."

The next witness was Bjorg from Skog, a dignified, friendly matron, a little out of breath from just being there. As an answer to what she knew about the differences at Syvendeaa, the late Jon's death, Bjarni's presumed murder of Jon, the late Gudrun's death, and her preceding sickness she said every time, "absolutely nothing."

Whereupon she went on puffing.

"Don't you know anything at all about the matter?" Judge Scheving asked, tired and irritated.

"Absolutely nothing," she answered, as calmly as before, "aside from some unreliable parish rumors."

"But I know that you were at Syvendeaa once last winter," growled the prosecutor.

"That's right," replied Bjorg with dignity. "Quite right. That was well along in the winter, that was. I found Gudrun in the kitchen and talked with her there. She complained a good deal; Bjarni wasn't good to her any more, she said, not to speak of Steinun. What words she used— that I don't remember. I don't have much of an opinion of that conversation. We were still living at that time at Melanes. And neighbors ought to leave one another alone— and their problems too. 'Why don't you go to the authorities?' I asked her. But she didn't dare do that, she said, for she'd been promised that if she talked she would pay for it with her life. And she asked me to talk quietly too; somebody could be eavesdropping down below; that had happened before. Some time later she dropped in at Melanes on the way home from church. But she didn't dare stop, she said, because she'd been told that she was to come home the same evening, or if she didn't she could just stay away. 'Well then, stay away,' I advised her. 'Yes— if the law only allowed that,' she answered. But it wasn't just the law alone. She said, too, that if all the tears she had shed that winter were gathered together there would be a lot of people amazed. 'Some day it will come out in the open,' she said. We didn't talk any more about those matters. And after that I never saw her alive."

"Who was it that told her she would pay with her life?" asked Judge Scheving.

"She didn't mention a name. I assumed she meant Bjarni and Steinun."

"Didn't you help Bjarni and Steinun lay Gudrun out in the coffin?" asked Judge Scheving.

"Yes."

"Wasn't there anything unusual to be seen about the body?"

"Poor Gudrun was already dressed in her shroud when I came. And since her face was so calm in death, it never occurred to me to look more closely."

"Did it occur to you that she hadn't died a natural death?"

"Maybe at first . . . but when I'd seen her I was sorry that I'd been suspicious. And it was best for her, it seemed to me—that she had been released from all her pain. As God is my witness, she looked as though she had found peace and quiet."

XXII

"Let's take a minute's breather," Judge Scheving burst out when Bjorg from Skog was out the door, whereupon he danced out into the room, stretched so that his bones creaked, and refreshed himself with various arm swingings and leg movements. "A man sits and gets old. Well, there's been enough hunting here, though it's doubtful to what extent these two can be called game animals. But it's stalking. I damned well don't like it . . . "

Monsieur Gudmund of Valdall, the defense attorney, who up to now had not uttered a word, cleared his throat ponderously and said, "The case was represented to me as though the fact that Bjarni and Steinun had killed Jon and Gudrun was something known to God and man."

Judge Scheving put an end to his gymnastics and listened attentively. When the defense attorney was silent he asked, "And now?"

"Well, now everything seems to point up the fact that not many know anything at all."

"You're beginning, in other words, to waver in your belief that the accused should be found guilty. Tell me—what do you think about Bjarni's explanation that Jon is supposed to have fallen at Rodeskred and have gotten away without breaking any bones?"

"I don't know the place. But Bjarni didn't say that he saw him fall. He didn't think he could follow his trail any longer—that's all. He presented a conjecture, in other words, that the man fell at that particular place. Isn't that a rather thin basis for an accusation of murder? Here at this court I have several times heard mention of the block, and I was astonished, because that's a serious device. I am assuming that we don't yet dispose of people's lives just on the basis of irresponsible conjectures."

"Bravo," Judge Scheving called out. "That's what I call a defense counsel. Isn't that just what I said would happen, Monsieur Einar—that it was going to be a hard squeeze for you to get the tongs on it unless you can get a confession? . . . Well, why don't you go on, Monsieur Gudmund? What about the powder that Bjarni salted the soup with?"

"In the first place, you can't put any particular weight on Steinun's declaration on this point, particularly since she herself took it to be a joke and didn't know what it was that Bjarni had in the paper," Monsieur Gudmund answered cautiously. "Unless Bjarni confesses, I'll regard that testimony as doubtful. Secondly, even if Bjarni that time should have attempted to remove his wife with poison, such an action renders it by no means impossible that she can, three weeks later, have died a natural death—which the last witness's declaration tends to substantiate, and which the coroners' attestation also by and large seems to substantiate. Up to now I have not heard anything in the court except loose parish gossip. Is the whole case anything else? I consider it, at the least, a grossly improper action on the part of the court to attempt to further disconcert the accused, whose composure is already shaken by the terrible suspicion and the solitary confinement, by feigning a confession from a person accused as a confederate, a confession which we all well know does not exist. The law should eschew proceeding against the accused with untruths."

"Not bad—really not bad," said Judge Scheving, and went thoughtfully back to his chair, "but when the one says that Gudrun died at the pens and the other says that she died on the way to the pens—what do you deduce from that?"

"I deduce nothing from that, tentatively, for one can express himself with enormous variety about the same matter. Least of all does such a discrepancy indicate that they had prior agreement about what they should testify, since they are not even in agreement about the place. Still, 'at' and 'on the way to'—can't they be brought into agreement? Steinun certainly bungled her statement a little. But it isn't easy to stand accused of murder—after having been suspected for months by everybody she met, been moved by force out of her home to another neighborhood, and finally even sitting in jail with irons on her wrists."

"Turning the charge right around—isn't that going a little too far?" answered Judge Scheving, raising his eyebrows sarcastically. "Possibly we ought to go on . . . Next witness."

It was Gudmund Einarsson—the young man who had been present at the finding of Jon Thorgrimsson's body—who was now let in.

He was thoroughly unhappy at being introduced as a witness; I thought that he would burst into tears at any moment. Some little remarks which I had heard now and then, but had never paid any attention to, came suddenly to mind. They said that Young Mundy had great difficulty keeping his eyes off of Steinun when they met.

When he was asked about what he knew of the difficulties at Syvendeaa, he answered in a whisper, "Not anything at all."

Monsieur Einar began to interrogate him about Jon's and Gudrun's deaths and Gudrun's attack. About them he knew nothing either. When the prosecutor went on anyway, he answered firmly, "In the last two years I haven't set foot at Syvendeaa. I don't know anything about these things. I live a long ways away."

"But you talked once in the winter with Jon Thorgrimsson—that I know," Einar Jonsson attacked him, his lower lip jutting forward.

Gudmund was silent a moment and then he answered, "That's true enough; it was a Tuesday evening at the beginning of Lent when he came to Stakk where I was visiting my aunt. We were alone a little while in the kitchen, Jon and I, and I asked him, without meaning anything special—the way you do with somebody—how he liked being at Syvendeaa. He said, 'I'd just as soon not talk about that, but it's enough to make me wish I was out of there—with my two kids; and I'd sure like never to have to see anybody from Syvendeaa again.'"

Gudmund Einarsson was silent; he had repeated Jon's declaration with his lips trembling alarmingly.

"Didn't he say anything more?" Judge Scheving asked interestedly.

"No; I got up as though I had to be on my way."

"Are you certain that it wasn't he who began talking about these matters?"

"No, it was me. For the time being I'd clean forgotten that I'd heard some talk."

"He didn't say which two of the five children he wanted to take away with him from Syvendeaa—and why?"

"No, because I went right away."

"You talked with the departed Gudrun too—didn't you?" the prosecutor asked when Judge Scheving made no sign of going on.

"Yes, just once—in a big hurry. I ran into her on the fields below Kirkjuhvamm, once, along toward the middle of March. She'd been to church in Baer and was on her way home. She asked me to come over and open a vein—for a pain in her back."

"Are you a doctor?" Judge Scheving interrupted, astonished.

Gudmund raised his troubled boy's eyes, looked Judge Scheving firmly in the face. "No, I'm afraid I'm not a doctor," he answered unhappily, "But I've read a lot of books, bought me some tools and I help people—as much as I can."

"So, plainly and simply, quackery?"

"I suppose you could call it that."

"And so Gudrun you didn't want to help. You said before, didn't you, that you hadn't been at Syvendeaa?"

"I told Gudrun, which was the truth, that I didn't have time because I had stock to take care of," Gudmund went on, somewhat more securely than before, "but if she wanted to go back and stay the night in Baer I'd be able to make it early the next morning and bleed her. She said that she didn't dare, because Bjarni and Steinun had forbidden her to spend the night away. They were afraid that she'd go and tell how they were behaving, she said. I'd rather not have heard any more about that: it wasn't any of my business. But I asked her anyway, 'So it's true what people are saying, that they've got their eyes on each other?' She said, 'That's not putting it too strong.' And after that we went on about our business, each of us."

"Didn't Gudrun say anything about their having threatened her life? Bjarni and Steinun?" Judge Scheving asked.

"What she said exactly I don't remember too well—outside of what I've already told you. Poor Gudrun didn't always hold her tongue; she used to exaggerate pretty much. It's possible that she did hint something about them threatening her life, if she was too free with her mouth."

"What was it that she wasn't supposed to tell?"

"She didn't tell me any more—I don't know any more," Gudmund Einarsson mumbled unhappily, and was let out.

"Well, now we have Jon Jonsson from Stakkadal himself," Judge Scheving exclaimed, as Jon from Stakkadal, short and fat and with a gracious smile in the middle of a wreath of gray flecked beard and hair—as though hidden at the bottom of a nest—picked his way across the floor. "Welcome, Monsieur Jon."

"Welcome, Judge—welcome, welcome," whinnied Jon,

gratified, and tried, with only partial success, to reach his hand across the table; "although it were to be wished that we had come together on a more happy occasion." And he added with a sigh, "Ah, yes . . . some are created for majesty, some for the fall."

"Very true . . . Well, what do you say, my friend, about these painful matters?"

Jon Jonsson found a nose someplace at the bottom of the nest, blew the nose, shook his head energetically, and replied, relieved, "Nothing, Judge, absolutely nothing—the Lord God he thanked for that. But we have it very good here in Sauthlauksdal, we witnesses, it would be a crime to complain. We have our keep paid, our inconvenience is compensated for, so I am told. I for my part thank my lucky stars that I came along. A man needs a little amusement and consolation now and again, Judge Scheving. My wife says the same thing. The two of us, we're not annoyed that you summoned us; on the contrary, happy and grateful, judge."

"That was to be expected of you, dear Jon . . . Tell me, Einar my friend—what were your intentions in summoning this fine, pleasant man?"

"Jon of Stakkadal has talked with the deceased Gudrun, I know. Moreover he is one of the last men outside of Syvendeaa who exchanged words with the departed Jon."

"You lie in your damned throat, Einar of Kollsvig, if you claim I'm supposed to have talked with the late Gudrun," Jon contradicted him cheerfully. "I haven't been at Syvendeaa in many a long year, and I've only seen her at church, never talked to her. Poor Gudrun was not one of those persons you would go up to of your own free will and say kitchy kitchy coo. But it's true enough, if you must know, that Jon Thorgrimsson came to me in Stakkadal a week before he died and asked me if I couldn't take him on as a hired man—him and three of his children. I asked him why he wanted to get away from Syvendeaa.

He answered that it made no difference why he wanted to get away, but away was what he wanted. And since his wife didn't want to go along with him they were going to have to separate. 'So Steinun is going to stay on at Syvendeaa?' I asked and he answered, 'yes.' And I said, as was the case, that I was too poor to think of doing anything like that, and besides we were short on space. So we didn't talk any more about it."

"Is that all?" Judge Scheving asked.

"As I told you before, Judge—I can't bear witness in this case."

"You don't know which three children he meant?"

"No, that I don't."

"Well, we can certainly let Monsieur Jon go. Possibly his spouse has something more to tell us."

"Gudrun, his wife, as round and friendly as her husband, was willing enough—but not very useful.

"Shall I confine myself to what I have heard and seen myself," she began cautiously, but with warm eagerness as though she did not regard it as strictly necessary. "If I'm to confine myself to what I've heard and seen myself then I don't know very much . . . "

"You'd do best to do that," Judge Scheving advised her.

Something died out in Gudrun's eye, and the glow in her bright cheeks paled a little; she swallowed what she was going to say and answered briefly, "Yes, well, I don't, as I said, know anything."

"Didn't you talk at all with Jon Thorgrimsson, the day he was at your place with your husband to talk about coming with you?"

"Nothing more than hello and goodbye. And he thanked me for the dried cod I gave him."

"Aren't you supposed to have been at Syvendeaa once last winter?" the prosecutor inserted meaningfully.

"That's true, but as God is my witness I spoke not one single word with poor Jon that time. But I did talk with Gudrun . . . When we were alone for a moment, she said,

'This winter, my dear namesake—it's the worst winter I've ever lived through.' 'Oh yes,' I said, 'it certainly is bad enough, everybody's complaining.' 'It wasn't the weather I meant,' she said then; 'it was the people.' 'Is it Bjarni—isn't he good to you?' I asked. 'Steinun is still worse,' she answered, 'because she's seduced him and turned his mind from me.' But then somebody came, and we didn't get to talk together again."

"When was it you came to Syvendeaa?"

"Sunday, about the first of March, so help me God."

The next in line was Rognvald Olafsson, Bjarni's brother-in-law, married to Gudrun's sister Ingibjorg. From nervousness and confusion he was near to falling over his own feet in the door opening, and the first of the judge's questions he answered with another question, "Is Bjarni going to find out what I say here?"

Judge Scheving slammed the table impatiently and replied sternly, "What you say can, depending on the circumstances, be laid before Bjarni, yes. But you will remember that you have given your oath, on pain of risking your eternal soul, to tell the truth and nothing but the truth. If you lie it will certainly go worse with you than if you hold to the truth. If I find you in a perjury, or even in a misleading statement, you will be punished right here in this court to the full extent of the law."

"Well—in the name of God," Rognvald stammered.

"Yes, you may well say that."

And then it developed anyhow that, either about the differences at Syvendeaa or about Jon Thorgrimsson's and Gudrun's deaths, he did not know the least thing. Only when the prosecutor asked him if, during the previous winter, he had ever talked with the late Jon did he have anything to tell.

"Ye-es," he said slowly, "true is true. Poor Jon came to me at Krokshus the middle of February and began to talk about wanting to find himself another place to live. He wanted to get away from Syvendeaa, he said. But Steinun wanted to stay, he said. 'You must be joking, huh?' I asked him then. 'You mean you really can't get along at Syvendeaa?' 'I've never been farther from joking,' he said. 'I'm in dead earnest.' Well, I didn't think I wanted to know any more. And he didn't tell me any more then, either."

"Is that all that you know about Jon?" asked Judge Scheving—and when Rognvald nodded he went on, "What do you know about the late Gudrun's death?"

"About her death I don't know anything," Rognvald answered emphatically, weighing every word carefully, "but I exchanged a few words with her once late in the winter. Or was it at the beginning of summer? She told me then that she'd never in her life had it as bad as she'd had it that winter. She'd gone through suffering before, all right, but that had just been physical, she said. Now she didn't know anymore whether she was dead or alive, if she was a human or an animal; because she couldn't speak one word with anybody, either when she went out or when somebody came to visit. They'd forbidden her, Bjarni and Steinun, and it wasn't so easy to put up with a situation like hers in silence and all alone; and she knew some people that wouldn't be sorry if one fine day she went the same way as poor Jon; and it didn't matter to her anymore one way or another what happened to her, she'd never have it good anymore, it was all the same to her . . ."

Rognvald stopped and dried his forehead. But when nobody gave any indication of helping him with a question he continued. "See, we didn't talk any more together that day . . . but I came there again—a few days later. In the meantime what had happened was that Gudrun had got mighty sick one evening—because Steinun had given her a ladle of soup that she'd put something dangerous in, she thought. What had saved her was throwing up the poison, but God only knew if she would ever be really well again—before that blessed time when you're finally cured of all sickness, she said. I thought I could see she

148

was pretty scared. And when I saw that, I got scared myself, I don't know why. The whole thing was so terrible, because when I asked her what evening she'd got sick she didn't give me any answer but she turned red; all of a sudden she stood without moving and held her breath, just as if she was standing and listening. So I hurried up to get away, because I'd got awfully scared. Nothing on earth could've got me to stay there any longer. I was quiet until I was out of sight, and then I ran. Ran till I fell . . ."

"What were you afraid of?"

"I don't know. I wasn't at all clear about that."

"Whom were you afraid of?"

"I don't know that, either."

"Had you been threatened?"

"No—no."

"Was there anyone that you seemed to think wanted to do you harm?"

"No, there wasn't anything said about anything like that."

There were a few more questions and answers. But Rognvald had no more to report.

I wonder if the others did not feel what I did—if we did not all sit there feeling the horror that had made Rognvald that day take to his heels.

When his wife Ingibjorg Egilsdottir, Gudrun's sister, walked across the floor with a woolen scarf over her head, a huge shawl wound around her shoulders, and coughing just a little, it was almost as though the departed Gudrun had risen from her grave to give testimony herself. I had never before noticed how strikingly the two sisters resembled one another—right down to the rise and fall of the voice that emerged from the shawls. Possibly it was the fatigue and lack of sleep, but I really sat there feeling uncertain and confused—sat there and looked to see if it was the hands of a living being that held the shawls together.

To the prosecutor's first question, which to my astonishment concerned Jon Thorgrimsson, the mummified figure answered, coughing, "He came to my home the middle of February, a good month before he died—poor man."

It was curious to hear Ingibjorg Egilsdottir talk about "my home," knowing that she and her husband were living in some miserable shacks at Krok—more like outhouses than human dwellings. Was it because she was Gudrun's sister that everything went so badly for her? Was bad luck inheritable? Or contagious? Like coughing? Like mankind's bodily sicknesses?

"Jon told me that every day at Syvendeaa was a trial for him, every night a torture," Ingibjorg reported tonelessly, coughing all the while. "But it didn't look as though he was going to get away from there, he said, nobody wanted to take him in. And he said besides, 'Death lies in wait here and death lies in wait there; if he doesn't come on his own, you have to call on him for help like a sleepy ferry man . . .' Yes, that's what he said. What he meant, only God knows."

"What do you think he meant?"

"I don't know."

About the situation at Syvendeaa she denied having any more specific knowledge. She had kept away from there lately, she said; she hadn't been there since the herds were collected last fall.

"I won't forget that day in a hurry," she said with a sigh. "I met my sister Gudrun up at the barn, she was busy collecting peat and stacking it. We went along home to the farm, and I went in with her because I'd asked her to give me a drop to drink. But suddenly, right while we were standing there, here comes Bjarni shouting, 'Yeah, there you stand blabbing instead of doing your work! Don't you think you're a little too old to goof off from your job—like some kid or other? Are we going to have rain in the peat? You're not going to be any better to look at, you scarecrow, if you have to burn wet peat all winter. And besides that, it'd be nice to be spared lies and slander in my own house.' . . . Oh, the way he went on . . . I'd never seen him sore before; I stood there like I'd been turned to stone."

"What did Gudrun say to all that?"

"She said next to nothing, the poor thing. She asked him to control himself and said that as long as she was mistress in the house she certainly had leave to give her sister a drink of whey, and to have a drink herself if she felt thirsty. But he shouted, 'Go ahead, swill the whey down, the both of you, you two witches, till you bust. Then maybe the poison will run out of you . . . ' Then I went. I didn't want to hear any more. She'd told me before that he wasn't as good to her as he had been. Now I'd seen and heard, both, how it was. Even if I'm just a poor woman, I've never been too poor to keep away from a place where I've been received with abuse."

"Did Gudrun say it was Steinun who was responsible for Bjarni's changed attitude toward her?"

"No, she didn't say that to me; I only heard that later. From someplace else. The way you heard so much anyhow, last winter, that you couldn't believe—or couldn't repeat. Particularly since the whole thing was gossip, up to last fall now—when poor Jon's body was washed ashore."

"What do you mean by that?" Judge Scheving asked quickly.

The figure in the shawls was silent.

"A dead body is of and by itself no proof."

The shawls began to move—stood quivering; a half choked voice issued from them. "If you can't even call for justice with a bare skull and an empty mouth, then . . . No, I won't say any more."

"But my good woman . . . what about your sister's body? You stood there yourself and looked at it, and didn't raise any outcry, isn't that true?"

"Yes, yes, I *saw* it."

"You were there when she was buried?"

"Yes, yes, I was there."

"Was there anything that indicated that she died by human hands?"

"I've never killed anybody! How should I know what killed people look like? . . . She had a bruise above her breast."

"Did you think that came from her having been murdered?"

"A person doesn't like to believe the worst . . . There were smarter people than I am there. They said that it could come from internal trouble and that you shouldn't suspect your fellow man without good reasons."

"Who said that?"

"Our Dean, the Reverend Jon Ormsson . . . "

Monsieur Einar from Kollsvig made a distinct noise with his big underlip. A by no means dissatisfied noise.

"Was it the Reverend Jon's fault that you didn't step forward with your suspicion?" Judge Scheving asked insistently.

"I didn't want to believe what I was afraid of . . . and what everybody was saying. So I tried to forget it. I didn't want to think about it at all. But as God is my witness, I haven't had a single peaceful night since . . . "

The figure in the shawls bent itself in weeping.

"You didn't object to her being buried," Judge Scheving reproached her mildly.

"I thought that if she was dead from poison then she would have to be green and blue all over," sobbed Ingibjorg. "When I saw her peaceful face . . . "

Judge Scheving shuddered; with shaking fingers he leafed though his papers, leafed through them over and over again.

"Do you know anything more you can tell, my good woman?" he asked gently.

But Ingibjorg had nothing more to tell.

When she was gone Judge Scheving called a recess, came up to me and pulled me with him over to a window.

"Do you know what, my dear Reverend?" he said, and

moved his thin shoulders as though he were shaking something off. "It pretty nearly seems to me that even more horrible than what has been done are the fantasies which the suspicions about it have awakened. The black thoughts and dreams that have been aroused can be washed away by only one thing. The two must die. I almost said: whether they killed or not."

I was silent.

"They must die," Judge Scheving continued with less heat but just as decisively, "unless you will talk with them and try to get them to tell the truth—*provisionally, just tell the truth*—decently . . . God in heaven knows, they'll have to deal with me; I will hunt them, I swear it to you, until I have them . . . they're guilty. You only need to look at them to know it. But of what? That's the knot. Truth is the best thing, in any event. But it is by no means indispensable. I'm really going to get them to confess . . . something or other that can part them from their heads . . ."

He was silent. I was silent. There was not a word on my tongue. Had the hunt not been under way a long time already? 'We cannot help one another—we can only kill one another . . .' Bjarni had said. I wonder if he had any notion how truly he had spoken.

"Think about that now," Judge Scheving concluded, after having stood a while, whistling between his teeth, making a peephole in the frost on the window. "You could possibly come to doing what is, in its way, a good deed. It's not a matter of indifference how even murderers die. We have to die, all of us, like what we—are *not*, men . . ."

He was already on the way back to his judge's seat, but he turned around and whispered to me, smiling privately, "Notice my round table . . ."

Once more he came back. "How have you been able to live in that hell—in that fire of fiendishness and malice—month after month," he whispered "It's a riddle to me . . .

153

You aren't infected yourself, yet—are you?" he asked, and inspected me closely. There was a certain hidden fear in his piercing, not quite certain, eyes. "I'll tell you—for my part I am pretty near to getting—desperate . . . I try to—amuse myself. To keep it at a distance. But do you find it amusing here? My head's swimming, right at the moment. This whole hopeless confusion of guilt and shame and terror . . . It's more than a man can breathe in . . . They must die."

"Whether they are guilty or not?"

"They *are* guilty. Even if they just possibly didn't kill. But they did. And what's worse . . . they bungled it."

He went back to his place and burst out bitterly, "Shall we try to get finished with these idiotic witnesses? We've wasted a whole day with listening to their twaddle. We've got one old hag left, I see; and then we have Monsieur Jon Palsson. All right. Let the hag come in."

Gudrun Bjarnisdottir, a poor, old, quivering thing, was led in. She had to lean over the table and bare her bloodless ear to be able to hear what the prosecutor's questions were about. Her answers she shouted back; the louder she shouted the more difficult it was to understand, toothless as she was, and with all the irrelevant smackings and slurpings she did with her tongue, her gums, her lips.

While she was being questioned I sat and looked a little more closely at Judge Scheving and his "round table." Thorberg sat motionless, sunk down in his fur, good-natured and dull—just waiting for a pick-me-up in the pauses between the witnesses. Monsieur Einar was no longer so arrogant in the lower lip—it had begun to hang a little and gave him a wounded expression, like an old horse who finds his load too heavy. The defense counsel sat with his narrow head thrust forward, a distinctly watchful look in his big blue-gray eyes, whose glance alternately brightened and dulled as though he were fluctuating back and forth between two equally weighty convictions. The three other jurists sat silent, with genial, lively eyes, ready to print their names in the register toward evening. And it was going to be evening very soon.

"Now we've heard enough of what you *don't* know," Judge Scheving, copper-red in the face, snapped at the old woman.

She did not hear what he said, but shuffled amicably nearer and laid her hand like a funnel behind her ear.

He repeated it and added impatiently, "What *do* you know about the case?"

"Nothing," she called back and slurped with her lips. "Not a thing."

"I thought you said before that you had talked with Gudrun?"

"Oh yes . . . yes—that's true. It was at church. She was taking Communion. Bjarni and Steinun were there too. That's the holy truth. That was—let's see—that was the third or maybe the fourth Sunday after Easter. I left the church right after Communion—had to step out a minute. Gudrun came behind me. 'You've been pretty sick, I heard,' I said to her. 'Oh yes,' she answered, and said that she couldn't understand how she could still be alive the way she had thrown up—blood and phlegm and pus. But that was nothing, she said, nothing compared to Bjarni not paying any more attention to her. 'My dear,' I said, 'but he's your husband.' 'No, he's not my husband any more,' she said, 'I don't think he cares any more about me than his dog; he probably thinks it would be the best thing for me to go throw myself into the ocean, and maybe I'll do that some day.' 'How does Steinun treat you?' I asked. 'She's nice enough to me since the day I got sick,' she said; 'but she's done the worst to me she could, taken my husband away from me and set him against me.' That's the holy truth. That's what she said."

Judge Scheving finished with her in a rush and asked to have the last witness brought in—Monsieur Jon Palsson.

My father-in-law whispered to me as he went by, "Bjarni would like to talk to you . . ."

That was what I had been waiting for . . . knew would come. But still I could not understand how I could remain sitting in the chair acting as though nothing had happened—how I did not sink through the floor. Because now there was no way out . . . It had to happen. And happen with my intercession. Faith in truth's strength and triumph, in its grace and its curative powers—at that moment it ebbed from me. Truth! Was not the need for truth one more of the thirsty werwolves of the mind? One of the most insidious, possibly . . . Truth! Was it not also one of existence's dark, hoarse, voracious vultures? Was not its law, like that of the rest of life—to multiply and destroy? . . .

New strength had come to Einar Jonsson, including his lower lip. Monsieur Jon Palsson was by no means his friend, still less an admirer of his. He knew it, and he reciprocated as best he could.

Questioned about the differences at Syvendeaa, Monsieur Jon replied that his farm now, as anybody knew, was twenty miles from Syvendeaa. "I wasn't ever a daily visitor there."

"Does that mean that in the interval in question you were never at Syvendeaa?" asked the prosecutor.

"That means that I don't consider myself competent to give testimony about the atmosphere in the house," Monsieur Jon answered steadily.

"You are aware that you are talking under oath?"

Monsieur Jon looked around, smiling. He said nothing.

Judge Scheving interrupted—asked: "Did I misunderstand you, Monsieur Jon, in believing you to feel personally convinced that this is a case of murder?"

"No, no, you didn't, Judge. Murder or manslaughter—I think so too. But unfortunately I am, for my part, in no position to help you particularly with any clarification of the crimes that may exist. For that you called up my colleague and your friend, Monsieur Einar from Kollsvig."

"Have you anything against telling me on what you base your private conviction, Monsieur Jon?"

"I base it primarily on a conversation I had with Bjarni and Steinun one Sunday at church. I told Bjarni that there might have been poison in the soup Steinun had given his wife—the evening she had had the nausea, which you certainly have heard about. He answered to this that it wasn't from that that she was dead. She got over that, he said. Then I knew where I had my man. And that there had been poison in the soup."

"Did you press him any further on it?"

"Oh yes, but he gave me the slip. They're dangerous, those two. But you'll get them all right."

"A confession isn't going to be easy to get."

"With Monsieur Einar at your side you can catch even wilier game."

"Wasn't Jon Thorgrimsson at your place, asking you to help him get away from Syvendeaa."

"If he only had been! I'd have done it at once, even if I'd have had to take that witch of a woman into my own house—for a while. No—but the late Gudrun came to me once and said that it would be nice if I were in a position to rescue her from Syvendeaa; her husband had begun to beat her and yank her around by the hair, she said. I thought she was lying, or at least was exaggerating. And I still think so. Bjarni may possibly have killed her, but I don't believe that he beat her or mistreated her. At that time I hadn't heard anything about—the situation there. So I said to her, that I just couldn't do anything about it; in any case she would first have to go to her minister; marital affairs belonged under spiritual matters, I said. That's the way it's always been in my time in our part of the country. Whether she then talked with the Reverend Jon—that I wouldn't be able to say."

"Why did you take Steinun away from Syvendeaa once last summer?"

"I had a perfect right to. I knew what I knew all right. Even if I couldn't, and can't, prove anything. If I had put it off, then she and her children would have been entitled to parish relief here, in Rodesand parish. That was a reason too. I was abroad early. I wanted to catch her in bed—with Bjarni. Well, it didn't work out that way. And yet she *had* slept there, she was getting out of bed just as I came into the house, and it couldn't be any other bed than Bjarni's. But foxes aren't to be caught like that, with bare hands. I'm beginning to get old, too."

Monsieur Jon had nothing more to tell; and Judge Scheving was just going to adjourn for the day, when the defense counsel remarked that he would like to object to the reliability of various of the testimonies delivered—at any rate as far as the statements of time were concerned. Gudrun Egilsdottir could not have been on one and the same day both home and away; in particular she could hardly have been encountered at church on days when there had not been any service held in Saurbaer.

If there had not been any confusion in the court before, there was now. Judge Scheving summoned the witnesses all together and worked on them like a mad man—until he eventually, to everybody's amazement, had got their times to agree. When they were gone, he turned without any preamble to me and asked, "Well, Monsieur Curate. Have you decided now to talk to the accused?"

"Under the condition that it can take place privately and without witnesses—and under the condition that the court will entrust them to me for the interval, without interfering with my actions," I answered, and to my amazement found my tongue sure and my voice firm.

"Orders will be given to the effect that you can take over the accused at any time—on your own responsibility," Judge Scheving answered, contentedly slamming shut the signed record.

With that, court was over for the day.

XXIII

Lantern in hand I went out into the black night. Usually when you go in the dark it closes tight around you, it even presses in on you so that you become dark yourself and can only remember light as a dream, distant and unreal. But if you have a light with you, then you stay within the circle of the light while the dark is forced to keep its distance, powerless—but still more impenetrable.

Before I looked up Bjarni I went to the barn where two men were guarding Steinun. She sat in the hay, huddled up, her arms propped on her knees, her head in her hands. She did not look up when I came—paid no attention; she might have been sleeping. But when I got a closer look at her, I could tell that her position was not that of a sleeper.

I referred to the order the guards must have got from the judge, asked them to take the irons off her and go. They watched me out of the corners of their eyes as they did it, had something to say to each other with their eyes too; then they left. I heard them whispering and laughing outside the barn. Then the snow crunched under their feet, fainter and fainter.

I had never before exchanged a word with Steinun alone. I sat down in the hay, having no idea what I should say, how I should begin.

"Well—am I free?" she asked slowly after an interval—in a dull voice.

She was sitting now with her head raised; but I did not believe that she either saw, heard, or felt what went on, her eyes were so fixed, her features so motionless.

I pulled myself together—said, "Hand irons we humans can lock on your wrists, and then free you from."

She still sat for a while motionless. Then she threw herself down suddenly in the hay, buried her face in her hands, and burst into tears. I had never in my life ever heard anyone weep as despairingly as that. It was a weeping without hope. I remembered the Reverend Jon's words—"He who dwells in his own heart . . ." Suddenly the poor woman rolled over on her side and sobbed, "I don't want to—die . . . I don't want to die . . . *I don't want to die.*"

Three times she cried out, each time louder and more wildly. Then her voice failed her. And she lay down again with her face in the hay and wept.

After a while her weeping subsided, perhaps because she heard me, too, sitting and weeping. Finally she was silent. And it was quiet in the barn; quiet in the low circle of the smouldering fan of light which the lantern emitted.

I began to speak—feeble words about death, which is inevitable whether man will meet it or not; of death, which is a touchstone of the human heart; of death, which is life's hope, confirmation; death, which is the crown of life.

She groaned; groaned like a tortured animal. And I was silent.

Since I did not seem to be able to give her any comfort, I told her that we could go—over to Bjarni. And that I could leave them alone tonight, in case they wanted that.

"Oh yes," she burst out, and got up.

And suddenly she fell on my neck, kissed me like a sister, kissed me and wept, embracing me and sobbing, "I always knew that you were the only good man in the world, Reverend Eiulv . . . Come on—let's go. Let's hurry up . . ."

And we went. Our steps creaked faintly in the soft snow. The darkness breathed softly, a black, invisible gust. The circle of light shot forward over the snow in small leaps. Steinun held my hand—suddenly she tightened her grip, "Maybe—it isn't so bad."

I walked talking with God—trying to draw Him down to me, down to us three, His neediest creatures. But somehow I could not get near to Him—could not feel His peace. And yet I felt myself in some fashion or other in His power. Incomprehensible art Thou, Lord, I thought, and Thou sendest me on strange paths.

"You've finally come," Bjarni sighed, when I, with the lantern before me, crawled in to him and his guards.

But at the same time he caught sight of Steinun, saw that she was going unfettered, was astonished and said nothing.

I asked the guards to free him and told them to go on about their business. A couple of them had been sleeping; they were not particularly eager to interrupt their sleep.

"Where are we supposed to sleep?" one of them muttered hoarsely.

I referred them to the barn where Steinun had been under guard before, and they went away sullenly.

Bjarni was rubbing his wrists, but he went on lying there as before, half buried in the hay. Then he put his hands back of his head, looked at Steinun, looked at me— and said after a very long interval, "I'd thought we were going to talk alone, Eiulv . . ."

"Have you got something to tell me that Steinun doesn't know or can't listen to?" I asked.

He was silent a moment. Then he answered with a groan, "No . . . but it's so hard . . . Everything's gradually got so hard, Reverend Eiulv."

Steinun had remained sitting by the door; she sat there with her head bowed, motionless.

"I thought I could give you the most help by giving you a chance to be alone with Steinun," I answered, as my heart suddenly filled with disappointment and bitter uncertainty. Had I miscalculated again? Could I no longer rely on my intuition? Was my faith in my own mind and God's guidance only a misreable self-deception?

"What was that?" Bjarni asked incredulously. "Alone?"

"Yes. In a little I'm going. But I'd like to remain nearby. Not to keep an eye on you, Bjarni, because I'm relying on you. But—in case you should have need of me."

"But what—what if we run away anyhow?"

"Where would you run to, poor devil?"

"Is it so that we can work out how to get our testimony to agree better—that you're bringing us together?" Bjarni asked suspiciously.

"How would I be able to stop that . . . if you yourselves haven't had enough of childishness?"

"Do you call it childish—to save your life?"

"I won't talk to you like this, Bjarni," I answered, and was encouraged in my despair. "I'm going now. I'll stay out there until dawn, unless you call me in first. But I want to tell you something, man, before I go, although you may have learned it yourself: salvation and damnation are not something outside. Salvation and damnation are in you yourself. That is your responsibility to God."

I went out into the night . . . Suddenly I was alone in the sheltering darkness, wonderfully alone, and God incomprehensibly near.

Without being able to explain it intelligently, I knew quite suddenly that I had done the right thing. Or was it merely my fatigue and the soft breeze that rocked me into the sweet deception of rest and sleep?

I was brought to consciousness by someone calling to me—a man's low voice. It could almost have been the darkness' own, it sounded so compounded of earth and blood. But then I suddenly remembered where I was and remembered Bjarni.

"I'm coming," I whispered back.

Stiffness and cold had crept over me and fastened themselves as a resistance to any change, a reluctance toward life, a reluctance to movement. But I pulled myself together, shook the clutch of the deadly hand of the cold off me, and crept in to the two in the barn.

When I came, Bjarni laid himself down again as he apparently had lain while I was gone—with his head in Steinun's lap.

He met my questioning glance with a pathetic little attempt at a smile, cleared his throat and said, "We can't talk any more—the two of us . . ."

They reached for each other's hands, and Bjarni stretched himself more comfortably—closed his eyes.

I crawled down in the hay to get a little warmth in my body. I met Steinun's look, which stayed with mine—warm and secure. Very soon I began to fall asleep. Then Bjarni whispered, without opening his eyes, but so awake that a start went through me and all my sleepiness and indolence fell away at once, "What have you done with Steinun . . .?"

I said nothing. I listened. My heart was hammering, hammering, full of fear and expectant.

"We were so scared," he went on, very softly—"especially Steinun. Now she's suddenly got to be the bravest of the two of us. We'll tell the truth, Eiulv . . ."

This time it was I who broke down. I wept a long time. A great and sinful bitterness arose in my mind, a bitterness with God. Why did He lay so heavy a responsibility on me? Why on me? But then I came to think of Young Olof whom He had given me, and of my church back home that He had given me too. And of my parish children who—young and old—would someday be gathered together under the sod in my churchyard, and whose peace in death it was my duty not to disturb, either with doubt or with sorrow. I thought also of the child that was soon to be born to me. And so my weeping ended in prayer and humble thanks. I promised God that I would live my life as well and as usefully as I could. And yet there was still something that smarted in my heart, smarted and burned. Was it my earthly impotence—here, where I wanted to help? Or a vague feeling of complicity—a guilt that would be difficult if not impossible to determine for myself, and for which I therefore did not know how I should make atonement?

Bjarni went on, "But we don't want to tell you anything, Eiulv, not now tonight. We've agreed on that. We'd rather tell—it—just once. How it happened . . . and then never again."

I said, "Bjarni and Steinun—you should know this: in any way I can be of help, you can rely on me."

"We know that," Bjarni answered calmly. "I have always known that I have a friend in you, Eiulv. Only I didn't know—what a terrible friend . . ."

Suddenly he was lying there weeping. We wept, all three of us.

And the night passed. That night that was like an abyss of misery, through whose impenetrable darkness faith and hope glimmered only faintly, like distant stars, like those frozen and glowing balls our blind dreams and feeble eyes grasp despairingly.

XXIV

In the morning's gray dawn, when I crept out of the barn, Bjarni and Steinun had fallen asleep. They were sleeping so heavily that they did not wake when I left. Judge Scheving would have preferred to wake them and interrogate them at once, but I managed to get him satisfied with setting a guard on the barn and waiting until they woke up by themselves. This wasn't done, however, until he had assured himself with his own eyes that they were in the barn, and that there was no other way out than the end door.

The court was convened and the procedures got under way. First, Jon Bjarnason was interrogated again; after that, Malfrith. The prosecutor wanted to know more exactly the reasons why the married couples at Syvendeaa had left their marriage beds the previous winter. Neither the man nor the woman, however, knew any more than they had already told.

Then it was finally the Reverend Jon Ormsson, the sinner's, turn.

The Reverend came, composed but mighty unsteady on his legs. Every emotion showed up at once in his old lameness. He brought along a long *pro memoria,* which he requested permission to lay before the court as a substitute for oral testimony. To letting himself be questioned he gave a flat no.

"This 'no' of the Dean I would like to have in that form in the records," Monsieur Einar stammered, red in the face—only with the greatest difficulty did he get the words shoveled out over his thick underlip.

"Wait a minute, Monsieur Einar, wait a minute," Judge Scheving admonished him cheerfully. "The Reverend Jon isn't actually the guilty party in this case."

"Who knows?" mumbled the prosecutor, offended.

"What did you say?"

"I said, 'who knows?' And I'll stand by it."

Judge Scheving laughed. A short, sharp laugh. Then he turned, still with an amused gleam in his eye, to the Reverend Jon. "Your *pro memoria* will be included in the file of the case, Reverend Jon. Would you like to read it aloud yourself? . . . On the question as to whether you yourself can be excused from giving oral testimony the court will take a position later."

Monsieur Einar straightened himself in his chair—said firmly: "Without regard to this *pro memoria,* I officially request that the Reverend Dean be fined for his defiant attitude toward his majesty's royal district court, and that the aforesaid district court officially order the aforesaid Dean to answer truthfully and in detail every question which I, as prosecutor, may wish to put to him."

"Every question relevant to the case, you probably mean," Judge Scheving interrupted smilingly.

"Certainly—relevant to the case. What is relevant to the case I will determine myself. If there are difficulties from the side of the court put in my way as prosecutor, I will file an appeal."

"We'll wait a little with putting that in the record," Judge Scheving decided sharply. "Now let's hear your *pro memoria,* Reverend Dean."

The Reverend Jon arranged himself more comfortably in his chair I had brought him, held the papers out at arm's length in front of him, and began: *"Pro memoria . . .* I am exceedingly astonished to have been invited by a summons to appear before this court to give testimony *pro officio* concerning the internal affairs of the people at Syvendeaa during the last and the preceding years; but I find it still more disconcerting that I have been summoned here to give testimony about any matter, great or small, which any person in question might have entrusted to me as his parish priest, on pastoral visits or other occasions, and which might serve to illuminate this criminal case, since it is written in the law that a priest, under penalty of losing his appointment, may not reveal what has been confided to him in secrecy."

The Reverend Jon let the papers sink, and paused. An effective pause. The jurors shot malicious glances out of the corners of their eyes at Monsieur Einar, who sat with a grim face. Even Judge Scheving looked as though he was getting some amusement at his good friend's expense.

The Reverend Jon Ormsson raised his *pro memoria* again—continued: "In any event, I consider it as my duty to throw any light which I may and can on the clarification of the case, and I herewith do this willingly, and would have done it without being summoned, whenever the court might have wished it. Once, last winter, the Deacons, Monsieur Olaf and Monsieur Thorberg, said to me that they had heard that the concord between the people at Syvendeaa was not as good as it ought to be; as far as I understood this, it had to do with the men, and also with the individual married partners; to which I replied that the deacons, within the framework of their official duties, should investigate the matter and settle it, insofar as they were able; which they neglected to do with the excuse that it would do no good unless I went along with them; which I was not in any condition to manage without great discomfort, with the weather and the roads the way they were, since I had all I could do to get to and from the churches on the rare occasion when there was a break in the weather, as old and tired as I have become, and suffering from affliction in my leg which has grown worse with the years."

"Hm—hm," Monsieur Einar cleared his throat, "Hm—hm."

The Reverend Jon raised his voice. "For the reasons

which I have just mentioned, I was prevented last winter from making a pastoral visit to Syvendeaa."

"Hm—hm," Monsieur Einar inserted again.

". . . as well as elsewhere in my parish, with just the exception of the few farms I managed to visit before the winter was on us. From another side, too, I heard, toward the close of the winter, vague rumors that everything was not as it ought to be at Syvendeaa; I then first heard whispers about a relationship between Bjarni and Steinun; but I did not hear it from people from the farm itself, or from others who could be assumed to know about it; it is definite that the departed Jon Thorgrimsson never mentioned to me anything, either of his disagreements with Bjarni, or of his marital discord, not even when he had business with me and we spoke together in peace and quiet a week's time before he disappeared. Later I did hear that he expressed to others something about the former. Along in the summer there was more and more mention made of the relationship between Bjarni and Steinun, until in August they were separated, and Steinun was moved to the parish of her birth; later Bjarni also confided to me that he had it in mind to marry her."

The Reverend Jon ended his *pro memoria* by entering a protest that this worldly court should have authority to inflict any kind of punishment on him whatsoever, or instruct him in any way, and he closed by calling upon God to witness the truth of his account.

"Well—what does the prosecutor think?" Judge Scheving burst out.

"If the Dean's protest against undergoing sentence by this court be legal, I have nothing to take exception to," Monsieur Einar answered wryly, "all the less since I in the summons expressly added: as far as the law permits . . ."

"A somewhat ambiguous phrase," Judge Scheving smiled and winked at the others.

"Possibly," Monsieur Einar replied, his underlip jutting.

"That's the way *I* meant it. For which reason I deny most expressly any implication that I in the slightest degree overstepped my authority by summoning the Dean. Furthermore, I as prosecutor insist that the court, in an *interlocutoris* or in the final decision, call attention to the Dean's dereliction, which was certainly known to us before—and which he now with his enclosure or testimony, or whatever it might be called legally, has more than sufficiently attested—so that his action or lack of action in the case can be evident. The officials who have authority, even over a Dean, can evaluate that themselves according to its deserts."

Judge Scheving reflected; whereupon he dictated the following ruling for the record:

"The protest included in the testimony of the Dean against suffering reproof or punishment from this court, irrespective of whether he might be found guilty in the neglect of his official duties or not, the court finds in accordance with the pastoral privileges and does declare the said Dean Jon Ormsson free from the imposition of any fine or punishment by this court for any neglect of his official duties such as might possibly be established in this case; but it does declare that it will include in the final decision of the court any neglect of pastoral duties which might appear, together with an appropriate communication to the proper authorities."

Judge Scheving turned to his jurors. "Are we agreed?"

They were.

The ruling was thereupon read, at the Judge's behest, to the Reverend Jon and Monsieur Einar, after which Judge Scheving asked them whether they wished to accept it or take exception to it. They were both silent.

Judge Scheving hid a smile behind his hand; then he asked, "Won't you give us permission, either, to question you concerning your part in viewing the body of the departed Gudrun Egilsdottir, Reverend Dean?"

169

Dean Jon Ormsson did not answer; instead he produced in silence some papers which turned out to contain a written, sworn testimony about the viewing of the body. This testimony the court ordered read; the Reverend Jon refused. About the blue spot at the collar-bone, it said that it was the same bluish color that can be seen on the face or lips of a dead or dying man; on the other hand, it by no means had the appearance of having arisen from a stab or blow, or of having coagulated blood below it; the belly had been swollen as though the woman were pregnant or had overeaten.

Judge Scheving let the Reverend Jon go while he interrogated the coroners, but he asked him to remain in the vicinity. He could make use of him. Whereupon the Sinner limped out, rather dejected and for the moment speechless.

Monsieur Sigmund, who was called in first, described in detail the departed Gudrun's corpse as he had seen it in Baer church that day; he also dwelt on the swollen belly. He mentioned, besides, three small blood blisters which he had seen just below the breasts—and which I, from the farther side where I was, might have overlooked.

"Didn't you find anything suspicious in the appearance of the corpse," Judge Scheving asked. "Didn't it occur to you that the rumors could be true—that Bjarni and Steinun killed her?"

"Yes, certainly, it seemed strange to me," Sigmund answered, his eyelids continually going up and down over his large eyes, "but the gossip ran that she had died of poison. And I thought that anyone who died of poison—would have to look different."

"Didn't you mention your suspicion to the Reverend Jon?"

"Yes. But the Reverend Jon said that the flesh often turned blue in death—at spots where in the living body there had been injury underneath. And the departed Gu-

170

drun had actually suffered pains in the chest—I knew that."

"What did you think was wrong with Gudrun, that her belly was so swollen?"

"I thought she was with child. Although I couldn't really believe that."

Olaf from Lambavatn described the departed Gudrun's body in detail, as Sigmund had described it. He too had noticed the three small blood blisters. But when Judge Scheving asked him whether the appearance of the corpse had not induced further suspicion in him, he answered mildly, "On the contrary . . . I had, until I saw the body, been convinced that Gudrun had been murdered. So I was really shocked to discover that she looked just like any other dead human being. Little blood blisters like that—I've seen them myself on living people. And I've often seen, on dead people, blue spots that didn't come from a blow, but from the sickness they died of. I can swear to this: the way poor Gudrun lay there that day, I felt convinced that she had died of the pains in the chest, and maybe of the stomach too—but certainly not of poison."

"Didn't it occur to you that the woman could have been pregnant when she died?"

"No, that possibility never occurred to me."

Monsieur Einar suggested pugnaciously to the court that the Reverend Jon Ormsson might be called in and questioned as to what reasons he had had for assuming that the departed Gudrun was pregnant. Judge Scheving acceded immediately to the prosecutor's suggestion. When the Reverend Jon was again standing before the court he said to him, amicably but pointedly, "There are some points in your written testimony, Reverend Jon, which I must request you to clarify more exactly. What proofs can you bring that the late Gudrun was pregnant when she died?"

"Proofs?" the Reverend Jon repeated, and his pale old face in the wreath of white hair slowly turned red; "Why should I need to prove what I've never said?"

"You used the words, that her belly was swollen as though she were pregnant," Judge Scheving burst out heatedly.

"As though she were pregnant or had overeaten," the Reverend Jon conceded. "By which I did not any more say that she was pregnant than that she had overeaten."

"No hairsplitting here now, cleric. This is a court here, not morning worship. Why *mention* pregnancy when you don't *mean* pregnancy. In testimony under oath."

"To give as exact a description as possible of the appearance of the corpse," the Reverend Jon answered stoutly.

"All right . . . Why didn't you mention in your testimony the three blood blisters which the coroners saw—underneath the breasts?"

"What blood blisters? I didn't see any blood blisters."

"You want to take exception to the testimony of the coroners?"

"Not at all. Since I didn't examine the corpse as exactly as they. But I want to take exception to your competence to question me in a tone as though I belonged to the accused in the case."

"The tone in this court *I* determine. And I alone . . . Are you aware of the responsibility which you assumed for yourself, in influencing the coroners and possibly preventing them from calling a doctor?"

"I did not influence the coroners in any way, and calling a doctor never came into question."

"Do you deny having explained away the marks of violence on the deceased?"

"I didn't explain away anything. What I did was explain that a blue spot like that—the only possible mark of violence that *I* saw—was not *infrequently* visible even on

172

the body of persons who had died a natural death. That I did say."

"Did you not say to the sister of the departed, that where one does not have a plain and unmistakable reason for suspicion that one should not believe the worst about one's fellow man."

"That is possible. It's even probable, although I don't remember. Do you think one should?"

"Hm—hm," interjected Einar Jonsson contentedly, "hm—hm."

"Did you say or did you not say it?" Judge Scheving asked, his voice shaking.

"That about the blue spot I said. It is possible that I also said the other . . . May I call your attention to the fact that it was I who had the coffin opened! Much against the promptings of my heart. May I further add that I asked those present to declare whatever they might *know* or merely have reason to *suspect* concerning the departed Gudrun's death; to which they either declared that they knew nothing, or were silent."

Judge Scheving pounded one fist on the table. "It is in any case to be regarded as irresponsible, under the circumstances, for you to have let Gudrun Egilsdottir be buried without having called a doctor."

The Reverend Jon shook his white head resignedly. "I will introduce as many witnesses as you could possibly wish, to show that it was quite impossible. There are, as you know, three long mountain passes to go over before you can reach a doctor. We were then in the middle of the thaw. None of the three stretches was passable by any but winged creatures. Besides that, the weather had suddenly turned very warm so that the corpse would have decayed long before the snow had melted enough to let the roads be traveled. Moreover, the parish people were not really fit for long trips—lean as they were from a hard winter's half starvation. And finally, it was the busiest

173

time of the year. Nevertheless, I wrote a letter to the then incumbent Judge David Scheving, in which I reported that case and invited him to determine how far he wished to proceed with it."

"I know that. When did you write the letter?"

"I wrote it the twenty-first of June, and it was sent from here to Skapadal the twenty-eighth of June."

Judge Scheving sat a while—dumb. Then he said, "You were, in other words, a week in getting it sent off. To the nearest farm. A letter which concerned a criminal matter ... Yes, that resembles all the rest pretty much."

"I request that the letter be included in the record," said the Reverend Jon quietly.

"Have you the letter?" Judge Scheving asked the prosecutor.

The prosecutor proved to have it. And he was glad of it, because the Reverend Jon began it by giving his firm opinion that Gudrun had died of the sickness which had troubled her in recent years, and that the rumors that Bjarni and Steinun were supposed to have killed her were nothing but parish gossip.

Judge Scheving must have forgotten that letter. At least he studied it with a certain astonishment. And then asked the Reverend Jon, almost friendly, "Is it really possible, Reverend Jon, that Bjarni and Steinun had the insolence to complain to you that they suffered damages to their good names and reputations by being exposed to the terrible suspicion which gossip had attached to them?"

"The circumstances are precisely as I wrote them," the Reverend Jon answered—drily.

"Obviously, Reverend Jon, obviously . . . But nonetheless I call that—more than bold. The two must certainly have been mighty sure that you would not, if you could help it, do them any harm . . . So it's like that!"

At that moment there was a thunderous knocking at the door. As soon as it was opened one of the guards rushed in and reported that the delinquents were awake. "Bjarni is standing outside," he whispered, nervous and breathless, and added that he had refused to let himself be bound, had gone at once to the house and asked to be interrogated—at once.

"Naturally," exclaimed Judge Scheving, his eyebrows shooting up into his forehead, and said nastily, "When it suits the convenience of the accused, why the court has to be at their beck and call; that's no more than reasonable. Ask the honorable murderer to wait a moment—and just omit the title."

Judge Scheving got up, went quickly over to the Reverend Jon, laid a hand on his shoulder—said, "Our little exchange of words we can't count as an interrogation—it won't be put down in the record, Reverend Jon. At least insofar as you will go along with my suggestion, which is this: that you tomorrow, together with the two coroners, give a statement in which you and the coroners make a joint declaration as to what was undertaken with regard to the late Gudrun's death, and why more was not undertaken in the matter."

With the last words he was accompanying the Reverend Jon to the door. Gently he pushed him outside. Then he quickly went back to his place.

XXV

I had thought that Bjarni would gain inner freedom and peace with his decision to tell the truth, confess his guilt. I had thought, too, that his newly acquired freedom and peace had made it possible for him to fall asleep and to sleep so deeply and so long. When I saw him again I was more inclined to believe that he had fallen asleep from fatigue. For the first time I saw him with bowed head; he kept his eyes hidden. On his way across the floor he staggered and nearly fell. Judge Scheving immediately gave an order to have a chair brought for him.

There he sat, collapsed, radiating silence as though he were dumb for all eternity. He sat there, a captive. It was deathly silent in the courtroom.

"Well Bjarni?" whispered Judge Scheving finally, and although it was only a murmur the words filled the narrow room—vibrated in it and kept on vibrating long after they had vanished.

Bjarni tried to speak, but no sound passed his lips. Then again he fell silent. And all of a sudden I understood. Understood that it could not be his conscience alone that tortured him. Understood that we had, sitting here in the midst of us a man who was on the verge of expiring from shame.

Now I do not dare reflect on the feelings caused by this understanding. Is shame worse than guilt? I may well have groaned to myself without knowing it, for Bjarni turned suddenly toward me, startled. And with forced courage—a painful, pathetic courage—he began to talk: "It was last winter . . . early in the winter . . . Steinun and I— we couldn't—we couldn't any more . . ."

Judge Scheving asked cautiously, "Do you mean, Bjarni, that in the beginning of the winter a carnal relation began between you and Steinun?"

"Yes—a little later . . ."

"You are remembering to tell the truth?"

Bjarni did not answer that. He went on, "It was from that that the whole trouble at Syvendeaa came . . . My wife's complaints against me . . . and poor Jon's quarrels with his wife. It was from that."

"They knew about it?"

"No, they didn't know anything . . . but they noticed something . . . they couldn't miss it I guess . . . Long before there was anything—they seemed to notice something. It was as though they pushed us into it."

"Long before there was anything, you say . . . Are you sure of that?"

"Oh yes; I know what I'm talking about. Because it was that—that caused . . ."

"Caused what?"

"No, it doesn't matter," Bjarni murmured tiredly. "I can't work it out anyhow. I never could."

"But your wife's and the late Jon's complaints didn't bear any fruit then?"

"Yes, they bore fruit."

"You didn't keep away from each other for that reason, I mean?"

"No . . . we didn't."

"So that was really the reason then that you couldn't get along with the late Jon?"

"Yes, that was it . . . Up to then we'd got along with each other pretty well. I let him complain, when he was in the mood. Didn't pay any attention to him. What did it matter to me? . . . But from that time on—it got worse. Worse and worse."

177

"The witnesses say that you always took Steinun's side when Jon quarreled with her—is that right?"

"That's right. It can't be anybody but my brother Jon, and then Malfrith, that testified to that; those two don't talk idle gossip. Or anyhow not my brother Jon . . . No, that's perfectly right. I got worked up every time he began. I couldn't stand to listen to him. I just couldn't . . ."

"That was your bad conscience, then?"

"What it was I don't know. But anyway it was these eternal scoldings that made me get the idea—of killing Jon . . . there were times when I felt inside me that I could have wiped him out—completely coldbloodedly . . . I really thought that."

"You even planned to get him out of the way?"

"I decided to kill him. I made up my mind. I talked a lot with Steinun about it."

"You were agreed?"

"We were agreed, yes . . . For a while we almost didn't talk about anything else. It was—it was like a dream."

"A dream? What do you mean?"

"Yes—I can't explain it . . . But we talked so much about it. I'd really made up my mind . . . I think."

"Don't you know?"

"The funny thing was, that I didn't do anything . . ."

"You wavered possibly?"

"No, I didn't waver; I don't think so; it didn't seem so to me. Just the opposite. It was just—I was waiting . . . I don't know for what."

"Did Steinun participate in these murder plans?"

"She took part. But I was a lot more eager. Maybe it egged me on, too, that Gudrun and Steinun had warned me against Jon."

"Warned you how?"

"They claimed they could see that he hated me. They told me that, both of them—several times. They said I should watch out for Jon."

"Was Jon a man you had to be afraid of?"

"Not man to man. Not in a pitched battle . . . But a man that hate has got a grip on is always dangerous . . ."

"Did you notice, yourself, that he hated you?"

"Yes, it was easy enough to see. But I wouldn't have paid any particular attention to it if I hadn't been reminded of it again and again. I might even have forgotten all about it."

"In what way could you tell that Jon hated you?"

"That's not so easy to say. From his whole manner. From his words. From the tone he talked in. I almost couldn't breathe around him. It was—unbearable . . ."

"Was it after a quarrel that you killed the departed Jon?"

"No—that happened another way."

"When did your last quarrel take place?"

"Oh—about three or four days before he died, I guess."

"What was the reason?"

"The reason was a ball of yarn that Jon cut to pieces to get at Steinun. When Steinun complained about it to him he answered with insults. He said, 'All threads aren't so important to you, you . . .' But that doesn't matter. I couldn't stand and watch that. And so then we were the ones that started to quarrel—Jon and me."

"Do you remember with certainty that that was your last quarrel?"

"Yes, for sure."

"Where did this quarrel take place, and at what time of day?"

"It was in the house . . . in the evening."

"And it ended up with your threatening each other?"

"Not that time, no . . ."

"But on other occasions?"

"Just once . . . if you can call it a threat. I said, 'It would be too bad if Steinun had to put up with your nonsense for long.' Jon said to that, that he hadn't thought that things would go on like this between us—very much longer."

"When, and in what connection, did these words occur?"

"I don't remember that."

"Was there anybody but you two present?"

"I don't remember that either . . . Steinun was probably around."

"Did it ever come to blows between you and the late Jon?"

"No, it didn't."

"Weren't you quarreling first—the day he died?"

"Not first, no."

"Will you tell us how it happened?"

"It happened like this . . . Jon had gone out before I'd finished eating. A little later I went. He hadn't got his sheep out of the pen when I got there. Our sheep pens, the men here know them, are alongside each other, halfway between the farm and the shore. So it worked out that without talking about it we drove our sheep together down to the shore; we were used to doing it that way when it was so icy. We had to watch out and sometimes help them along, one by one. I could see all right that Jon had a nastier look in his eye for me than usual, that day. That was plain enough. We each had a staff to help us, and I noticed that he kept himself behind me all the time. So I gradually began to suspect him of having something in mind. So I kept my eyes open too, kept one eye over my shoulder all the time. We did almost get down to the shore all right, but I mustn't have kept my eyes open so well any more—because suddenly he's standing right behind me with his staff raised and saying, 'Now I'm going to do what I've been wanting to do.' But I was faster turning; I ducked his swing and drove my prod right straight at him. I didn't have any intention then—of killing him; I just hit. It hit him on the cheek and he fell down dead . . . The shaft had broken in two in the middle."

"What kind of a staff was it? What has become of it?"

"It was my aspen, that I said afterwards I had loaned to

Jon because it was better than his . . . I threw the pieces out in the water to get them out of the way. Threw them out as hard as I could, and I haven't seen them since."

"Well—and then what?"

"Well—when I saw what I'd done—I took the body and threw it into the ocean too. Out from the cliff alongside the boat shed."

"Wasn't there any sign of life on him?"

"No, at least I assumed Jon was dead . . . I really didn't think of anything at that minute but getting rid of him, and you can hardly say that I *thought* about that. It was almost like a nightmare when I got busy wiping out any traces. I had first and foremost to hide what I'd done."

"Jon's staff—you took it home with you . . .Why?"

"I didn't do it for any reason, I guess. Not right away. I probably just thought that since I'd left home with a staff in my hands—I ought to come back with a staff in my hands too . . . It seemed less noticeable, in a way."

"When you came home then was when you invented the story that Jon had gone over to Skor?"

"Yes; I told that to the others. But Steinun I told the whole thing to—the way it had happened. Except I didn't really tell her the whole thing . . . Just that I'd killed Jon."

"Doesn't it seem to you afterwards that it was pretty unbelievable—what you told the others?"

"Yes, pretty much . . . But it was mostly Steinun too that thought it up. Everybody knew that Jon was nearly out of hay at home. So it seemed to me right away that Steinun's idea was pretty good, and I didn't think any more about it—just said that it had happened like that. To tell the truth, I just couldn't think of anything myself right then. I wasn't used to lying. I was almost inclined to let on I hadn't seen Jon after I left home in the morning. But you can see the sheep pens from the farm. And Steinun said, which was true enough, that somebody could have seen us going together down toward the shore. Just thinking about how bad it would have gone for me if I

had met any of the others before I met Steinun, I was relieved and happy to be able to say that Jon had gone over
to Skor. When I met my brother Jon at the door I was in a
hurry to tell him what Steinun and I had just agreed on. I
even made out that you could still see Jon, so that maybe
my brother could imagine that he'd seen him go across
too. But that didn't work. He couldn't see anything. There
wasn't anything to see."

"Why didn't you tell the truth about your encounter?"

"I couldn't. Nobody would have believed me. Especially not when I had thrown the man in the water. And then
when I carried him down to the ocean—all I was thinking
of was getting rid of him. Now that he was finally dead . . ."

"It was therefore to conceal your misdeed that you invented the lie that he had gone over to Skor and fallen?"

"Yes, what else . . .?"

"And since then you never saw the departed Jon?"

"Oh yes, worse luck. He wasn't the kind you could get
rid of."

A little spasm went through Bjarni as though he were
going to burst into tears. Time after time he would shudder. Then he would sit quietly again. Judge Scheving
gave him a little rest. Then he asked him, "Not the kind
you could get rid of, you said. Why?"

"Yes . . . Because the day after—when I was driving the
sheep down to the shore at the usual time—I found him
washed up on shore . . . It made me so uncomfortable to
see him again. I just didn't know what to do about it. If I
threw him in the ocean again—maybe I'd find him here
again tomorrow morning. Maybe every morning. I
couldn't stand thinking about it. So I took him—and carried him up over the slope . . . over to a place where I
knew there was a deep snow drift under the ice. Then I
cut a hole in the ice, dug a grave in the snow; I laid him
there . . ."

"How long did you have him lying there?"

"The whole winter . . . till the breakup last spring."

"So into the month of June? Possibly till just a few days before your wife died?"

"Yes—that's right."

"What was your idea in burying him there?"

"Why, I had to hide him."

"But the snow would melt sometime; you knew that. And could melt very quickly. What then?"

"Yes, what then . . .? That winter wasn't one of those that make you think that spring would ever come . . . I couldn't imagine summer anymore; and green grass . . . until it was there again."

"You don't mean that you thought that Jon could go on lying there in the snowdrift until doomsday?"

"What I knew, what I thought . . . I'm just telling what happened. I buried him there."

"And had him lying—a corpse—the whole winter—right across from your farm?"

"Yes—right across from the farm."

Something was happening in Judge Scheving, something dangerous. But he controlled himself; he conquered it. Contented himself with hammering his fist on the table, hammering and hammering.

"And then when the snow melted," he asked, his voice rough, "what then?"

"Yes—Then there wasn't any other way . . . He had to go out into the ocean again."

"To wash ashore—the day after?"

"No, because I'd got to thinking about a rock point, where there's a current. I carried him there. It was a long way . . . and let him slide in off there."

"This time you let him slide; before, you threw him?"

"Yes—that's the way it was."

"And after that you didn't see him again?"

"Not before in Baer church—washed up into the shallows . . . the day I was arrested."

"And Steinun—did she know all about this?"

"Yes, she knew."

"Did she help you?"

"No, I did it alone."

"Didn't she see the body either?"

"No, never."

"Well . . . And what about the hole in the neck of the corpse?"

"I don't know anything about it. The hole isn't my work."

Judge Scheving sat silent for a moment. The glance that rested on Bjarni was not merely bitter—that would have been understandable, although he sat there with the responsibility of a judge—it was malignant and threatening. Not a spark of mercy was to be seen in it. It was clear to me that Judge Scheving did not believe Bjarni. Did not want to believe him. I did not understand that, because I believed him. Unconditionally. Moreover, Judge Scheving did not seem to be alone in his doubt.

The prosecutor sat with a marked disbelieving expression on his large lower lip. But you could say that he, in comparison to the defending counsel, whose confidence in Bjarni's truthfulness was completely destroyed by his open confession, looked convinced. The rest of the farmers sat dead still with shocked, and at the same time ravenously inquisitive, eyes. Only the fat Jon Thorberg wiped, now and then, a gentle, brandied tear from his chin.

Judge Scheving said, squeezing the words between his lips, "So when Jon was once again sent on his way—it was then you decided to kill your wife besides?"

"I really couldn't help—that it happened," Bjarni answered, but his voice failed him—he had to repeat it.

Judge Scheving half rose in his chair as though he were going to attack Bjarni, jump on him. He shouted, "Speak louder, and speak the truth."

Bjarni did not seem to notice his fury at all. He cleared his throat willingly, attempted to speak louder. "But Steinun went on with it . . . She said that Gudrun had to be got rid of . . . It wasn't going to be only her husband that would be killed—she said. There were times when it seemed as though she couldn't forgive me for having killed Jon—her husband. I didn't understand that, because I knew that she'd loathed Jon for a long time. I knew that. And they were forever quarreling . . . So it couldn't be true that she was angry with me—because I had killed him—could it? But there were times you could think so . . . Whether she still loved me—or whether she maybe mostly hated me now afterwards . . . I asked God about it often."

Judge Scheving dropped his fist when Bjarni mentioned the name of God. He sat biting his lips, silent as a stone.

Bjarni groped for words. He went on. "We wanted so much to have each other—as man and wife—Steinun and I. To be really married to each other. We'd often talked about how good we'd have it . . . All our children . . . we could keep . . . And live alone together . . . at Syvendeaa . . . which is isolated and off the beaten path . . . But I—had a horror of the idea of killing Gudrun, both because she was a woman . . . And now I knew too what it was—to kill . . . knew that it doesn't do any good . . . But Steinun—she still didn't know it. She hadn't killed anybody yet . . . You can't imagine that."

Bjarni was silent, groaned quietly. A groan as lonesome as death itself, lonesome and hopeless. And then he started again. "But Steinun went on with it . . . she went on. It isn't my idea to complain about her. Because as I said—she didn't know yet what it was. And the greatest guilt is still mine—really all the guilt. If for no other reason than because I'm a man. But—that's the way it happened . . . Maybe I shouldn't have told it. But I don't want to lie anymore . . . The fact that Jon, her husband, was lying out there right outside the farm—killed by me . . . She just seemed not to be able to forget it. I couldn't either . . . Not for one minute was it out of my mind. Not even at night. Not even in dreams. But it affected her entirely differently than it did me . . . I'd rather—never have touched anything dead again. And I didn't want, didn't want to have to—kill again . . . And yet—it didn't make any difference on the other hand . . . now . . . But do it with my own hands—do it myself . . . I couldn't do it. So— when Steinun went on with it—I mixed some old rat poison and some copper filings from Jon's smithy—mixed them together and gave it to her, in a piece of paper. Then she couldn't say any more that I didn't want to . . . When I'd done that I went and hoped—and wished—that she wouldn't use it . . . And the opposite I hoped too, and wished; both ways . . . A few days went by. There were several times I was just going to ask her to give me the paper back . . . but then I didn't, because if she didn't dare do it now—and it looked as though she didn't dare— she couldn't complain to me afterwards that I'd kept her from it . . ."

"You're a good liar," Judge Scheving hissed. "It was you yourself gave your wife the poison."

"Why should I lie?" Bjarni answered wearily. "One thing is just as bad as the other . . . Anyhow she didn't die from the poison we gave her. She only got mighty sick— got some terrible vomiting spells . . . lay there vomiting most of one night. But then she got well . . . then we were back again where we started with our plans . . . me and Steinun. Back again. Only what had happened now was— that we had given ourselves away . . . which could get dangerous . . . and got dangerous . . . Gudrun couldn't have missed getting suspicious, and if anybody came she spoke right up about her suspicion. Any old time. When she was away from home she told anybody who wanted to listen that we'd poisoned her . . . which was true. But having it told didn't help much. We had to be prepared for people believing her . . . What should we do? Why didn't she keep quiet?"

"Why didn't you keep her home then?"

"Because—because we wanted so much to be alone . . ."

"Why didn't you hurry up and really kill her? Since that was the idea."

"Because—I couldn't bring myself to do it."

"You finally did though?"

"Yes—finally."

"And it was Steinun, you say, that convinced you to do it?"

"Well, convinced . . . We didn't have an easy time of it talking to one another any more: it turned into nothing but threats. Steinun threatened me the next time a stranger came to the farm to take him over to the snow grave—where Jon was. And loan him a shovel. I almost wished she would do it in earnest. But then it seemed to me that —it was all for nothing . . . But I couldn't leave off hoping, either. When spring came . . . then it seemed to me anyhow—that it could be done . . . Then I began to believe again that Steinun and I maybe could still get along together. If Gudrun died . . . or if she went—and stayed away. Went and drowned herself. Or just ran away from the farm . . . When she was supposed to go out and talked about staying overnight I'd say to her, on account of that, 'Either you come home this evening—or else you stay away.' Right up till she was back home again I went on hoping that she—wouldn't come . . . If she'd stayed away— then everything would have been all right. I thought. As right as it could be . . . after what had already happened."

Judge Scheving leaned over and said, hoarsely, "Let's get back to the subject . . . Saturday before Whitsun, that is, Saturday the fifth of June—you killed her?"

"Yes . . . I was up early that morning . . . up and outside . . . to get the milkers home that hadn't come in by themselves. It was agreed that as soon as I had got them together Gudrun and Steinun would come down to the pens and milk them. When I had the sheep together in the pen . . . Steinun came . . ."

Bjarni was silent. He sat there, collapsed, hiding his face in his hands. Sat weeping very quietly.

Judge Scheving asked, "Possibly you had decided to celebrate Whitsun by sending your wife down the same road you had sent Jon Thorgrimsson—the Thursday before Easter. The Reverend Jon will perhaps see a kind of piety in this . . . Go on, man."

"A little later . . . A little later we saw Gudrun come from the house, down . . . Then Steinun said, 'Now you can choose—either, or. If you don't do it I'll turn you in.' I said: 'Do it yourself' . . . 'I can't alone,' she answered . . . Gudrun had sat down—on the path. I went then—up there. Well—I ran . . . When she saw me coming—she got up . . . I grabbed her around the neck with one hand, hit her with the other in the back so that she fell . . ."

"Did she say anything when you came?"

"She said, 'Are you going to kill me?' When she was lying there—I pressed both hands down on her face—held her mouth and nose . . ."

"With the intention of killing her?"

"Yes . . ."

"And Steinun?"

"She held her arms—clamped them tight to her sides—so she couldn't thrash around."

"She must have fought to get free?"

"No—she lay completely still . . . When I took my hands from her face because I thought she was dead—she wasn't dead yet . . . She looked at me . . . move she couldn't . . . but her eyes followed me . . . Steinun—went home then— got a blanket . . . We put her in that . . . and carried her home."

"Was she dead by that time?"

"No—not quite . . . We laid her in her bed . . . She died there . . . A little later—we closed her eyes . . ."

"And then?"

"Then Pentecost came . . . The fourth day of Pentecost I went and got our neighbor, Bjorg from Melanes; I asked her to help us lay Gudrun in a coffin."

"Coffin—where did you get that from?"

"I built it myself . . . during Whitsuntide."

"Why did you call on outside help? Was that to ward off possible suspicion?"

"It was for that, yes . . . It seemed to me to be best for somebody to have seen Gudrun . . . before she was buried."

"And Bjorg—did she get suspicious at all?"

"Bjorg knew me well . . . No, I don't think that she did. But you'd better ask her about that . . . The day after that, I brought the body to the church and said that she'd died of pains in the chest . . . which people knew she suffered from."

Judge Scheving had the record of Bjarni's confession read slowly, word for word, after which he asked if he acknowledged his confession—in that form. Bjarni nodded dully.

"Let's get a confession in plain words," burst out Judge Scheving impatiently, and dictated for the record the following question: "Did you, Bjarni, the first of April this year kill the late Jon Thorgrimsson without cause?"

Bjarni lifted his head and answered—a little astonished, "Certainly I had the bad luck to kill Jon Thorgrimsson; but you can't say it was without cause, because he without any provocation from my side was raising his staff before I hit him."

Judge Scheving ignored his answer, apparently—went on dictating, "Did you, Bjarni, afflict on the departed Jon the wound which was established on the body washed ashore?"

"No."

"What was your intention in giving Steinun the copper filings with which she poisoned your wife?"

"So that Gudrun would die of it," Bjarni whispered.

"Did you, Bjarni, strangle and thereby murder your wife, the departed Gudrun Egilsdottir?"

Bjarni collapsed all at once into sobs, but only for a moment. Then he took his hands again from his face and answered composedly, "Yes—that I confess . . ."

"Did you, Bjarni, have any other accomplice than Steinun?"

"No, none."

Judge Scheving regarded Bjarni silently. Then he said— in another tone: "Tell me, finally, don't you find that it's almost as much of an unlikely explanation that Jon Thorgrimsson should have attacked you, as that he should have fallen over at Rodeskred and have come off without broken bones."

"All I've done is tell the way it happened," Bjarni answered in distress.

"Can you give any reasonable explanation for a man you could do anything with you wanted to, since you were much stronger than he, attacking you?"

"No I can't."

"Have you a scar to show?"

"No."

"Were you hit by anything?"

"No, he didn't manage to hit me."

"Have you given the same explanation to anybody before today?"

"No, because I haven't told anybody how it happened."

"Don't you want to tell the truth at all?"

"I am telling the truth."

Judge Scheving jumped up and pounded the table. "Take this bastard out and put him in irons."

Bjarni got up, went wearily toward the door. His glance caught mine. But dully, almost as though he did not grasp who I was.

XXVI

Steinun stepped in the door erect and defiant, too erect and defiant for her bearing to be really genuine. She was very pale; to my worry and sorrow I read fear in her eyes. It was well hidden, but it was there. A peculiarly wild and vague fear—such as you meet in women or womanish men.

Judge Scheving leaned back in his chair; he had grown tired. He made no move at all to interrogate her, just sat and looked at her. There was this time a certain shyness in his glance but no discomfort of any kind. Since the prosecutor in the meantime did not seem to have any intention of stepping in, Judge Scheving set him in motion with a glance.

Monsieur Einar regarded Steinun with hostility, and as an introduction put a question about her relationship with Bjarni.

Steinun, who had been standing and looking down, raised her eyes full of contempt for him and admitted calmly that that was the way it had been.

"How often did you have intercourse before Bjarni killed Jon?"

"I didn't keep count of it."

"In other words, very often?"

Steinun was silent a moment, then she said casually, "Yes, very often."

"When did it begin?"

"Sometime last winter."

"When?"

"After the beginning of winter."

"And that continued then?"

"It continued, yes. Right up until the thirteenth week of summer when I, without being asked and against my will, was moved with my children away from Syvendeaa."

"Did you conspire with Bjarni against your departed husband's life?"

"Yes."

"Did you agree that Bjarni should kill him?"

"Yes."

"Did you egg him on to do it?"

"No. I didn't."

"But you knew ahead of time that Bjarni was going to kill him?"

"I knew that he intended to kill him but I didn't know when."

"Did you know how he intended to kill him?"

"No, I didn't know that. He hadn't talked about it. But as soon as he came home that day he told me—that Jon was dead now."

"What did he say?"

"He said that he had killed my Jon."

"How had he killed him, did he say?"

"Hit him with his staff in the head. And afterwards thrown him in the water."

"Didn't he tell you what had happened before between them?"

"No, he didn't."

"Didn't he tell you, either, that Jon had attacked him?"

"No."

"Didn't you ask him about what happened?"

"No, not at all."

"Is it possible that you didn't inquire about the circumstances of the murder?"

"Since Bjarni didn't tell anything on his own, I supposed he just didn't want to talk about it."

"Weren't you curious?"

"I'd rather not have known. I knew enough."

"What did you know?"

"That he'd hit him on the head and thrown him in the water."

"Didn't you give Bjarni any help in killing him?"

A sudden terror seized Steinun—she burst out, her teeth chattering, "No!"

"Where were you when it happened?"

"I was home in the house."

"Where in the house?"

"In the kitchen—the halls—at the door; how would I know?"

"You were walking around nervously, maybe?"

"Why should I do that. I didn't have any idea that anything was going to happen that day."

"Didn't you help Bjarni bury Jon in the snowdrift? Or with carrying him there?"

Steinun closed her eyes a moment; then she answered dully, "No, he didn't ask me for help; and I didn't offer to help him, either."

"Would you have helped him if he'd asked you to?"

"I'd have done anything that Bjarni asked me."

"What did he do with the body?"

"When Jon washed ashore the day after, Bjarni buried him in the snow. He was lying there a while. Until Bjarni threw him back into the ocean, then, in the spring."

"You didn't take a boat? You didn't row him out to sea?"

Steinun shook her head. "Who can say such a thing? There wasn't anything like that at all. That didn't even come up."

"Didn't Bjarni say that he'd stabbed Jon in the chest before he fell?"

"I can't believe he did that. Because he told me after he'd thrown him into the ocean a second time that it didn't matter if he washed ashore; you couldn't see on him that he was murdered; there wasn't any visible mark."

Judge Scheving cleared his throat, which Einar Jonsson seemed to take as a request to change the subject—he asked, "So you also talked with Bjarni about killing his wife, the late Gudrun?"

"Yes—once my husband was killed."

"Hadn't that been decided before?"

"No. But if he could kill my husband he could kill his wife, too, I guess."

"It was you, though, that gave her the poison—a good month before she died. Bjarni explained that."

Steinun reddened, was silent a moment, and then answered—suddenly uncertain and fumbling for words. "That's true too . . . that is . . . I didn't know what it was that Bjarni had put in a piece of paper—so that I should give it to Gudrun . . . And I hid it for two days—before I gave it to her . . ."

Steinun was as altered as though time had been turned back a few days. It could hardly be only because she was now ashamed for having falsely charged Bjarni of being the one that had put the poison in the soup. More likely it was one of those jumps in time and mind which are so frequent in human beings: you need only remind them of an earlier mood or get them to remember it themselves, and all at once they are changed, transported into the old situation with its sensations, attitudes, and conditions. Certainly it was something like that which happened to Steinun now. The fear, which in the night had expressed itself in her desperate cry—that she didn't want to die—had lain in wait the whole time. Suddenly it overwhelmed her. She was not herself any more. The terror of the flesh had got its claws into her.

"Didn't Bjarni tell you what the paper had in it?"

"No, he didn't. He didn't say a word about it . . . Maybe he said—root powder, I think he called it."

"Didn't he call it rat powder?"

"That's possible. Yes, I think so . . . But I said I couldn't remember."

Judge Scheving leaned forward over the table, asked slowly—and pointedly, "Didn't Bjarni tell you that it was—lethal?"

Steinun, who had turned pale by now, reddened again, helpless: obviously she could not make up her mind about how much she should admit, could not see where she should draw the line between truth and fiction. Finally she mumbled uncertainly, "He said that—sure . . . He said that, that he thought so."

"All right. What was your intention in getting Gudrun to eat the poisoned soup?"

"It was Bjarni's intention that Gudrun should die from it."

"Not yours?"

"Ye—es . . . Yes—mine too . . . But she didn't die. She recovered."

"We know how that went . . . Tell me, it was you that got Bjarni to kill her?"

"No, no . . . Not at all."

"Not at all? . . . Didn't you help him kill her?"

"I only held her arms . . . He ordered me to do it. I didn't dare do anything but obey him. He was so angry . . . That—I can't be beheaded for that?"

Judge Scheving's eyes wavered.

Steinun broke, suddenly, as though she were lifeless; her knees gave way, her hips gave way, and she collapsed. The back of her head hit hard against the floor.

I helped bathe her temples with water and force a little brandy in between her teeth; little by little she came back to life. She got a chair to sit on, and Judge Scheving began again. He questioned her about all the details of the murder of Gudrun; her explanation agreed exactly with Bjarni's. Except that she denied, and kept on denying, that she had asked him to kill Gudrun that day.

That, she had never done—not since the day they gave her poison—she continued to insist. When Judge Scheving ended by asking where her and Bjarni's children had been when they did it, she was silent—and then she whispered, "They hadn't got up . . ."

Judge Scheving stroked his forehead—asked softly, "How was the relationship between your children and Bjarni?"

"The boys hung on him," Steinun answered tonelessly, "Particularly Svein—the oldest . . . He was always with Bjarni whenever he got permission. Since we were moved over to Hrisnes in the summer he goes around singing all the time, 'My friend never comes—my friend never comes' . . . 'My friend'—that's Bjarni."

She burst into sobs suddenly, wildly and hopelessly. It sounded like a pup half barking and half whining.

"All right, bring Bjarni in," Judge Scheving drowned her out, "We have to get settled which of them is telling the truth."

Steinun started in the chair. "Oh no," she pleaded despairingly, "Do you have to . . ."

XXVII

Bjarni was already standing in the room.

He was calmer than before, a lot calmer. This time he did not only see me—he greeted me, as well, with a nod intended to be brave. However, the look he sent me was stricken and ashamed. But it was obvious that he had made up his mind. He was not going to evade any more. He had—conquered . . . As far as a poor, weak human of fearful flesh and blood can conquer. He put himself by the side of Steinun—there was, in spite of his impotence, something protective in his attitude—and he looked down at her.

She remained sitting as she had been, collapsed, without raising her face to him. But she had stopped weeping. His eyes and features seemed to dull a little in disappointment. But he stood calmly.

Judge Scheving let him stand a moment; regarded him carefully. Then he began, "Steinun Sveinsdottir denies that she, at any time after the day you gave Gudrun the poisoned soup, asked you to kill your wife."

"Why are you denying it?" Bjarni asked, softly and sorrowfully.

"You will direct your answers to the court," Judge Scheving ordered sternly. "What do you say to that?"

"That it's true," Bjarni answered defiantly.

Steinun shook as though with cold. She burst out, "No, don't believe him. He's lying . . . *He's lying.*"

Bjarni started. He was on the point of giving an angry answer; his features changed, darkened, until it looked as though black blood would burst the skin. Then he mastered his emotions—contented himself with shaking his head. And said nothing.

"Do you admit that you lied?" Judge Scheving snapped at him, breathing hard.

Bjarni was silent. Tried to talk, was silent again. Then he said, "I told the whole thing exactly as it happened. I won't lie any more, not even to save Steinun—and anyhow it's too late. I thought that we were agreed . . . Steinun has just got scared. She'll still get straight in her mind what's true."

Steinun shrank, began to rock back and forth on her chair like an old woman, wailed, "Oh—oh . . . Why are you telling a thing like that, Bjarni . . . Oh—God . . . Why make me more miserable than I am? . . . Haven't I gone through enough for your sake, don't you think? . . ."

"How often did you—altogether—ask Bjarni to kill Gudrun?" Judge Scheving asked, moved.

"Only twice . . . Only twice . . . And that was before I gave her the poison."

Bjarni shook his head, disheartened. His perplexed eyes were fixed on me—he who knew nothing and dared not advise him, either by word or gesture.

"Why did you want to have him kill her?"

"It wasn't only I. He wanted it himself, too."

Judge Scheving shot back impatiently, "Yes, yes . . . But why did you want to have her out of the way?"

"So that we could get married to each other . . . That was the reason; we couldn't do it as long as she lived. And besides, she went and told everybody that we mistreated her and that we—were living together. It was on account of her gossip that we were separated later and never—got each other. How many times I said that that's the way it would go . . . as long as she was allowed to go on."

"Didn't you say, that day at the pens, that Bjarni could choose between killing Gudrun now or having you tell that he had killed Jon?"

"No, no . . . I never said those words."

"Those were just the words you did say," Bjarni said with a sigh. "Because they were the words that made me go out of my head."

"What're you lying for? . . . You called on me yourself . . . You said yourself I should help you."

"Yes, that's true enough. But that was afterwards. You remember that all right. That was after I'd answered that you could kill her. Don't you remember that? Don't you remember that you said, 'I can't do it alone?' It was then I said, 'Good, come on' . . . and ran on ahead. Don't you remember that?"

"No!" shouted Steinun, "No, no. You mustn't believe him. It's all made up, the whole thing."

"Don't you remember, either, that you told me that we'd never have a better chance—because the kids were asleep, you said . . . Have you forgotten that?"

"No—I remember that all right . . . It was just something I kind of said."

"Don't you remember either how often you said that Gudrun was going and talking—everywhere . . . and was slandering us? And that it would end up by our getting into trouble—if we didn't shut her mouth? Forever . . ."

"Oh—Maybe . . . Why are you reminding me of all that?"

"Well, then you must remember too that I yelled to you that morning, 'Now I'll get her mouth shut all right—so you don't have to worry about it anymore.' . . ."

Steinun only wept. Wept and whimpered.

"I'd have gone without telling about your part—why didn't you ask me in time?" Bjarni said—calmed by her little confession, "but you must be able to see that it's too late now . . . Why did you let me believe that we were agreed last night? I was so glad that you were going with me . . . even into death . . . But I can go alone, too."

Steinun sat collapsed—she only wept.

Judge Scheving gave orders to have her taken out.

When she was gone, he said to Bjarni, "Why won't you admit, Bjarni, that you stabbed Jon to death?"

"Because I didn't."

Judge Scheving had the coroners' report read, after which he directed at me the question as to whether I for my part acknowledged that I had thought it was from a stab in the throat that Jon had died.

"I thought that," I answered, "but the hole in the neck was less visible when we viewed the body a second time."

"We know that . . . But admit now, Bjarni, that you stabbed Jon!" Judge Scheving exclaimed.

Bjarni looked me in the eyes and answered quietly, "I did *not* stab Jon. I don't know anything about that hole . . . I'm not saying that to make myself less guilty. Kill him I did. And that I admitted. I thought he was dead—from hitting him with the staff. But if he wasn't dead when I threw him in the water . . . I think—it's still me that drowned him . . . If I'd stabbed him I would have admitted that too . . . As well as all the rest."

"Are you going to go on insisting that he had raised his staff against you before you struck?"

"Yes; because it was him that was going to hit me—otherwise it maybe wouldn't have happened that day."

Judge Scheving was foaming. "That's pure nonsense, the whole thing. Evasions, man. The murder was planned —you've admitted that . . . You'd decided to kill Jon Thorgrimsson—long before."

"Yes, that's true . . . I thought he had to die."

"Why?"

"I've already told you that. We'd come to hate each other . . . That came from my relationship with Steinun."

"You didn't think it was bad enough that you slept with the wife? The husband had to be killed . . . And your own wife—what was your idea in murdering her?"

"The real reason was probably my desire to marry Steinun."

"Desire—uh huh . . . desire . . ."

200

Judge Scheving pounded his fist on the table. "Bring the woman in."

Steinun had to be supported by her guards this time. She was in no condition any more to keep upright by herself. They got her sitting on the chair, but they could not let go of her and leave, she would have fallen.

Judge Scheving asked her, "How could you go along, Steinun, with Bjarni killing your husband?"

"All I felt then was coldness and hatred for my husband," Steinun whispered barely audibly—with long pauses between the words. "For a long time there hadn't been anything between us—but anger and insults—me and my husband . . . And he'd begun to threaten to beat me too . . . ever since I was little I've been so scared of—anything that hurt . . . I wasn't sure but whether he might maybe come to—killing me . . . He'd turned so queer . . . so different . . . Besides—I loved Bjarni . . ."

"What was your intention in planning and in helping Bjarni carry out the murder of his wife?"

"Because I loved him . . . and I wanted us to be able to get married . . . All my misery comes from my love for Bjarni."

Steinun collapsed in hysterical weeping. Judge Scheving had her taken out again. Immediately after that he turned Bjarni over to his guards and adjourned the hearings.

XXVIII

Before I went to bed that evening I was out with the prisoners. Steinun was apparently calm again. But as soon as she saw me she burst into tears.

"You must forgive me," she whispered, weeping, "I'm no good for anything any more. I'm so miserable . . . so miserable."

I laid my hand on her head. "Poor Steinun," I said. "There is only One who can give you strength. Only God can give you strength. If you seek Him—and want Him . . . Then you will find Him—in your heart."

When she had cried a little she asked—with a voice I remembered having heard a long time ago, "Won't you tell Bjarni? . . ."

"No messages are to go between the prisoners," one of the guards firmly interrupted the conversation.

"That order's no longer valid," I replied. "There has been a full confession."

"I take my orders from the judge only," he retorted.

"Then get him," I said.

But he would not do it.

"What is it I'm supposed to say to Bjarni?" I asked Steinun.

"Ask him for me if he won't forget me—the way he saw me now," she whispered, and her eyes were burned out—dead. "Ask him if he won't try to remember me the way I was once . . . The time—he liked me . . . The time he—loved me . . ."

I stood there not knowing whether I should go or stay.

Steinun was silent a moment, then she whispered, still softer, "Because I'm—simply not like . . . like everybody must believe. I've done—terrible harm . . . But I'm not like that . . . It just all—happened . . . Anybody who wants to know me—has to have known me—the way I was then . . . That's what I'm like—inside . . . Jon—that was just like not having a husband. But I didn't know that—not then . . . It would have been the best thing if I'd never found out about it . . . Happiness—you don't get it with a hard hand, Eiulv."

I left, frightened and chilled. In her words there had been something foreboding. Something that reached to me. An evil prophecy . . . Just that, that she had mentioned me by name . . . Her fate, as it had developed and would develop, touched me. Was woven together with mine. Were all men's fates woven together? Was a man blind if he did not see this? Insensitive if he did not feel it? . . . Yes, that was it. I knew that suddenly . . . And there I stood—in the midst of a threatening, endless blackness. In the midst of blood and horror and the numbing tolling of a sinful heart.

Bjarni smiled when he saw me coming—now he could smile again. "I'll carry it out all right," he said, "my part . . ."

Then the little light in his eyes died out. "I shouldn't have said anything about Steinun . . . Maybe I could have saved her. Isn't it possible for her to get off with a prison sentence, do you think?"

I knew it was hardly possible. So I answered that it was pointless to conjecture about a verdict that had not yet been given. After that I told him what Steinun had asked me to say.

He fell into thought . . . After a great while he said, "It's true—she was a different person . . . before. There shouldn't ever have been anything between us. I knew that . . . Will you try to understand if I tell you that Jon, and especially Gudrun, were very much to blame . . . I'm not saying that to justify myself. I've come to terms with myself; I—don't seem to be living any more. But that is the way I felt . . . The misfortune was that Steinun and I didn't meet each other when we were young."

I did not want to tell Bjarni that life was hardly as simple as he seemed to think. Perhaps he found some strength in imagining a life together with Steinun—from childhood. A more innocent dream, or a purer one, he could hardly dream, now. And our inner peace depends on the dreams we have—on the kind of life dream that is ours. I listened therefore only with patience to him, and said nothing. The only thing I could do from now on for Bjarni was just to listen to him.

"If you've given your life and your blood you can't give more—can you?" he went on. "But what about the hereafter? . . . Are Steinun and I going to meet Jon and Gudrun there afterwards? Are we going to be married to them there, maybe?"

"Don't think about that, Bjarni," I replied. "Believe me; you leave your clay behind you in more than one sense."

"But—you'll know each other—won't you?"

"Your tribulations, when you are born into the heavenly kingdom, will be no greater than the time you were born as a baby on earth."

"There isn't waiting there—as hard a life again? Do you think?"

I said, "Bjarni . . . We, who can't even imagine for ourselves foreign lands and people—how should we be able to fashion reasonable pictures of the life beyond the earth's matter? But close your eyes without fear—when the time comes. And go erect with your head up, man. You have sinned; we both know it, you and I. But you have confessed your sins and are taking the penalty of the law with your head up. And you are not doing it only because we men have the power and the duty to judge you. You have realized, yourself, that by shedding blood you harvest death. You have repented. And repentence gives reconciliation. Be at peace."

Bjarni was silent for a long time. Then he said, "If it's true that you can wash away dishonor by dying with honor—then God will have no reason to be ashamed of me . . . I'll give Him a sign."

With these words of Bjarni it became clear to me that I might just as well give up talking. He understood me only in part. And certainly I him only in part, too.

. . . I had gone to bed and put the light out, when there was a knock at my door and somebody stuck his head in and asked through the darkness, "Are you sleeping, Reverend?"

It was Gudmund Scheving. I hurried to light the lamp, asked him to sit down. He was not quite sober.

"I hope I'm not disturbing you too unreasonably," he said, and sat down with a weight that seemed all out of proportion to his thin body. "They're so god-awful boring, all of them. The whole court. The jurors, the defender, the prosecutor. They *bore* me . . . And you just can't sleep—the night before you execute a man. Even if it's a scoundrel like Bjarni—along with his guilty trollop . . . Oh, Reverend Eiulv. Tell me, am I bothering you? Have a drop . . . But I *had* to run away, you know. It's all right for them to be silent—in court. They ought to be. And I don't mind doing all the talking myself. I don't mind it. But you know what—you can't talk to the silent . . . Tell me something? Did you ever see the like of that scoundrel? The like of that cold-blooded, stupid, nerveless animal . . . He went ahead and stabbed the man down, no matter how the hell he carries on about it. And then he buries him—over across from the farmyard. And then sleeps the whole winter with his wife—wall to wall with the corpse, so to speak. And bed to bed with his own wife. Whom he finally strangles—by holding her mouth and nose—since she won't die from his damned poison."

"Did you consider, Judge, that if Gudrun died of strangulation her face could hardly have been as pale as it was, and as composed?"

"Who says it was pale?"

"I say it, who saw her myself."

"You think he killed her some other way? Maybe even more bestial?"

"I think she died of terror—that her heart just stopped. She wasn't strong."

"No, Lord, no . . . No spirituality here, I beg you. Are you going to start now—like the Reverend Ormsson—with innocence and all that? No, my spiritual friend, that won't do—not with Gudmund Scheving. You stay in your black shirt and keep your trap shut about things you don't know anything about. Can't you understand? The man confessed . . . Perhaps that escaped your attention. Watch out that I don't charge you. For bribery, or anyhow corrupting a servant of the law. Did you talk with Bjarni about that? No? That's good. May I solicit you not to do it. Otherwise I'll see you come to regret it—just between us."

"Is that a threat?"

"It's a suggestion. So don't talk to Bjarni. Not about this."

"Maybe I won't. In any event it will be because I myself consider it proper to be silent. Consider it best for Bjarni."

"Consider all you want to, as long as you're quiet about it. Oh, Reverend Eiulv—man's motives . . . I'm not much older than you, and yet I could tell you such things about that matter as you hardly know, or are aware of. I wasn't born yesterday. Man's motives . . . Chaos, I give you my word. Chaos that even the Devil himself couldn't find his way through."

"Such as your reason for being so hard with Bjarni, you mean?"

"You looking for trouble? . . . I do believe the man's snapping back."

"You don't believe him even when he's telling the truth. Why don't you believe him?"

"A man like Bjarni can't tell the truth . . . That is, can and can't. But he doesn't do it. By God, he doesn't do it.

Steinun, now—she tells something more like the truth. She lies so obviously that in its way what she says is true. Bjarni on the other hand—him you can't figure out. You never know when he's lying and when he's telling the truth. Or in what mixture he's lying and telling the truth. But that he is lying—that's certain. Believe me. We Schevings haven't been jurists and criminologists for nothing—and criminals if you please—for generations . . . Dumb—that we aren't . . . But he's going to lose his head. And his right hand. And be nipped with red-hot tongs. The animal."

"Is this the way justice looks," I asked, "behind the mask?"

"That's the way it looks, yes . . . I'll be glad to show you the paragraphs. I don't intend to excede my authority in the slightest—if it's that you are getting at. I will confine myself precisely to justice—as they call the law in divine, or shall we say Jon Ormssonish, simplicity. I'll bet you any amount you want that I'll get my verdict—essentially unaltered—through all the appeal courts. The Supreme Court included. Shall we risk a few farms?"

"No thank you."

"Then keep your tongue in check better next time, you spiritual father. If you hadn't served my purposes in this case . . . Well man—no, no threats."

"It wasn't you I was serving," I answered, and raised myself up in the bed. "I was serving, as well as I knew how to, my Lord, who is God."

"On such a lofty and vague dignity neither the King nor the law nor my own humble self make any demands, Sir. Well here's how . . . I've never asked where the brandy was distilled. As long as it was there."

"Is it impossible to spare Bjarni? At any rate, from torture?"

"Did he spare anybody else? . . . See, see—you're not saying anything . . . No, but Steinun will get off—by losing her head . . . Lighter than that neither one of them can get off. Except by the King's grace. And that's not very large. When—a recommendation . . . can't be included."

"And there can't be?"

"There can't, no. We have too many isolated farms here in Iceland. Although probably not any more isolated than Syvendeaa. We can't get people used to a thing like slaughtering whatever home folks, one way or another, get in their hair a little. No, we can't . . ."

XXIX

It is man's fate to look forward to one day with longing, another day with horror. Yet the day is always the same— and never the same. Not once is the day that rises over men the same day for even two of them. So manifold is the mind, so variously does the individual's plight shape itself. Therefore the quaking heart seeks constancy, and must seek it. Must seek it behind things, seek it with God. Everybody, everybody seeks it. Even the Unbelievers, who, like Gudmund Scheving—as he confided to me that night—have no hope that God is anything else but man's dream of constancy, which they yearn for with every fiber and find nowhere.

It was so still at the house, the fourth day of the court. All the witnesses were gone—down to the two coroners, who, together with the Reverend Jon, had been instructed to present a written account of what they had undertaken and not undertaken after they had viewed in Saurbaer church the earthly remains of the departed Gudrun. They did it, as soon as the court was convened; whereupon they too rode home.

It was so still at the house.

Even in the room where the court was working hard at composing the verdict there was only an occasional sound to be heard.

Actually—actually it was only Gudmund Scheving who was working. He had certainly let the prosecutor cast the sentences of the verdict according to the paragraphs he had indicated to him, and himself put the words in his mouth about "lamentable deed of villainy," "painful death," and more of the same. But the only part of the prosecutor's contribution that was completely his own had to do neither with Bjarni nor Steinun: it had to do with our good Dean, Jon Ormsson. Judge Scheving had certainly also listened patiently to the defender's harmless contribution (especially after having heard the introductory words which ran: that he by no means wanted to minimize the nature of the loathsome crime that had been committed by the two guilty parties) which concluded with a quiet recommendation that the case be pursued under less severe paragraphs than those to which the prosecutor had referred—he citing as mitigating circumstances Jon Thorgrimsson's "constant insults," "the absence of a timely pastoral visit and forceful admonition on the part of the ecclesiastical authority," together with the intelligence that it was understandable that everything had happened as it happened "when you consider the violence of feminine lust." But it was Gudmund Scheving who composed the decision. He alone.

He had sat down at the table, busy and in good spirits— with the pale autumn sun falling through a dew-covered window onto the papers. You could not tell that he had sat up most of the night. When he was thinking and not writing, he drummed his fingers, tapped his feet, or occupied himself with something else cheerful and noisy— whistled cheery melodies, or gargled hymns in his throat, with a sound having some resemblance to a reed organ.

Now and then he would toss a question out into the air. If he did get an answer—he did not hear it anyway, for he was only asking himself. He was not accustomed to asking questions of others. At any rate, not to getting their answers. He asked his books too. He had bookmarks inserted here and there; the case appeared to have been well thought out—whenever he had found time for it. He found immediately what he was looking for every time— paged forward, paged back, compared; thumped the book on the table, whistled a phrase thoughtfully—and picked up the pen.

Still the whole day went in composing the decision. Not until sundown did Judge Scheving manage to get it finished and agreed to by the jurors. By then it had got too late to deliver it that same evening to the accused.

But finished it was . . . Gudmund Scheving nailed it down. With a fist on the table. Whereupon he leaned back in his chair and said, "I'm tired now . . . and happy."

The last you could see on him, but not the first.

Suddenly he sprang up from the chair, danced out into the room with Jon Thorberg—whose heavy fur coat had room enough for both of them—singing:

> Drink, brothers, drink, for now you can feel spring's breath,
> Kiss, brothers, kiss, and hunt out a girl today,
> Drink, brothers, drink, for it's thirsty work waiting for death,
> Kiss, brothers, kiss, for the lips and the flesh decay.

XXX

And verily there came the Reverend Jon, our Sinner, to sit
"in the pew," as he called it, with a murderer and evil-
doer, to hear a verdict read, a twofold sentence of death,
in which his name expressly and by no means to his favor
or advantage was named—several times. Condemned he
certainly was not. But he was the only one who wept.

Bjarni and Steinun were not led into the court that
morning "free and unencumbered," as the order had read
when they had been summoned to the hearing. Judge
Scheving had them stand fettered while the sentence was
read.

The Reverend Jon Ormsson put his chair between the
prisoners. It was probably what he had meant by sitting
in the pew with them, and he sat there weeping, with
Bjarni standing on his left side and Steinun on his right.
Already before Judge Scheving had begun, Jon Ormsson
was sitting and weeping; weeping humbly and simply—
like a child. And like an old man.

Bjarni and Steinun, on the other hand, stood there both
motionless. That they were standing there fettered, and
not being questioned any more, seemed to keep them
from understanding fully how serious the matter was for
them. And Bjarni seemed gradually to have become perfectly calm. But we had all been worried about how
Steinun would take her sentence.

We could have spared ourselves the worry.

Because whether Steinun now fully understood what
was going on or whether she did not understand it—she

stood there with her old bearing. A bearing I so well—in a sudden flush of youthful recollection—remembered. Her bearing from "before." Perhaps she was standing there as though asleep; standing and waiting to wake up. Wake up from the whole evil and improbable dream. Wake up and become—herself . . .

Judge Scheving read first the justification for the sentence, and then the sentence itself—coolly, impartially, and yet quickly; almost hastily. Neither by tone nor tempo did he emphasize any word or expression. It was as though he had quite forgotten the zeal and passion with which, the day before, he had undertaken the composition of this same sentence. Or at least as though he neither fully understood nor acknowledged what was written. Perhaps it was accidental. Gudmund Scheving was a capricious man. When it was not a case of money.

He went through the case in detail; laid the blame on the Reverend Jon Ormsson expressly for not having made the charge against the culprits already on the death of Gudrun Egilsdottir; gave explicit justification as to why neither his uncle, Judge David Scheving, to whom the Dean had written his "vague and misleading" letter, nor he himself, who was the newly appointed judge, had undertaken any action—on such a vague basis; and went, after that, over to a description of the course of the trial as it had developed during the interrogations. He demonstrated that Syvendeaa—that "isolated and desolate" place where, aside from the two married couples, only two adults lived the time the first murder was committed, while there were when Gudrun was killed, besides the guilty parties, only children on the farm—had by its situation facilitated the plans for the murders and favored the possibility of concealing them so long. Whereupon he went through the circumstances that had, bit by bit, brought the truth to light; the community's knowledge of the quarrels at Syvendeaa; the rumors of "illicit relations" between Bjarni and Steinun; Jon Thorgrimsson's announcement of his distaste for staying any longer at the farm; Gudrun's sudden violent sickness and the suspicion that Steinun had poisoned her—which Gudrun had made no secret of; Gudrun's persistent reference to the relationship between Bjarni and Steinun, and her account of their having threatened her life if she revealed anything about the situation in the house; and finally the washing ashore of Jon's body, in which a hole was found, apparently produced by a powerful blow—which blow, oddly enough, Bjarni would still not admit. There was certainly neither a corpus delecti nor any eyewitness account to rely upon, since both of the victims were long since lying underground, and only the guilty parties had been present when the ghastly deeds had been done; but there existed both the guilty parties' full confession, which they had deposed after the minister Eiulv Kolbeinsson had converted them from their defiance and original, not wholly consistent, denials. The case could therefore be regarded as completely cleared up, not only with respect to the guilty parties' illicit relationship but also with respect to the murder of both of their spouses: first the murder of Jon, in which Steinun's guilt was confined to complicity while Bjarni was the sole perpetrator; after that the "incredibly vicious murder of a poor sickly woman," in which they were both implicated as accomplices and perpetrators.

When Gudmund Scheving had gone this far and before I had heard the sentence itself, I knew that he had not said any more to me than what he could, and intended to, back up: however the sentence might run it would, with a justification like this, not be reduced in any court of appeal. That was certain.

"Affirmed and attested," said Judge Scheving, suddenly finishing the preamble.

He paused for a moment. Whereupon he read on—with the same haste and indifference in his voice: "Bjarni Bjarnason shall for committing the act of murder on Jon Thorgrimsson on the first of April, which act in spite of the form of the confession cannot possibly be regarded as having taken place in self-defense, and for a uniquely godless act of murder on his innocent wife, Gudrun Egilsdottir, whom he on the fifth of June killed with the intention of subsequently marrying Steinun Sveinsdottir, be nipped three times with red-hot tongs, have his right hand severed from his body while alive, and thereafter his head with an axe, both of which parts are to be erected on a pole over the body, which is to be buried at the place of execution. Steinun Sveinsdottir shall, for conspiracy in and knowledge of her husband's murder, and conspiracy in and attempt to commit the murder of Gudrun with copper filings, together with aiding and abetting her murder on the fifth of June, lose her head, which shall be cut off with an axe and erected on a pole, while the body is to be buried at the place of execution. The property of both, real and movable, shall be forfeited to the King."

The rest of the verdict—the longest part—was a review of the Reverend Jon Ormsson's and the two coroners' situation, a review which resulted in the coroners' being absolved, while the court, "questioning its authority" to judge a partly spiritual matter, referred the Dean's probable responsibility to "the decision of the bishop."

When the verdict had been read, Judge Scheving asked the criminals whether they acknowledged themselves satisfied with it or whether they wanted to appeal. Neither Bjarni nor Steinun made any answer to the question; it seemed to leave both of them quite untouched—as if it were not even directed to them. Often, before, I had been distressed during this case, but certainly never as in that moment. The defense stepped in before Judge Scheving could dissolve the hearing. He advised against appeal, but he advised petitioning his Royal Majesty for pardon. The criminals did not answer this either, not before they were expressly and repeatedly asked. Then they finally agreed, dully.

After which Judge Scheving, "since there were no further matters to consider," dissolved the court.

The Reverend Jon Ormsson rose, made the sign of the

cross on the condemned, first on Bjarni and then on Stein-un, murmured something, said with his old, worn, minister's voice, "We'll probably not see each other again . . . "

And limped out.

When the prisoners were taken out I went over to Judge Scheving.

"Now the two of us have killed, too," I said.

"There have to be human sacrifices in all ages," he smiled indulgently back, "in one form or another."

. . . There is not much more to tell.

Bjarni and Steinun were taken to Haga, the Judge's farm where they were to be guarded until the sentence, since it was a death sentence, had been confirmed by the superior court and laid before the King.

Steinun I was never to see again. But I talked twice more with Bjarni.

Saturday, the fifth of February the next year, there was a soft knocking on my windowpane where I was sitting writing in my study. My son Hilarius, three weeks old, was sick that night. I was late in preparing my sermon, therefore. So soft was the knocking on my window that at first I did not know whether there was somebody knocking, or whether the noise came from something or other hanging on the wall and set moving by the wind.

When the knocking meantime was repeated, it occurred to me that I had heard that Bjarni Monday night had escaped from Haga. . . . It was he.

"What do you want with me, Bjarni?" I asked him when I, troubled and uncertain of my duty now, had brought him into my room.

"Nothing," he answered, and smiled—a lonesome smile, a dead man's smile. "I just wanted to say hello to you . . . friends are scarce."

"Why did you escape?" I asked uneasily.

"Not to escape my sentence—don't believe that," he replied wearily—and as though disappointed. "More to show them that their little irons aren't what can hold me—that I'm not staying with them for that reason . . . Besides, I get a kick out of seeing my fellow men again. Seeing Skor Cliffs . . . Seeing Syvendeaa."

"You've been there?"

"I went through the rooms, yes. Sat a while in the living room . . . In the moonlight . . . Sat there till I seemed to begin to hear the others."

"Didn't you meet anybody? Didn't anybody see you?"

Bjarni shrugged his heavy shoulders. "I've got to have food; and shelter . . . sometimes . . . The farmers—They're so willing to let me have both. And besides they give me good advice and offer to help me to get away. Far away."

Again he smiled his lonesome smile. "They're all so afraid that I'll kill them . . . "

Bjarni stood up, walked restlessly back and forth a bit, went on—bitterly. "Well, let them be afraid. They don't even dare earn the twenty rigsdaler that've been put on my head. They're such cowards . . . Since yesterday I've been living in the barn at Jon of Maberg's place—an honest man. He wasn't mixed up in my case. He's poor and has children; it's him I'd like the most to have the money. Now I'm just waiting for him to turn me in. And he'll do it . . . Probably tomorrow, even. At least I didn't dare postpone this visit any longer."

The night passed. As even dark and heavy times do. Bjarni said, as he left, that he would come again the next night—if Jon gave him the time. Which he probably wouldn't do.

He was right. Early Sunday morning Jon of Maberg came to the barn with some men. And Bjarni was taken back to Haga.

A good two years later I talked again with Bjarni. It was a summer day. He and Steinun by this time had been recently moved to confinement in Reykjavik. Their case had finally gone through all the appeal jurisdictions. The sentence in Bjarni's case had been increased; he was to be nipped five times instead of three. Moreover, his dead body was to be put on the wheel.

Just before I reached the town, our capital, I saw some

people riding in front of me jump off their horses and each throw a stone on a cairn. It was a new cairn. When I came to it immediately after, I did what they had done.

Although I had a lot of business, my first visit was to the prison. I would have no peace until I had visited my two poor parishioners who—year in and year out—had to wait for so terrible a death.

Something had happened to Bjarni. I saw that at once. He had grown gray.

Not that he had turned white-haired or white-bearded. But everything seemed to have faded on him. Most of all his eyes.

He was sitting on his bed. It was deathly still in the prison. The other prisoners were out working.

"I'm too big a scoundrel myself to go with them," he smiled.

I asked what had happened to Steinun.

He looked up at me quickly, "Steinun—you don't know? . . . She's dead. Did you come by a cairn alongside the road?"

"Yes . . . I threw a stone on it myself."

"You couldn't know whose it was . . . It's already got a name. They call it the Steina cairn."

"How did she die?"

"Of fear—I think . . . That was when she heard that we were to be sent to Norway to have our heads chopped off. Then it just kind of came over her . . . uncontrollable fear and weeping. Then she died . . . They couldn't get anybody here for the job. I suppose you knew that. Except an old, gray-haired Northerner. He was so decrepit, the poor old boy, that when they made a test he couldn't even hit the block . . . Well, he said, he'd manage—when he had to."

Bjarni of Syvendeaa laughed; and then he added—half in admiration and half as a sigh, "They're tough, the Northerners."

That was the last time I saw and spoke with Bjarni. The

ship that was to take him to Kristianssand was already lying at Havnefjord. It was an expensive trip for the government. More than two thousand Rigsdaler were paid out all in all to get Bjarni's head off his shoulders. An enormous sum. And a sum which—it seems to me—could have been better used for the benefit of mankind and the glory of God.

A very young minister—Hjort Jonsson—went with him to Norway, so that the condemned man could have the consolations of religion in his own tongue before his torture by hot iron and his death by cold steel. That was the only grace accessible to Bjarni.

The young minister—of whom I heard after his return that he could not quite get over the bloody event he had had to witness in the course of his official duties—I invited to my house in Baer at Rodesand. We got to know each other well. He told me a lot about Bjarni, both about their association on board ship and Bjarni's final journey. What had made the greatest impression on Hjort had been Bjarni's calm "right up to when his head rolled and the blood spurted from his slaughtered trunk."

"I don't understand how a man can die like that," he would conclude. "Is it possible not to be afraid of such a death?"

In the beginning Hjort wept almost always when he got to telling about these things. He was, after all, a young man—almost a boy. Sometimes he would rave about the spectators; they had stormed the rock where the block was set up, he said; many of them had fallen and hurt themselves badly.

"The only one who didn't scream and shout was Bjarni," he used to add. "You can't have been at something like that without afterwards feeling guilty of murder . . . "

"He was remarkable—Bjarni was," he said another time. "Did you know him, Reverend Eiulv? Did you *understand* him? . . . Like now that time at the block—maybe I didn't tell you. Suddenly—just as his hand was chopped off—he

lifted his arm up . . . What do you say about that? . . .
Right up. Why do you think he did that?"

"That was the sign," I answered.

. . . These useless sheets—they are my confession. They
are my sermon to you and over you, Hilarius, my son, a
poor and sorrow-laden father's address.

My friend Amor Jonsson and my beloved wife Olof—
will I dare show them what I have written here? And if I
do—will they be able to tell me what part I have in the
evil that happened that time? What, and how much?

But I will never be able, certainly, to understand the
whole thing. Not until my God—may He be merciful to
me—on the promised day of judgment reveals it to me,
poor Publican.

ut supra

PUBLISHED IN THE
NORDIC TRANSLATION SERIES

From Denmark
H. C. Branner, *Two Minutes of Silence*. Selected short stories, translated by Vera Lindholm Vance, with an introduction by Richard B. Vowles. 1966.

Jacob Paludan, *Jørgen Stein*. Translated by Carl Malmberg, with an introduction by P. M. Mitchell. 1966.

From Finland
Hagar Olsson, *The Woodcarver and Death*. *Träsnidaren och döden*, translated by George C. Schoolfield. 1965.

Toivo Pekkanen, *My Childhood*. *Lapsuuteni*, translated by Alan Blair, with an introduction by Thomas Warburton. 1966.

F. E. Sillanpää, *People in the Summer Night*. *Ihmiset suviyössä*, translated by Alan Blair, with an introduction by Thomas Warburton. 1966.

From Iceland
Fire and Ice: Three Icelandic Plays, with introductions by Einar Haugen. Jóhann Sigurjónsson, *The Wish* (*Galdra-Loftur*), translated by Einar Haugen. Davið Stefánsson, *The Golden Gate* (*Gullna hliðið*), translated